W9-BAS-221

For Better,
For Murder

FORTHCOMING BY LISA BORK

For Richer, For Danger

LISA BORK

For Better, For Murder

A Broken Vows Mystery

MIDNIGHT INK
WOODBURY, MINNESOTA

First Edition
First Printing, 2009

Book design and format by Donna Burch
Cover design by Kevin R. Brown
Cover Illustration © Sean Harrison
Editing by Connie Hill

Midnight Ink, an imprint of Llewellyn Publications

Library of Congress Cataloging-in-Publication Data
Bork, Lisa, 1964–
For better, for murder : a broken vows mystery / by Lisa Bork. — 1st ed.
p. cm.
ISBN 978-0-7387-1866-8
I. Title.
PS3602.O755F67 2009
813'.6—dc22
2009014088

This is a work of fiction. Names, characters, places, and incidents are either the product of the author's imagination or are used fictitiously, and any resemblance to actual persons, living or dead, business establishments, events, or locales is entirely coincidental.

Midnight Ink
Llewellyn Publications
2143 Wooddale Drive, Dept. 978-0-7387-1866-8
Woodbury, MN 55125-2989 USA
www.midnightinkbooks.com

Printed in the United States of America

ONE

I WAS ONE STEP away. One step—one sale, in fact—from becoming a successful businesswoman in Wachobe, New York. An insignificant achievement to some, but a meaningful one to me. On the other hand, one misstep and my business would be on the brink of bankruptcy. That's why I wore my dress boots today.

The ice and snow outside my window didn't say dress boots. They said thermal insulation with leak-proof rubber. The weather also didn't say "drive a hot new Ferrari" like the one under my showroom pin lights. But I'd snatched this Italian stallion out of arid Scottsdale, Arizona, and had it delivered here to my sports car boutique with one of my best customers in mind. Because I liked to think I knew a thing or two about desire. The need for the fast lane. The hunger to show the world what money can buy. The longing for a pre-owned but pristine F430 Ferrari Spider. Most men would be happy to take it out on the wet roads and see if they could make it hydroplane. I counted on Mr. Hughes of the Hughes grocery store chain to take the step and pay to become that man.

I crossed the showroom floor with my hand outstretched as he stamped snow off his Gucci loafers. "Mr. Hughes, I have a beauty to show you."

His frosty fingertips squeezed mine with genteel pressure. "I was delighted to receive your call, Miss Asdale."

The phone on the showroom reception desk rang. Mr. Hughes glanced toward it before continuing, "There's nothing like Italian engineering."

"Exactly. Please, come take a look."

The phone rang a second time as I ushered him to the Ferrari. "This is a 2006 Rosso Corsa Spider with only fifteen hundred and two miles. The previous owner was a collector. Notice the—"

"Excuse me, Jo." My mechanic, Cory Kempe, stood wiping his hands on a grease rag in the doorway between the showroom and the garage. He was three inches shorter than my five-foot-four, and wiry with porcelain skin, poodle-tight auburn hair, and girly eyelashes.

"You have a phone call. It's urgent." He wiggled his eyebrows, a signal that the call was about my sister, who currently resided in the state psychiatric center.

Calls about her were always deemed urgent by the person making them, usually her. I didn't always agree, but I would have trouble remembering the Ferrari's selling points if I didn't verify that was the case this time.

Mr. Hughes gestured toward the phone. "Please. I'll take my time and look the car over."

"Why don't you start with the interior?" I whipped open the passenger door, hoping a waft of Italian leather would help clinch the sale.

A man's body flopped out headfirst, his skull hitting the floor with a thump.

I yelped and jumped back a foot.

Mr. Hughes jumped right along with me, stretching his arm in front of me.

My gaze flickered between the dead man's vacant eyes and the knife in his chest. Bile backed up in my throat, washing my tongue with its bitterness. I recognized him, even though his face was twisted in shock and pain, eyes bulging from the sockets, his fingers spread wide as though pleading. Blood had drenched his green-and-white-striped sweater and stone-colored chinos. Round drops of it spotted his tan loafers. For one wild second, I considered pulling the knife out and trying to restore him to the healthy, smiling man I remembered.

The phone buzzed, signaling I'd left my call on hold too long. It jolted us into action.

Mr. Hughes did not get to be the CEO of a major chain without the ability to remain cool in stressful situations. He raised one of his plucked and trimmed white eyebrows, studied the body, and held out his hand.

"I seem to have caught you at a bad time, Miss Asdale. Perhaps I can make another appointment for later in the week."

After my damp hand met his remarkably sweat-free grasp, he bowed his head, clicked his heels, and departed into the early December snowfall, leaving me suspended in the Land of Oz. I wished I had the option not to get involved, but this house had landed squarely on me.

"I'm sorry, Jo. Did I chase him off?"

I tore my gaze from the dead man and lifted it to Cory's questioning face.

"No. We … ah …" I gestured to the body.

He crinkled his brow and jogged across the showroom to investigate. When he caught sight of the corpse, he froze. His mouth opened. He sucked in air.

I decided I'd better be the one to summon the police.

I darted around the front end of the car and ran for the phone in my office. Line one blinked red. I pressed line two and dialed 911. The operator's nasal tones filled the line. I took a deep breath.

"This is Jolene Asdale from Asdale Auto Imports. I just found a dead man in one of my showroom cars. He's been stabbed. Can you send someone right away?"

"Yes, ma'am. Hold on while I contact the officer in your vicinity."

It was a matter of seconds before she was back. "Would you like me to stay on the line with you until they arrive?"

"No, thank you."

I heard the operator's admonition not to touch anything as I switched to line one.

A dial tone greeted me on line one. Just as well. Even my sister couldn't upstage a dead man.

I rejoined Cory, who had found his wind and was now leaning to the left with his head upside down in order to get a better look at the body. "Isn't that—?"

"Yes."

We took several steps back and stood silently side by side, unable to take our eyes off the scene. Questions ran through my mind. Why had someone killed him? Why here? Had he suffered? Who would tell his family? How would they take it?

I looked up when the Chief of Police for Wachobe rushed through the showroom entrance, bent at the waist with both hands in front of him as though ready for guns blazing. But Walter wasn't armed. He wasn't even in uniform. His navy sweat suit had baggy knees and what appeared to be a bleach spot on the sleeve, making him look more like the fifty-something wrestling coach he was than the Chief of Police. His gaze darted around the room and came to rest on Cory and me.

I gave him a tentative wave, uncertain of the protocol.

He straightened, walked over, took one look at the body, and vomited on his Converse sneakers.

Cory looked away.

I patted Walter's back. "We know it's horrifying."

He hung his head, either in agreement or shame.

A red and white sheriff's car skidded to a halt on the sidewalk in front of the shop minutes later, lights flashing. Deputy Ray Parker entered the showroom in his perfectly pressed gray uniform with matching ski jacket, immediately taking up all available space with his six-foot-three, 220-pound frame. His nose twitched when he reached our little group, but if he noticed the vomit on Walter, he chose not to comment.

He tilted his head and looked at the body. "Isn't that—?"

"Yes." I hissed the word, causing Walter to jump. While the four of us didn't know everyone who lived in Wachobe and certainly not all who passed through, we knew each other and the dead man.

"Any idea how he got here?"

I knew Ray was talking to me. "None."

"Why's he dead?"

"I have no idea." I couldn't imagine a less likely or more unjustifiable murder candidate.

"Who killed him?"

"I don't know. I opened the car door and he fell out."

"All right. Cory, are you at all involved in this?" Ray fixed his steely stare on Cory, who raised his hands in surrender.

"Not me!"

"Then you can head into the shop for now. Take a look around and see if you notice anything out of place, but don't touch anything."

"Yessir."

"Walter, the restroom is in the corner. You might want to freshen up before the rest of the crew gets here."

Ray didn't wait for a response before turning to me.

I couldn't meet his eyes. It was hard to live in the same town as my almost-ex-husband. It was even harder now not to step closer to him in the hopes he would put his arms around me and make this whole nightmare go away. Ray was good at things like that.

He pulled out his wallet. "Darlin', would you mind going to get me a venti caramel macchiato?"

I imagined I heard feminists gasping, but Ray was not the stereotypical male chauvinist in uniform. Quite the opposite, in fact. He only called me by my given name when he was mad or feeling the urge, neither of which were likely right now. He did need a cup of coffee in the morning, especially after coming off the overnight shift as I suspected he had. He also knew me well enough to realize another dead body in a car would remind me of the worst day of my life, a day I tried to push farther back in my memories with each passing year. I realized he was being kind by removing me from the crime scene.

I accepted the ten and tried not to notice that Ray still carried a picture of me in his wallet, my college yearbook picture with the long brown curly hair he loved so much, the hair that gave me the Valerie Bertinelli look. Her picture hung on the inside of his locker door all through high school. Both pictures were of pretty girls with sparkling eyes and thick eyelashes. I didn't know if Valerie still had her sparkle. I lost mine around the time she ditched Eddie Van Halen, and my hair had been cut off years before to the businesslike bob brushing my chin now.

"Thank you." Ray squeezed my shoulder before turning his attention to the dead man.

As I crossed Main Street to the Starbucks, I tried not to relive the tingle that had run down my spine at his touch. I hadn't been touched in years. Entirely my own fault, of course. I'd had offers, more than I could recall. I was just not that kind of girl. I was a good girl, not out of religious principles or fears of STDs, but out of self-respect and a desire for happily ever after. Well, that and an irrational fear of pregnancy.

I placed Ray's order and listened to the whoosh of the coffee machines, trying to think of anything else but the dead man in my showroom. His tortured gaze was now burned onto the back of my eyelids. I took a deep breath to cleanse away the scent of death. Although I never drank coffee, I enjoyed its aroma. It reminded me of Ray.

I shook my head, amazed and rueful that a few minutes in his presence had shaken my resolve. He was the only man I ever loved, but he had one or two traits I couldn't overlook, let alone love.

A man in line jostled me. I shifted to give him better access to the napkins. The coffee house was full. I glanced at the inhabitants, passing over and returning to the perfectly coiffed blonde sitting by the fireplace. She looked up and leapt to her feet, dashing over to join me. My heart sank.

"Jo, how are you? Still dating that accountant—what was his name, again? Tim Lapham?"

"No, we're not dating anymore. Not for months." And not ever again. Tim now lay dead on my showroom floor—from all appearances, murdered—and I had no clue as to why. I decided to keep that information to myself, not only because Celeste was a champion gossip, but also because it didn't feel like my place to announce the news, especially before Walter or Ray informed Tim's ex-wife and children.

"I didn't think so, not after the way you were fighting." A smug expression settled on her face.

"Fighting? What are you talking about, Celeste?"

"Last week. You and Tim were standing in front of your showroom window. Your arms were waving and his were waving, and then you hit him."

My jaw dropped. Celeste managed the Talbots next door. I bought most of my size eight clothes there as a concession to my status as a businesswoman in this community. I figured the clothes made it seem like I had good taste, because in the moments when I was most honest with myself, I had to admit that after thirty-seven years I'd only developed good taste in cars. Maybe I'd shop elsewhere now that I knew she spent her work hours spying on me.

"Celeste, we were discussing zoning. I was pointing to the street, Tim was pointing, and I bumped his arm by accident."

"Well, the way he jumped back, I thought you'd struck him." Celeste folded her arms across her chest and continued, "A couple of the other shopkeepers thought the same."

"No, Celeste, you all misunderstood." I had been on quite a rant that day, directed more at the town than Tim, though. I didn't even remember all of what I'd said, and to someone looking through the window at us, it probably had seemed heated.

"Okay, fine. Seen Ray lately?" I heard the interest in her voice. She'd be happy to become the second Mrs. Ray Parker. I, on the other hand, went back to my maiden name right after we split.

I could see him through the front window of Starbucks, leaning against his patrol car and talking on his radio in front of my shop, which butted up to the sidewalk where several interested onlookers had gathered.

My sports car boutique sat smack dab in the middle of the town's main street, the only cedar-shingled building on the west end before the quarter mile of original and picturesque brick and clapboard structures dating to the 1790s. That was what Tim and I had been discussing. Some of the town mucketymucks thought my business stuck out like a marigold in a pansy bed and wanted to see it relocated to a back street, killing any walk-in business possibilities. And in a town like Wachobe where lakefront property sold in the millions and rented for thousands a week, the average window shopper might have the bucks to stroll in and buy a Ferrari.

Celeste turned to see what had captured my attention. "What's going on?"

I accepted the caramel macchiato from the barista and held it up to Celeste's inquiring face.

"I gotta run. This is for Ray."

By the time I crossed the street and handed him the coffee, Celeste had her nose pressed to the window of Starbucks in just the right position to superimpose her face over the face of the mermaid stenciled on the glass. Ray hooked his radio to his belt, took a sip and followed my gaze to her.

"Isn't that siren in the window Celeste Martin?"

I nodded.

"Well, if the shoe fits ..." Ray took another sip before announcing the coroner's ETA of thirty minutes. Wachobe had to rely on the nearby big city for those services. "The crime scene techs will be here in fifteen."

Ray set his coffee on the roof of his patrol car and reached inside. He withdrew a dark green parka from the front seat and put it around my shoulders. I wished he had some slipcovers for my leather boots which were now two inches deep in slush.

"Tell me what happened."

He sipped his coffee as I told my brief tale. He asked a few questions I didn't have answers to. Then he sighed, creating a cloud of condensation in the frigid air.

I tilted my head way back so I could look into his eyes. "What?"

"I'd tell you *what*, but if you recall the last time I did, you ran my toes over with the Porsche and filed for divorce."

How quickly we fall into our old familiar patterns. But now was not the time. The dead man inside merited all our attention. And something else I'd forgotten ... oh, yes, Erica.

I took the parka from my shoulders and held it out to Ray. He accepted it without further comment. I sidestepped the gawks to march through the shop's front door, accidentally whacking Walter, who was standing guard. I apologized and headed for my office.

"Jolene, you can't come in here." He dogged me across the showroom. "There may be fingerprints in your office. Evidence. You're going to mess it up."

This from the man who regurgitated on the crime scene. "I'm going to sit in my chair, Walter. I already sat in it once this morning. I also used the phone. I promise I won't touch anything else. I swear." I closed the door to my office in his face, blocking him and my view of Ray, and dropped into my black leather executive chair with a squeak, folding my hands in my lap as a precaution. I would never thwart the law intentionally, but I would thwart Ray.

The first time was six years ago when I invited my sister, Erica, to come live with us. She suffers from bipolar disorder and was often suicidal. Although Ray never said a word, I knew he resented her constant presence in our lives for the next three years. Even I felt relieved when she was admitted to the state psychiatric center, where she'd resided on and off since then.

I dialed the psych center now and asked to be connected to her floor. Tommye, the head nurse, answered the phone.

"I think Erica called me this morning. I didn't get to the phone. Is everything okay?" Out of the corner of my eye, I saw Ray, Walter, and a handful of men I didn't recognize surround the Ferrari.

"No. She's hallucinating again. The voice is telling her you're in danger. I let her call you so she'd know you're all right."

"I'm sorry. I had a ... situation here. Where is she now?"

"The doctor sedated her. She's sleeping peacefully."

"Tell her I'll come by later, okay?"

After thanking Tommye, I dropped the phone in the cradle and watched Ray at work. He paid no heed to the gawkers outside my showroom window, and I could tell the guys from the coroner's office listened to him with respect. Everyone listened to him with respect—except me.

In fact, I'm sure if asked, he'd say I tried to turn him into road kill.

TWO

Two hours later, after Tim Lapham's body had departed in a black nylon bag, Ray tapped on my office door and stepped inside. I had a Windex bottle in hand, wiping residue from fingerprint dust off my laminated wood desk. I'd had to be fingerprinted to eliminate my prints from the crime scene, a rather unsettling experience. All I wanted to do was lock up, go home, and fool myself into believing all this never happened, but I knew Ray's questions were just beginning.

Ray rested his shoulder against the door, all masculine and muscled. "Have lunch with me. They opened a new Italian restaurant in the old carriage house. I've heard the food is good."

"No thanks. I can't eat. Not after—" I jerked my chin toward the showroom.

"They have chocolate chip cannolis covered in fudge sauce."

I glanced at him out of the corner of my eye. "How do you know?"

"I know." He straightened and opened the door. "And I need to know everything you know about Tim Lapham. You can tell me at lunch or at the station where I'll eat from the vending machines. Your choice."

I took my black wool coat off the brass stand in the corner of my office. Ray was a dedicated, hard-working public servant who deserved a decent meal at least once a day, and I still remembered the time he got salmonella from a vending machine sandwich. Nasty. And he did name three of my favorite things: a new restaurant, Italian food, and chocolate.

When we reached the sidewalk, Ray opened the passenger door of his patrol car and looked at me expectantly.

"I'll drive myself."

"You'll have to park on a meter or in the municipal lot. It'll cost you, if you can even find an open spot this time of day."

I got in. He slammed the door. Wachobe was the western portal to the Finger Lakes region, an upscale tourist village highlighted by a heavily populated seven-mile-long diamond-clear lake, abundant shops, fine restaurants, and a dozen wineries. It was a picture postcard village that had attracted the likes of the Roosevelt family and the Clintons, with a year-round population of roughly 2,700. That number almost doubled in the summertime and fluctuated daily with visitors from all over the country and businesspeople from the two cities that squeezed our township like bookends. We were also a village that knew how to make a buck. Parking for Main Street and its offshoots was metered only—fifty cents for the first hour and ten every hour after. They were a gold mine.

I returned the waves from two members of the Dickens Christmas cast strolling by arm in arm. The man wore a black top hat and a gray coat with a velvet collar, the woman an emerald green dress and matching cape with black velvet trim and a black bonnet with netting.

As a member of the merchant's association, I helped fund the annual Dickens festival. The cast appeared on the streets Saturdays and Sundays from Thanksgiving until Christmas, providing a two o'clock choral concert at the park gazebo both days. Father Christmas sat on the steps of the VFW Club and dispensed treats to all good girls and boys. At the library, Mother Goose read stories to the children. Free horse-drawn carriage rides were available on Main Street, and roasted chestnuts, hot cider or chocolate, and donuts were given away at various stores around the village. The event brought in hundreds of tourists each year. The official lighting of the village tree would occur tomorrow night at the gazebo, complete with caroling and a visit from Father Christmas. Even the weather had cooperated this year, dumping an early foot of snow on the ground. I wondered if the murder would affect this year's celebration in the few weeks left until Christmas.

Ray negotiated the weekend traffic with ease and found the one available space with his usual magnetic attraction.

The new restaurant had opened in a two-hundred-year-old carriage house, allowing for a long, skinny dining room with booths lining the walls and a row of hardtops running down the middle. Traditional red and white checkerboard tablecloths covered their surfaces. A brick oven roasted pizzas at the rear of the room, blocking the view but not the mouthwatering aromas of the main kitchen beyond it.

I ordered the lasagna. Ray ordered the gnocchi with spicy Italian sausage and sweet peppers. I sipped my Pepsi and waited for the interrogation to begin.

"Tim wasn't killed in your car. The body was in an advanced stage of rigor mortis, probably locked into a seated position before it ever entered the building. We only found traces of body fluids on the seat." Ray peeled the paper lids off two creamers and dumped them in his coffee.

I wasn't sure what bothered me more—the reference to Tim as a "body" or the discussion of his fluids over lunch. Or maybe it was the thought that the Ferrari had taken on a whole new definition of used.

Ray started firing off questions. "Who knows your alarm code?"

"Cory. You. Erica. The alarm company."

He gave me the look, the incredulous, you-are-so-naïve look. "You haven't changed it in all these years? It's the same one your dad set up?"

"Why would I change it?"

Ray seemed pleased for some reason. "Okay, so we don't know who your dad might have given the code to, right?"

"Right."

"Did you ever hire a cleaning service?"

"No, I'm still mopping the floors." My customers were the most meticulous people. I only had to do it once a week to get the dust from the corners. It saved me money to do it myself, and money—specifically my lack of it—was my number-one business concern. Until I found a dead body. Money had now dropped to number two on my list of woes.

"Any new customers lately?"

I had a face that was way too easy to read. The "Duh, it's December" thought in my brain must have displayed in neon lights, because Ray frowned before he continued.

"Cory says he hasn't brought anyone by the shop. True?"

I thought a minute. Cory had a long string of love interests, all strapping males who loved to sit in my sexy, high performance cars. They loved to make out in them too, if I didn't keep watch and rock the car on its chassis in warning. But I couldn't think of anyone within the last three months. Winter was Cory's slow season too, with the nearby Broadway quality professional theater on hiatus. A skilled amateur actor, he often played a teenage boy in the theater's productions. "I can't recall any. Did you ask him?"

"Yep. He said he hasn't had his engine lubricated since September, and he needs an oil change soon."

September? What did he have to complain about? My engine had seized years before that.

Ray continued, "Have you had any problems with anyone? Noticed anything suspicious? Someone new hanging around? Phone calls? Funny looks? Footprints in the snow? Anything?"

I shook my head. "Sorry. This whole thing comes as a complete shock."

The waitress arrived with our salads and a basket of bread. Ray slid the basket over to me first. I munched a leaf of lettuce as he continued his barrage.

"Tell me everything you know about Tim."

"Tim is... was thirty-three, divorced from Becky with two children. Mark is eight; Emma is six. They had an amicable relationship and shared custody." I rushed on, hoping to avoid any opportunity for Ray to compare our situation to theirs. "His parents live in Florida and he has a brother in Poughkeepsie who is also an accountant. Tim lived in a second-floor three-bedroom apartment on Rose Street, in the home with the beauty shop on the first floor. His landlady runs it."

The waitress delivered our dinners and cleared the salad plates. I took a few bites of the delicious but thermonuclear lasagna while Ray devoured half his plate of gnocchi.

"Tim was a certified public accountant. He had private clients plus he did the books for the village. We voted for him, remember? And he was on the zoning board."

Ray nodded and kept on chewing. Apparently I hadn't told him anything he didn't already know because he hadn't even removed his notepad from his pocket yet.

I took a few more bites as I searched my memory. "He had the kids Tuesday and Thursday nights. Usually he took them out to dinner, then back to his place for homework. They stayed overnight with him on Saturday. He took them to dinner and a movie. He bowled on Wednesday nights. During tax season, he didn't see the kids except for Saturday. He liked opera."

Ray raised his eyebrows. He knew I hated opera.

"What else do you want to know?"

Ray wiped his lips and dropped his napkin on the table. "The important stuff, Jolene. What kind of car does he drive?"

"A silver Ford Focus. He bought it last year."

"Sporty." Through the sarcasm I heard Ray's message loud and clear—this guy wasn't right for you, Jolene. "It wasn't in your parking lot. Who were his clients?"

"I don't know."

"Did he ever seem stressed about anything while you were dating?"

"No. He was always very pleasant."

"Pleasant." Ray made it sound like a slur. "Did he mention other girlfriends or past relationships?"

"Just that he'd dated a few people, but no one special."

"Any names?"

"No."

"Did he sleep with them?"

"I don't know! I didn't ask."

"How many dates did you have with him, including our high school reunion?"

I tried to read his face and failed. I hadn't been able to read it that night, either, when I walked in with Tim. "Five." And I kept them all short to avoid getting involved. I knew Tim wasn't right for me, but I was lonely.

"Did you sleep with him?"

"How is that important?"

"I need to know if he was promiscuous. Maybe an irate ex or boyfriend stabbed him."

Could a man even be promiscuous? I thought that term was reserved for women only, but I didn't quibble. "No, Ray, I didn't sleep with him. He never tried to get past first base." I put my fork down on the table with most of my lasagna uneaten.

Ray eyed my plate. "Are you going to take that home?"

"No."

"Can I eat it?"

I handed it to him and watched him devour it, wondering what he would ask next. It bothered me that this murder had put me in the position of having to lay myself bare to him once again.

When the waitress reappeared with the check, Ray waved it off. "Add a chocolate chip cannoli to our order, please."

She hovered uncertainly, perhaps sensing tension in the air. "For here, or to go?"

I opened my mouth, but Ray got his words out first. "For here. Thanks." He waited until she walked away. "Tim's office is on Vineyard Street, right?"

"In one of the old mansions." Wachobe had lots of old mansions, some dating to 1796, homes where pre-Civil War reformists had lived. They contrasted nicely with the modern million-dollar mansions, euphemistically called cottages, ringing the lakeshore.

The cannoli appeared. Ray motioned for the waitress to set it in front of me. I didn't want it at first, but the smell of the fudge overcame me. I picked up the fork on my side of the plate—the waitress had thoughtfully supplied two so we could share—and scooped up the cheese and chips overfilling the end nearest me. I chewed, trying not to let my happiness show. Chocolate was definitely a comfort food.

"Good, eh?" He picked up his fork and reached across the table to dig in, although he left the last bite for me. Since we were no longer a couple, I didn't even mount a fake protest. I ate it. His amusement at my restored appetite showed in his eyes. I felt a pang of regret. Sometimes I missed that look in his eyes.

He paid the check, snagged a couple mints for us from the dish by the register, and escorted me out the door. We drove to the shop in silence. I guessed he'd run out of questions. I didn't have any answers anyway. In fact, the whole day had been so surreal that I didn't believe Tim was truly dead.

Ray backed into the driveway so my car door was closest to the shop entrance. Always the gentleman. I turned to look at him.

"A couple more questions, darlin', just for the record."

"Yes?"

"I heard you and Tim had a fight last week, and you punched him."

"I did not!"

Ray rubbed his chin, scraping over the rough of his whiskers and sending tingles up and down my spine. "Several people mentioned it to me earlier this week. You didn't mention it at all."

Okay, I could see how that might look bad. I scrambled to explain. "Tim and I were talking about zoning and aesthetics. I asked him why the paint on the historic buildings can be peeling but my storefront has to be pristine and why the board approved the modern money-making parking meters but frowned on my flashy modern cars." I realized I sounded resentful and stopped to take a deep breath. My father had taken a lot of heat from the town over the years about his "eyesore" garage. I often wondered if it had contributed to his fatal heart attack.

"We were standing in the front window of the showroom. I was pointing to the street, he was pointing, and then I bumped him. It was not a fight. It was a discussion. You know I'd never hit anyone."

Ray cocked an eyebrow.

I searched my memory. No, I was sure I had never hit him. Never, ever. I was not a violent person. "What?"

"You did wrestle your sister into the closet and leave her there for six hours."

I felt my face burn red. "She planned to go out and pick up another guy from another bar and get AIDS or something. I saved her from herself."

"She could have hyperventilated and died in there."

"Well, she didn't. And she forgave me. Besides, it was temporary insanity. You know me better than that."

Ray stared out the windshield. I wondered if he was recalling the time I ran over his toes.

He had pressured me for years to have a baby, though he'd known before we got married that I didn't plan to, fearing the child would be mentally ill like my sister and my mother. He told me we could face it. I told him I didn't want to. He said he loved me. I said not enough. After ten years of marriage and six years of tension, the ulcer in my stomach had eaten its way up to my heart, leaving a hole Ray couldn't fill. When Erica entered the psych center after her third suicide attempt, I'd had enough. I met Ray in the driveway with my suitcase one night and handed him the divorce papers. Then I leapt into my Porsche and tried to pull out of the driveway. I ran over his steel-toed shoes by accident when he tried to stop me. The next day I found the signed papers on my desk at work. He left a note that read "I've seen you show more respect for roadkill."

I decided to remain silent. Those were isolated and unfortunate incidents. He must realize Tim and I did not have the years of history behind us to generate such emotion. Of course, Ray knew the sports car boutique meant everything to me, since it used to be my father's auto repair garage. I wondered if he knew about the zoning board's grumblings that I should move my business from Main Street to a less visible location and about Tim's tacit agreement.

"Where were you last night?"

"Ray!" Crushed, I couldn't find the words to respond, nor could I believe how stunned I was to realize his opinion of me still meant so much.

He raised his hand to placate me. "I wouldn't be doing my job if I didn't ask and enter the information into the record."

I took a deep breath and a leap of faith that he still believed in me. "So you're going to handle the investigation?"

Ray shot me the look again. "Did you want Walter to do it?"

Although Walter Burnbaum was the Chief of Police, his primary service to our tiny community involved the collection of parking meter fees and writing the associated parking tickets. He did get to participate in a major statewide drug bust a few months ago. I think he drove the paddy wagon with a couple of the culprits inside. The village got a giggle out of his boasting, especially since rumor had it the scales his son kept in his bedroom were not for weighing justice.

"Of course not." I struggled to recall the prior evening, now faded in the light of recent events. "I left here at five, stopped for two slices and a salad at the pizzeria, and went home to watch HBO."

"What movie was on?"

"*Pride and Prejudice*."

"I know you love that."

He knew because we went to see it together for our anniversary, one of the last joyous times we spent together. He called me Mrs. Darcy for a week afterward. I smiled at the memory.

Ray leaned over and, for one wild moment, I thought he was going to kiss me. I smelled the sweet peppers on his breath. I closed my eyes. Nothing. I felt the rush of cold air as he pushed open my car door. I opened my eyes to find his face five inches from mine. He had that amused look in his eyes again.

I scrambled out of the car, my face hot with embarrassment, and said, "Thank you for the ride. And thank you for lunch." I was a very polite girl. I minded my manners even when I hoped the sidewalk would sink and drag me down into the center of the earth.

He tipped his imaginary hat and drove off toward the sunset.

I watched until his car disappeared, my lasagna churning in my stomach. A murder and a lunch date with Ray all in one day. It was a lot to process. At least Tim's death was in capable hands so I could grieve for him without concern for justice. But I had the uneasy feeling Ray might be back with more questions, questions I needed better answers to in order to stay off his suspect list. I couldn't just say "trust me" to this man I'd left after promising to stick with him through the good times and the bad.

And, after seeing Tim's dead body this morning, bad had taken on a whole new meaning.

THREE

THE PHONE RANG WHEN I entered the showroom. I grabbed the extension near the door.

"Ms. Asdale, Brennan Rowe here. Any word yet?"

Mr. Rowe had asked me to find him a special 1957 Mercedes-Benz 300SL roadster to add to his ample car collection. I'd heard a rumor one would appear on the auction block soon, a six-cylinder four-speed with tan exterior and green interior, in mint condition, just like he wanted. He called me daily now, lest I forget. He'd authorized me to bid as high as three quarters of a million dollars, including the bidder's premium. I wouldn't forget. I couldn't wait.

"Not yet, Mr. Rowe, but soon, I think."

"Leave no stone unturned, Ms. Asdale."

He didn't have to tell me that. For me, it wasn't the car. It was the thrill of the hunt. And the thrill of the bidding, just like at a Sotheby's auction. I now checked the auto auction house's website twice a day. I wanted to be the mysterious bidder phoning in the winning bid. I wanted the dollars I paid for premium cable access at home and in the office, the only access that provided the SPEED channel, to pay off for me big time. Mr. Rowe had promised me a five thousand dollar broker's fee. It wouldn't be as much of a thrill as being the bidder on Howard Hughes' 1953 Buick Roadmaster, which sold four years ago for $1.6 million at Barrett-Jackson's third annual Palm Beach auction, or the bidder on the 1966 Shelby Cobra 427 Super Snake, which sold at auction in January for a record-setting $5.5 million. But it was close enough for this small-town girl.

I checked my desk for messages, then strode into the shop. Cory's legs were sticking out from underneath a DeLorean DMC-12, identical to the one in the movie *Back to the Future*. Many car aficionados estimated six thousand DeLoreans, which began production in 1981 and ended shortly thereafter, still existed today. A few of us who shop the market on occasion knew for a fact how many were still on the road, but we were an exclusive club.

"Cory? Any messages?"

He dug his heels into the floor and rolled out from underneath the car on his mechanic's creeper. "All three of the television news channels called, asking for an on-camera interview. I made appointments for myself at three, four, and five o'clock. They're going to set up in the showroom by the Ferrari. This may be my big chance to get on Broadway."

"You're shittin' me."

"I am, but that's another dollar for the can. You sound like a garage monkey."

I had enlisted Cory to help me stop swearing by charging me a dollar each time I slipped. I'd learned to swear at the feet of the master—my dad, who had raised me from age twelve. Lately, Cory tended to encourage me. I suspected he was saving for a Ferrari of his own. "What did you really say?"

"No comment. No comment. No comment."

"Good. Thanks. Listen, can you assume your salesman look? I have to go see Erica. She's hearing voices again that say I'm in danger."

"Sure." Cory unzipped his navy coveralls and kicked them with precision onto the workbench three yards away. Now he wore tan chinos and a baby blue pinstriped dress shirt, untucked of course. He pulled the protective covers off his loafers and stripped the surgical gloves from his delicate hands. A long time ago he'd figured out the gloves were the best solution for keeping his hands pure white for the stage. Scrubbing with D & L hand cleaner and a nail brush daily had been murder.

"The caroling is at two, if you want to lock up for half an hour to join in." I knew no one would be shopping for cars at that time, and Cory had the purest tenor tones of any singer I knew. He'd put the paid cast to shame. Maybe someone would follow him back into the shop to compliment him and end up buying a car. I could use the cash. I had a sinking feeling the loan on the Ferrari would be outstanding for some time to come.

"Great. I wanted to check out the chestnuts."

With anybody else, I'd think free roasted nuts, but not Cory. "Okay, but no necking in the cars."

He lowered his chin. "Yes, Mommy."

I smiled so he wouldn't know the pain the nickname caused me and darted out the door.

It took forty-five minutes to reach the city and the psych center, even when I pressed the pedal of my black 1990 Porsche 944 S2 a little harder than the speed limit and the road conditions allowed. A smooth-riding car, the Porsche had been a graduation present from my father. He'd bought it from an insurance company after it had bounced off two trees and a Winnebago. He did the restoration work himself. I would've preferred a red 911, but he insisted this car would serve me well. So far, it had. It had inspired me to change the garage to a sports car boutique after his death, much more fitting for Wachobe's upscale image and its zoning board's vision, or at least so I'd thought at the time.

I made the turn onto the psych center's main drive. Erica resided on the fourth floor of the state facility—the tower as it was referred to. Sometimes she even thought she was Rapunzel. She had the long blonde hair for the role, but not the kind and gentle demeanor. Often, she was angry and demanding, alienating her peers. Always, she was incapable of holding a job, although able to obtain one during her manic periods. The telephone calls to her co-workers at all hours of the day and night usually did her in. Her compulsive spending sprees left her homeless, which was why Ray and I took her in. We could put up with her headstrong behavior, her massive collection of wine corks and bottle caps, the many nights we found her rutting on the couch with some loser, and her constant refusals to take her medication on the days she felt "good." What we couldn't take were the multiple suicide attempts which occurred, oddly enough, as her depression lifted and her activity levels increased.

The psych center tried medication, electroconvulsive therapy, and psychotherapy. None of them worked for long. She'd been in and out of here for three years now, long enough for me to know all of the staff on a very personal level. I believed Erica actually preferred living here now, and I sometimes wondered if her suicide attempts merely paved the way for her to return here after she'd struggled on the outside for a while, like a perpetual parole violator.

Tommye hugged me as I stepped off the elevator, and I smelled Chanel No. 5 and ... peanut butter. I released her squishy, comforting body and looked at her freckled brown face and warm chocolate eyes.

"Wheels, it's been too long."

Tears smarted in my eyes. "How is she?"

"I just gave her the dinner tray. She seems rational. She knows you're coming." Tommye and I walked in step down the hallway. "She kept asking me what time."

"I'm sorry it took me so long. I had quite a day."

"Want to talk about it?"

"No, but thanks." I knocked on Erica's door and swung it open. "I'll stop by on my way out."

Erica's walls were covered with pictures of butterflies cut from magazines and a few she'd drawn herself. I'd admired them until I learned she coveted their short life span. She wasn't in bed. Her half-eaten tray sat at the foot of it. I knocked on the closed bathroom door. No response.

"Erica? Hey, I'm here."

Still no response. I turned the knob. She wasn't in there. I bent down and looked under the bed. Nothing but dust bunnies. An ounce of my lasagna washed back up my throat, leaving a fiery trail. I headed down the hall to the recreation room, which held three other patients, a television, and a Ping-Pong table, but no Erica. When I asked if they'd seen her, they all shook their heads.

I jogged down the hall, looking in every room and startling one of the occupants into choking on his cherry Jell-O. I apologized profusely. I raced to the nurse's desk, where Tommye now stood.

"She's not in her room. She's not in the rec room either, or any of the other patients' rooms."

Tommye held up her index finger. "Did you check the broom closet? I caught her and Sam in there the other day, doing the wild thing."

"Who's Sam?"

"Samuel Green. He's a new patient. Good-looking boy, but a sociopath. Stabbed his mother in the hand when she tried to serve him pork chops."

Tommye hustled down the hall to find the closet empty.

"Okay, Wheels, now let's not panic. I'm going to check the floor again."

Ten minutes later, no Erica. Tommye sounded the alarm and the staff began a floor by floor search. It took an hour, and they didn't find her. They did notice Sam was missing too.

One hour after my arrival at the psych center, I conceded defeat and called Ray.

FOUR

Ray appeared at the psych center twenty minutes later. He interviewed the staff and the seventy-year-old retiree who passed for security at the front door, asked for a description of Sam, and disappeared outside to search around in the light snow that had begun minutes after I dialed his number.

I watched out the lobby windows. He returned ten minutes later and stamped snow off his shoes.

"I found two sets of tracks exiting the rear entrance and heading toward the woods. They ended roadside. Looks like maybe the two of them hitchhiked or arranged for a ride. I'm going to take the patrol car over to the neighborhood and knock on a few doors to see if I can find someone who witnessed them getting into a car."

"Should I come with you?"

He laid a comforting hand on my shoulder. "You've had enough excitement for one day. I'll call you as soon as I learn something."

I trudged into the elevator and got off at the fourth floor to collect my coat from the nurse's station. Tommye's shift had ended an hour ago, and she had left on time, eager to get home to the pot roast she left in her slow cooker and unfazed by yet another unscheduled release. The psych center had them at least once a week. One time I picked up a naked woman walking down the major roadway leading to the psych center drive. I returned her here. Where else could she have belonged?

In the car, I listened to the news, fearing I would hear about a daring Bonnie and Clyde robbery at the local 7-Eleven. Erica had robbed stores before when she was loose and manic, mostly shop-lifting food items. I didn't hear about any robberies. I did hear about Tim Lapham's murder and the scene of the crime—Asdale Auto Imports, owned by yours truly, who had "No comment." Cory must have fielded a few more phone calls in my absence. I clicked off the radio.

My cell phone rang. I swerved to the side of the road. Angry motorists honked as they swept past me, rocking the Porsche with their draft. It was against New York State law to drive and talk on the cell phone at the same time. Ray would be all over me if I got a ticket. Besides, I wanted to hear what he had to say.

It wasn't him. It was my best friend, Isabelle Branch. "Hi, Jolene. Where are you?"

"In my car."

"Are we on for lunch tomorrow?"

"I guess so." I gave her the short version of the untimely death of my ex-beau, Erica's great escape, and my reluctant reliance on Ray. As I articulated the situation, my shock and denial hit home, and my hand shook, bumping the phone against my cheek.

"Do you want me to come over?"

"No. I'm fine." I wasn't, but I could pretend with the best of them.

"Well, if you're sure. But call me right away if you need anything. I'll let you go now, but meet me tomorrow for lunch. Meantime, lock all your doors, and don't let Erica bring the sociopath into your apartment."

That would be hard to prevent. Erica shared my apartment during the periods when the doctors released her with their assurances she was fit for society. She had her own key and knew where I hid the spare.

I put the car in gear and traveled the next twenty miles in a haze of delayed post-traumatic stress, concerned for Tim's children now without a father, for the town with a killer on the loose, for Erica who had undoubtedly hooked up with another loser, and for what I'd lost with Ray. Selfishly, I also grieved for the loss of my peaceful life of work and home, where each day had blended into the next without much drama, rumor, or fanfare, all things I liked to avoid. This morning, it seemed as though the trumpeters had announced the arrival of a whole new era, one I feared would be my undoing. When I reached my driveway, I realized I couldn't remember looking at the road since Isabelle's call.

I called Cory at home to tell him about Erica and to thank him for locking up. He'd been with our family and the shop in both its incarnations for ten years. Nothing about my family surprised him.

I passed the evening watching SPEED-TV and trying to blot out Tim's face in death. I was unsuccessful. His twisted expression flashed over and over in my mind. I continued to wonder why anyone would want to kill such a nice man.

Ray called at ten o'clock. "Darlin', I can't find her. I need sleep. I'll try again tomorrow after Tim Lapham's autopsy."

I almost dropped the phone with that mental image. Instead, I clenched it in my hand to prevent myself from shaking again. "Okay. Thanks for trying." I hung up.

Erica had been missing more than she'd been present in the last three years. She would surface soon enough and the state would expect me to pay her bill to hold her room in the meantime. The dead man in my showroom, one I had dated however briefly, filled my thoughts as I put on my pajamas and lay down for the night.

Images of Tim's twisted face and blood-soaked body flashed before me again. The fact that he wore no coat bothered me. It had been below zero last night. He wouldn't have wandered out without one.

I felt sad for his family. I wondered if Walter or Ray had been the one to tell his wife, Becky, and how she took it. I should call her his ex-wife, but I knew Becky would probably still see herself as joined to him, just the way I felt about Ray and me.

I felt a little nervous about unlocking the shop tomorrow, dreading an encore. Why did the killer pick my sports car to dump the body? It couldn't have been an easy feat to carry Tim's dead weight into the showroom and set him inside the car.

Who did Dad give the alarm combination to? The alarm company didn't track activations and deactivations, but I knew the killer had to have turned off the alarm. I'd entered the code as always when I arrived at the shop this morning at nine forty-five.

My off-hours visitor had known the code, and I had no idea who it could be.

—

Sleep did not overtake my worries until around three a.m. Every creak in my house made me bolt upright in bed. Every scrape of a blowing tree limb sounded like an intruder breaking in. Around one a.m. it had occurred to me that the killer might have wanted to frame me or Cory for murder, but I couldn't think of any reason someone would want to do such a thing to me. And Cory, well, he was a lovable puppy. Everyone seemed to enjoy him.

In the morning, I wore jeans with a bright red turtleneck and a Christmas-tree-patterned cardigan to the shop, trying to cheer myself up. I avoided looking at the spot where Tim had last lain.

I tried to pay bills, but the balance in my account couldn't cover all of them. I spent twice as much time as usual running the numbers because of my lack of sleep and dire thoughts. Every noise in the building sent me rocketing out of my chair to investigate. I finally relaxed when I looked up to catch a handful of crime scene tourists peeking in my window and pointing to the Ferrari. Who would dare harm me with an audience?

My cell phone rang at eleven o'clock. I flipped the top open but didn't recognize the number.

"Ms. Asdale, Brennan Rowe. Any news yet?"

"Not yet. I checked the website this morning. It's still not scheduled for the block."

"Very well. I trust Tim Lapham's murder isn't going to put a crimp in our deal."

"Ah no, of course not. I'm right on top of things."

"Excellent. I'll call again tomorrow."

I started to remind him it really wasn't necessary to call me daily, but he hung up too fast. Then I wondered how he got my cell phone number. I certainly never gave it to him. And why would Tim's death put a crimp in our deal? Brennan Rowe was obsessed. After I got his car and my money, I hoped never to hear from him again. But in the back of my mind, I wondered if he'd heard the rumors of my fight with Tim and thought I might be the guilty party. I couldn't bid from behind bars, now could I?

At noon I rose, pushed in my chair, and put on my coat to cross the street to the Coachman Inn, a historic village landmark. The inn served breakfast, lunch, and dinner, operated paddle boat dinner cruises on the lake, and rented tastefully decorated rooms with comfy four-poster beds and gas fireplaces.

In the lamp-lit, pine-floored entryway, Isabelle threw her arms around me and hugged me in a rib-cracking embrace. She and I had roomed together for six years at college while we pursued our undergraduate and masters degrees in business. I loved her like the sister I never had. Effervescent. Sociable. Fun. Thank God she took a liking to me too. She'd even been brave enough never to question me about my mother's death and to stay at my house with Erica and my dad, who defined eccentric. She was also the only one in my life who never called me by a nickname. I liked to think that meant she took me seriously.

We had to wait a minute to be seated. Isabelle took our coats to the coatroom while I remained in the entry, glancing at the framed photographs of the lake scattered on the walls. A beautiful tall woman with long brown hair entered the restaurant and stopped dead, staring at me with recognition in her eyes. I gave her my best sales smile, uncertain if she was a customer's wife. She walked over and extended her hand to me.

"Catherine Thomas."

"Jolene Asdale." I didn't recognize the name or her face, but I shook her hand with my firm businesswoman grip. "I'm sorry. I can't place you."

Her eyes widened. She backed away. "My mistake. I thought you were my lunch date."

How awkward. I made a sympathetic face as though anyone could have made the same mistake, but when her real lunch date, a woman with blond hair and Botox lips, entered minutes later and they exchanged air kisses, I knew she'd lied. Isabelle reappeared as the hostess called for us.

I grabbed Isabelle's arm. "See that woman with the long brown hair by the door? Do you know her?"

Isabelle took a backward glance before following the hostess into the windowed dining room. "Nope, but did you see the rock on her finger? Gorgeous. Unusual setting. Looks like one we had in our jewelry store a few months back. The one…" Isabelle shoved me into the seat facing the rear of the room so she could face the entryway.

"Hey!"

"Why are you asking me about her?"

"She acted like she knew me and seemed surprised I didn't know her."

Isabelle leaned out of the booth to watch as the hostess seated Catherine Thomas diagonally across the room from us.

Isabelle tapped my fingertips with hers. "I have a bad feeling."

"What do you mean?" My stomach did a little flip-flop.

"I wasn't in the store the day the ring sold, but one of the clerks said a large, good-looking man bought it, a man in jeans and a Meatloaf T-shirt."

A man fitting Ray's off-duty description. I swiveled in my seat to look at Catherine Thomas and caught her looking right back at me. I jerked my face away. "Isabelle, does she bear any resemblance to Valerie Bertinelli? Tell me the truth."

Isabelle didn't even bother to look at Catherine again. "Yes. And I remember something else the man told the clerk."

"What?"

"The clerk asked him if he was planning to propose. The man said, 'For now, it's a reward for time served.'"

I digested her statement in silence. Well, okay, then. I snapped open my menu, the tremor in my hands rendering it unreadable.

Isabelle pulled the menu down onto the table. "You don't want to talk about this?"

"I do not. We're here to talk about advertising, remember?" Isabelle owned an advertising agency in the city. Her husband, Jack, owned a jewelry store, which was why Isabelle attracted attention wherever she went. Only the best gems would do for Jack's queen. Today she wore a white gold and pearl necklace to die for, with matching earrings and bracelet, of course. Isabelle's flat face and mousy brown hair tended toward homely, but with the jewels and a swipe of makeup, she was radiant. Needless to say, both she and her husband understood about catering to the finer tastes in life, too.

"Okay." Isabelle proceeded to fill the air with talk of demographics and quarter-page ads, thirty-second television commercials, and website presence. I heard almost none of it, instead picturing Ray on his knees in his favorite twenty-year-old Meatloaf

T-shirt, sliding that rock onto Catherine Thomas' finger. And worse, me admitting to him I'd never returned the signed divorce papers to my attorney for filing. Technically, we're still married. Honestly, I hadn't returned them on purpose. Even though we had irreconcilable differences, I wasn't quite ready to scoop up the road kill and incinerate it. And I certainly didn't want to be rushed.

Halfway through lunch, Isabelle stopped talking advertising and started to tell me about all the cute things her three-year-old daughter, my godchild, had been doing. I nodded and smiled, hopefully on cue, but I couldn't get my mind off Ray and this mystery woman. When we left the restaurant, I almost paid the wrong check, because I couldn't recall what we had ordered for lunch.

"You didn't hear a thing I said." Isabelle tucked her arm through mine as we crossed the street toward the band gazebo to hear the Dickens choral concert.

"I'm sorry. I'm going to do whatever advertising you think best. You decide and let me know."

"Okay, but I prefer to make joint decisions."

"Objection noted."

"Are you sure you don't want to talk about Ray? You've obviously been thinking of nothing else."

I squeezed her arm to let her know I appreciated her concern. She knew I wouldn't talk to her about him. Ray was my first best friend. I never talked about him with anybody. It would be disloyal, even now.

"What about filling me in on Tim Lapham's murder?"

Now that I could do. As we sat on a park bench and waited for the concert to start, I told Isabelle everything I knew. It didn't take long.

She gazed out toward the expanse of the lake, which glistened in the afternoon sunlight, and a waft of cold air blew strands of hair across her face. She swiped them back into place. "I can't figure out why anyone would go to the trouble of placing him inside your car."

"Me neither."

"Do you think it's a warning of some kind? The old horse-head-in-your-bed? You do have some customers in that line of work."

The thought hadn't occurred to me. Brennan Rowe came to mind now. He owned a construction company that built most of the new cottages on the lake, and people were forever making jokes about what he might be hiding in the foundations.

"I can't imagine what this body could be warning me about. Selling cars? Dating divorced men? Not changing my alarm code?"

"Okay. Well, your showroom is right in the center of the village. Maybe it's a warning to someone else. A see-what-I-can-get-away-with kind of thing."

"Maybe."

"Who did you acquire the car for?"

"I thought Mr. Hughes would like it, but he hasn't committed. It's not likely he will now."

"Well, he's certainly got the bucks." Isabelle did his advertising.

I didn't reply because the Dickens cast converged on the white-painted and garland-draped gazebo from all sides in a blur of red, green, and gold costumes, singing "We Wish You a Merry Christmas" and drowning out any possibility of further conversation. As we sat through all six of their numbers, I pondered Isabelle's ideas.

Only Cory and I knew that I'd purchased the Ferrari with Mr. Hughes in mind. I hadn't told anyone about his ten a.m. appointment. But maybe Mr. Hughes had. He had been ruffling a lot of feathers lately with the notion he was looking for a lot in Wachobe to build one of his nationally acclaimed grocery stores on. Tim had been on the planning board, which would have to give building approval for the store. They had denied Mr. Hughes' petition once. Could that be the reason for Tim's murder?

My cell phone vibrated. I pulled it out and walked away from the concert to answer.

"Darlin', a convenience store between Wachobe and the psych center was robbed last night by two individuals wearing ski masks. I saw the security camera footage. I'd like you to tell me if you think Erica is one of them. Can I pick you up?"

"I'm at the gazebo concert with Isabelle."

"I'll be there in ten."

FIVE

Isabelle hugged me goodbye and wiggled her fingers at Ray through the windshield of his cruiser when he pulled up to the curb. He gave her only a curt nod in reply, which should have concerned me because Ray loved Isabelle. But I wasn't thinking of anyone but Erica when I hopped into the front seat of the car. I did draw a few suspicious stares from the choral crowd still lingering in the park. Maybe they didn't know criminals don't get to ride in the front seat. Or maybe some of them had heard the rumor about my fight with Tim. I pushed the thought from my mind and tried not to look guilty.

Ray made a U-turn right in the middle of Main Street. Nobody dared to honk at him, but I could see a few other motorists shaking their heads in disgust. I slid a little lower in the seat.

"The camera in the parking lot of the store shows a Lincoln pulling up. Two passengers got out at the store; a third remained in the driver's seat. I couldn't make out any of the driver's features and the license plate is caked with road spray. I think it's a black

Lincoln, although the video is black and white, so it might be another dark color. Know anyone who drives a Lincoln?"

"Not off the top of my head."

"All right. You can look at the video and tell me what you see."

We drove the rest of the miles to the convenience store in silence. I felt acutely uncomfortable for three main reasons: my sister was a suspected felon; my husband was engaged to another woman; and until Tim's death, I hadn't spent this much time with Ray during the last three years.

For the first six months after I left him, if I spied his patrol car coming my way, I'd dart into the nearest store or hop behind a tree. That ended when he called me to ask about the house. My father had left the family home to me, so I'd actually left Ray and my house. Ray called to ask if I wanted him to move out. But I couldn't live there—too many memories of him, not to mention the ones of Erica lying in the bathtub naked with her wrists dripping blood onto the ceramic tile and my mom in the garage. Anyway, I told him he could stay if he wanted to pay the utilities and keep up the yard. He did.

After that, we'd run into each other on occasion and exchange awkward pleasantries or he'd call me to ask if I thought it was time to repaint the trim or the wrought-iron fence surrounding the property. I'd go over to look, but I could never quite meet his eyes, although he had no trouble fixing his on mine. And I had to call him a year ago when Erica released herself from the psych center the first time. I found her sitting in my living room three days later with a bloody lip and a black eye. She'd tried to turn a trick and gotten beaten up in the process. I called Ray to file a report and also to take her back to the psych center. She was always more cooperative for Ray.

But Ray's company hadn't been too hard to take the last two days. It almost felt like we were still married, except for the image of Catherine Thomas with her legs wrapped around him that kept pushing its way into my mind.

Ray pulled into the parking lot of the 7-Eleven and parked at the edge of the building. "Let's go."

I slid out of the front seat and followed him inside, the smells of burnt coffee, roasting hot dogs, and B.O. assailing my nose. I slipped and almost took a nosedive on the slush-covered tile floor, wrenching my back as I struggled to recover my balance. A swarthy man behind the counter looked up as we approached.

"Abigail, can you come watch the counter, please?"

A young woman with a silver nose ring, brush cut, and spiky eyelashes appeared, her frayed pant hems mopping the slush puddles as she approached and passed me. She had a vibrant tattoo of an eagle on the back of her neck, and her belly had a telltale mound to it, her ring finger noticeably bare. I wondered exactly how old she was. She took up the position next to the cash register, and the man, whose name tag said Bobby, led us into the storeroom.

"Bobby, can you show Jolene the video, please?"

Bobby patted a ripped black vinyl chair in front of a thirteen-inch television. I sat, realizing the B.O. scent emanated from him. Ray's cell phone rang and he flipped it open, moving away from us. Bobby pressed a couple of buttons and the grainy video filled the screen.

Two individuals wearing camouflage hunting outfits and lighter-colored solid ski masks entered the store. They toured the aisles separately before making their way to the counter where Bobby stood waiting. The front of the taller one's jacket bulged forward as though maybe hiding a pointed gun. Bobby rapidly emptied the cash drawer into a shopping bag and held the handles out to the taller one. Both of them turned tail and ran. Bobby then picked up the phone and started dialing.

Ray snapped his phone shut and returned to my side. "What do you think?"

"It could be anybody. I couldn't see enough to recognize her walk or anything. And the insulated suits mask their weight."

"All right. Bobby, I'll take the tape with me this time."

I followed Ray out of the store and climbed into his car, feeling both relieved and disappointed. Relieved we couldn't pin this one on Erica, not yet anyway, but disappointed not to have a lead as to her whereabouts. "Is that your only lead on Erica?"

"So far." Ray pulled out of the lot and gunned the engine. "Do you know a guy named Fitzgerald Simpson, a.k.a. the Beak?"

"The Beak?" I laughed nervously. "Was he the driver of the getaway car?"

"No. He's the guy who left his fingerprints in your Ferrari. At least one fingerprint."

"Where?"

"On the inside of the driver's door. It's the only clear print we found in the car."

"I never heard of him." I knew Cory had detailed the car after it arrived at our shop, so any fingerprint on it should be new. But if Cory had done the job while watching his favorite soap, *The Young and the Restless*, he might have overlooked a spot or two. Cory had a thing for older, distinguished-looking men with power, and the guy who played Victor Newman on the show for a quarter century held his undivided attention for one hour every weekday.

"Simpson's wanted in Arizona for assault with a deadly weapon. He's also got a rap sheet that includes attempted robbery, bribery, and a ten-year prison stint."

I preferred to think Cory missed the print. "Cory detailed the car, but maybe he didn't wipe that area."

"Maybe. Who'd you buy the car from?"

"A collector in Arizona. No one special."

"His name, darlin'. I need his name."

"I don't remember. I didn't meet him. I conducted business with his chauffeur. I've got the owner's name on the paperwork at home, though."

"Let's go pick it up."

When Ray pulled into my driveway, it occurred to me I had never invited him here before today, but he knew I lived in this particular 1870 white Victorian on Wells Street. Just one more of the many things he knew.

I unlocked my apartment's front door and smelled food. Food I hadn't cooked. Food I hadn't eaten. I kept those thoughts to myself as I darted across the oak floor and the gold and maroon Oriental carpet to my rolltop desk, shuffled through my file drawer, and pulled out the name of the Ferrari's previous owner. I copied it onto a piece of paper to hand to Ray, while surreptitiously surveying my living room. The white couches and floral-patterned accent chairs looked the same as when I left this morning, but I thought I smelled coffee and a whiff of cigarettes. Erica had been known to take a drag now and then when I wasn't looking.

"Thanks. Do I smell coffee?" He headed toward the kitchen, slipping his jacket off his shoulders as though he intended to stay awhile.

I chased after him and froze in the doorway.

My kitchen cabinets were still white. My countertops were still blue. But my Pfaltzgraff dishes were no longer stacked neatly behind the glass cabinet doors, and my CorningWare was not hidden away in the cupboard. It sat crusted with yellow gunk on my stovetop, my kitchen table covered with bowls of half-eaten macaroni and cheese, plates with torn bread crusts, and cups of coffee, including one with a big lipstick imprint in Erica's signature color—cotton candy pink. I counted. Four bowls, four plates, and four cups.

I stepped into the kitchen and spotted my spare key on the corner of the counter nearest the back door. Erica, Sam, the driver, and someone else? The wild card factor. I looked at Ray, whose eyes were still glued to the table.

"Did you have guests for lunch, Jolene?"

"No. It must have been Erica and her friends."

"You didn't have lunch with her?"

"No. I had lunch with Isabelle. You know that."

His expression softened a little. I had him there.

Ray set his jacket on the back of a chair. "Have you seen her since she left the psych center, Jolene?"

"No."

"Aiding and abetting a felon is a serious crime, whether they're mental patients or not."

I couldn't believe my ears. "I know that, Ray. But you don't even know for sure Erica was involved in the robbery at the 7-Eleven. You're just assuming it was her."

"I'm considering her history and looking at all the possibilities." Ray stood with his feet shoulder-width apart and his arms folded across his chest, his most intimidating deputy sheriff pose. "I need to ask you a few more questions about Tim Lapham."

"Okay." I was thrilled with the change of topic since I didn't like his accusatory tone with regard to the last one.

"Becky says you and Tim went to Vegas together over Columbus Day weekend."

I gasped. "We did not."

"I checked with the airline. You were both booked on the same flight for Chicago."

"I went on to Arizona ... to look at the Ferrari."

"Did you see Tim on the flight?"

"No, but it was full. I was one of the last people to board and someone had already grabbed my seat. I had to get the flight attendant to oust the guy."

Ray's eyes were locked on my face. I couldn't read his expression. He was too good at his job. Good cop, bad cop, whatever-you-need-me-to-be cop. After a minute-long staring contest, I started to fidget. "Are you doubting me, Ray?"

He relaxed his arms and picked up his jacket. "I'm doing my job, Jolene. My job is to ask all the questions. Becky's statement brings a lot of questions to mind, especially coupled with the scene between Tim and you over the zoning board issue."

I felt a lump form in my throat. "You are doubting me."

He slid his jacket over his shoulders, the shoulders I had rubbed for him almost every day for ten years. "I'm asking the questions; that's all, Jolene."

"I am ... I *was* your wife, Ray. You shouldn't have to ask those questions."

His eyes met mine again. "I wouldn't be the first guy who found out the woman he married wasn't the person he thought she was."

I parted my lips to reply, but the huge swelling in my throat prevented me.

Ray walked out the door.

It took me all of a minute to pick up the phone and call my lawyer.

SIX

Cooler heads would prevail. Greg Doran was the best lawyer in town, maybe even in the Finger Lakes region. I found his words somewhat reassuring, although I could sense his amusement over the phone wires.

"Jo, you're not a suspect. Ray's just doing his job. Have you ever given him any reason to doubt your honesty?"

I supposed it would be safe to confess to Greg that I did cover up for Erica after she helped rob a mom and pop movie theater twelve years ago, but I didn't. I'd confessed it to Ray before we got married, including the fact that I reimbursed the theater anonymously, so he'd know what kind of a girl he was throwing his lot in with. He didn't seem too concerned at the time, but I suspected it had been in the back of his mind today.

"But why did the killer put Tim Lapham in my Ferrari?" I was an innocent bystander. Why drag me into it, unless the rumored argument with Tim made me a likely suspect? I shivered.

"I didn't know Tim personally," Greg said. "I'd only be guessing, but I'm absolutely positive Ray does not think you're involved in Tim's death. If he does arrest you, *then* call me right away."

"Okay." I curled the phone cord around my fingers and took a deep breath. "You know the paperwork for our divorce?"

"Yes." Greg's voice was soft now.

"It still needs to be filed, right? Before we're officially divorced? I mean, technically, we're still married right now, correct?"

"Correct."

The muscles in my stomach tightened and I felt like I might throw up. "Maybe it's time to file it."

Silence filled the line.

"Greg?"

"I'm here, Jolene. Why now?"

This confession was hardest of all. "I think Ray asked someone to marry him."

"He did not."

My hackles rose. "How do you know?"

"Because I know Ray. He would never do that while he's still married to you."

"But he signed the papers three years ago when I left him. He doesn't think we're still married."

"Jo, Ray knows you're still married."

"How do you know? Have you talked to him about it?"

"I don't need to talk to him about it, Jo. It's Ray. He knows the law. Why don't you think about it a few more days—maybe even talk to him about it, eh?"

I hung up the phone feeling unsettled, mostly because Greg had to hammer the truth into me. Ray did know everything, and I didn't have the guts to talk to him about it. I would have to talk about my feelings, which was always hard for me. Of course, my role models had been two parents whose idea of sharing their feelings was saying "I love you" when they tucked me in bed at night.

The need to know more about Catherine Thomas ate at me. I pulled up the white pages on the Internet and set out to locate Catherine Thomas' den. I was pretty certain she didn't live in Wachobe—the townsfolk would have never overlooked her with Ray and missed the opportunity to fill me in. I checked the city west of us. Nothing. Then I checked to the east. Bingo. The listing indicated she was a criminal lawyer. That made sense to me. Ray spent plenty of time testifying in court. Undoubtedly, that was where they'd met. But how would I ask him if he needed me to finalize our divorce in order to marry her? Maybe sometime during his next interrogation of me would be a good time?

I decided to do what any sensible, mature woman would do under the circumstances.

I baked chocolate chip cookies.

While they baked, I washed my CorningWare and my plain white dishes and put them back in their cupboards. While the cookies cooled, I walked the four blocks to the shop to pick up my car and to buy a fancy box from the gift shop two doors over. Then I went home, loaded the cookies into the box, drove over to Becky Lapham's house, and knocked on the door to express my condolences in person—and ask her what the hell she was thinking when she told Ray I went to Vegas with Tim.

Little Emma answered my knock and all my determination left me. She was a tiny thing, all blue eyes and blond curls in a denim jumper and white tights. Very China-doll-like.

"Hi Emma, I'm Jolene Asdale. Do you remember me?" I met her once at the park with her mother, before Tim and I dated.

She shook her head and started to close the door.

"Wait! I brought you some cookies. Chocolate chip. Is your mother home?"

The door swung open wide. I stepped inside as Emma ran down the hallway screaming, "Mama. Mama."

Becky Lapham appeared with both Emma and Mark hiding behind her. She wore black pants and a black turtleneck. I realized I should have changed out of my colorful Christmas ensemble. I wrapped my black coat around me and hoped she'd forget her manners. She didn't.

"Jolene, how good of you to come. Let me take your coat."

I looked around for somewhere to set the box of cookies and decided to hand them to Mark, a handsome blond boy who came up to my chin. He accepted them and dashed down the hall with Emma in hot pursuit.

"Kids, what do you say to Ms. Asdale?"

"Thank you" floated out of the kitchen in stereo.

Becky took my hand and led me into the living room where I perched beside her on the olive camel-back sofa. "Really, it was good of you to come."

"I wanted to tell you how sorry I am about Tim. If there's anything I can do for you or the kids ..." I'm not very good at these types of social situations, or social situations in general. I only knew Becky slightly. She'd been two years behind me in high school, as had Tim. Tim had been my younger man. But Becky and I shopped at the same stores, so we chatted on occasion.

She tipped her head in acknowledgment and squeezed my hand. "No, there's really nothing. I spoke to Bill Young at the funeral home. Tim's funeral is tomorrow at ten a.m. My parents are flying in from Florida today. They'll be here by five. It's all been quite a shock, but the kids seem to be handling it well. It's not as though they got to see Tim every day."

I nodded in a way I hoped would seem understanding.

Becky continued, "It's weird. You're one of the few people who have come to visit except for the next-door neighbors. I got a few phone calls. I don't know if it's the fact we're divorced or the fact Tim was murdered that's keeping people away. Even at church this morning, no one had much to say to us, not that they ever do." She released my hand and raised her hand in the air as she shrugged. "I guess I don't blame them. I'm not sure how to handle it all either. I'm not his wife anymore."

"No, but you're the mother of his children."

"True. His parents are too ill to travel, so it will just be my family at the funeral."

"Cory and I will be there."

"Thanks. Ray told me you found Tim in a car in your shop, just sitting there?"

I wondered how much Ray told her and kicked myself for not asking him. "Yes. I have no idea how Tim got there. The alarm was on when I unlocked the doors."

"It's bizarre. I can't imagine who would have wanted to harm Tim. I keep thinking it had to be someone from the city who craved the sensationalism and thought we were too backwater to catch him."

Wachobe wasn't the boondocks. With the amount of money and people cruising through this area, we had everything a city had, just on a smaller scale. But Becky's guess was as good as mine at this point.

Becky tipped her head to listen to the laughter coming from the kitchen. "Sounds like they're enjoying your cookies."

She leapt to her feet. "I'm sorry. Can I get you something to drink or maybe snag one of the cookies for you?"

"No, thanks. I just wanted to stop by and express my condolences. I don't want to keep you." As I said this, I knew I should stand and say my goodbyes. Thankfully, when I didn't, Becky sank back onto the sofa beside me so I could pose the question pressing on my mind. "I wanted to ask you about something Ray said."

"Sure. What is it?"

"Ray said you thought Tim and I went to Vegas together over Columbus Day weekend. We didn't. I wondered where you'd gotten the idea we had."

Becky's face burned red. "I'm so embarrassed. I repeated what Tim told me. He must have lied to me." Her brow furrowed and she wrung her hands. "I can't imagine why he would lie to me, though." After a moment, her face brightened. "Except he knows I've always liked you. Maybe he went with someone else I wouldn't have approved of?"

"Maybe. He never mentioned anyone else to me, but we only had five dates. I don't feel like I knew him well."

Becky let out a nervous giggle. "We were married for eight years, and I don't feel like I knew him well either."

"Really?" I found it comforting to know someone else had unresolved marital issues. Some divorcees were alarmingly clear about the faults of the men they referred to as their rat-bastard ex-husbands. I, on the other hand, could fault Ray for only one thing, trying to push me into doing something I didn't want to do. Try as I might, I couldn't hate him for that.

Becky smoothed an imaginary crease from her pants. "Really. Tim was secretive. He went out every once in a while without telling me where he was going, and he didn't like it when I questioned him when he came home. He didn't talk to me very much. It drove us apart. That, and all the hours he worked. And his bowling. He never wanted to miss bowling, even when it fell on the night of our anniversary. For me, that was the final straw." Becky's voice broke and tears streamed down her cheeks. "Look at me, speaking ill of the dead. What kind of a person am I?"

Becky began to sob in earnest. I held her hand and passed her a few tissues, wishing I could do more. She pulled herself together after a couple of minutes and apologized.

"Don't be sorry, Becky. You've had a huge shock." I rose to my feet. "Please call me if I can do anything for you or the kids. I'd be happy to help out in any way."

"Thanks, Jolene. It's good to know I still have one friend."

As I backed out of her driveway, I pondered her statement. Where were all the people she called friends? She'd been a quiet girl in high school, but likeable. I knew she hung out with Sally Winslow and Chrissy Martin. Why weren't they at her house now, holding her hand instead of me? They all had kids the same age and went to the same church. Had Tim's murder tainted their family forever, like my mother's suicide had tainted mine? I hoped not. Tim's children were too young to have to suffer the stares and whispers until they could graduate from high school and run off to hide in college. Maybe they'd just become thick-skinned like me and not worry about what other people thought anymore.

At least, I'd never worried before. Today, I was a little worried.

I'd never been implicated in a murder before.

SEVEN

I CALLED CORY AS soon as I got home to let him know I'd committed him to appearing at the funeral. And I did mean appearing. He got all excited about picking out the correct wardrobe and rehearsing his lines. He'd come across as Tim's oldest and closest friend, I had no doubt. But Becky would also feel better after she'd seen Cory. He had the gift.

"Cory, I have to ask you about the Ferrari."

"I'll clean it up. Don't worry, Jo."

"Thanks, but that's not my question. Ray said they found a fingerprint on the interior of the driver's door. A fingerprint belonging to a guy known to reside in Arizona." I kept his name to myself. I wasn't sure if what Ray told me had been in confidence or not.

"I could've missed a spot. The car was so clean when it arrived that I didn't worry too much about it."

I hung up, relieved that the Beak probably wasn't wandering around our heretofore unsuspecting village but frustrated since we didn't have a clue as to who killed Tim.

I warmed to Becky's idea of an outsider looking to make a big splash in the newspapers. For all I knew, someone had been following me around for weeks, waiting for the right opportunity to learn my alarm code. All he would have needed was patience and a pair of binoculars. He would have looked like any other tourist surveying the lake as he spied on me through the showroom window.

I wanted to talk to Ray again and vindicate myself of the Vegas accusation as well as feel him out about Catherine. I knew where to find him. The annual Christmas tree lighting festival started at seven p.m. in the park. Ever since we were sixteen, Ray and I went to the ceremony together. Actually, the last three years we'd arrived separately and ended up standing together without talking much, but still, together. It was our tradition.

At a quarter to seven, I put on my black wool coat and my black leather gloves lined with rabbit fur, left my apartment, and walked the three blocks to the park, which was blanketed with fresh powder. It was also full of children giggling and darting between the legs of chatting adults and the smells of hot chocolate, roasted chestnuts, and popcorn. Salivating like Pavlov's dog, I took up a position at the end of the hot chocolate line. The two women in front of me turned around.

"Oh, Jolene. There you are. How are you, you poor thing?"

Celeste's blond curls were partially hidden by a pale blue wool beret. I knew the model in Talbots' storefront window sported the same one, and Celeste had the matching scarf and gloves as well. Her companion, Mindy something, had on the same set in pale pink. All frightfully fashionable, especially blended with their perfectly made-up faces. I plucked a stray hair off the sleeve of my coat and formed a polite response.

"I'm fine, Celeste. How are you?"

"Shocked. We can't believe the news about Tim Lapham's murder. And to find him in your showroom" —Celeste's voice rose an octave as she held the "ooom" in room and I realized she'd attracted the attention of the crowd around us— "you must be devastated."

"I'm very sad for Tim's family. I'm sure the rest of the village is, too." With my peripheral vision, I saw a few of the older women nod and turn away. The rest of the crowd averted their eyes as though avoiding a train wreck.

"Oh, yes, of course." Celeste leaned in to my ear. "Who does Ray think did him in?"

"I really can't say." I meant I didn't know, but Celeste grabbed my forearm as though she thought I meant I knew but couldn't share.

"Was it his wife?"

"No."

"His partner?"

I tried to extract my arm from her grasp. "No."

"Did Ray ask you about the fight you had with Tim?"

"Celeste!"

She had enough sense to look embarrassed but not enough to stop talking. "But it was someone from here, right? Or is Ray looking for a drifter?"

"Celeste, I have no idea who killed Tim. I don't think Ray has a suspect identified yet either." Unless it was me and he just wasn't saying so.

Mindy tugged on Celeste's sleeve as the line moved forward, saving me from further inquisition.

I got my hot chocolate and moved as far away from Celeste and Mindy as possible. Christmas was still my favorite time of year—the wreaths with red velvet bows, the evergreen scent, the sparkling white lights, and the atmosphere of goodwill toward man—even though it hadn't always brought me good cheer. I wasn't going to let a gossip monger like Celeste ruin it.

As I sipped, I scanned the crowd, looking for Ray. He was always easy to spot, standing at least a head taller than any other person. I didn't see him. As the carolers converged on the gazebo from all sides, singing "Oh, Christmas Tree," I tried to join in the festivities, oohing and aahing as the tree lights flashed on and cheering as jolly Father Christmas rang his bells and ho ho ho'd his way through the townspeople, passing out candy canes to the little ones.

But I felt abandoned as the high school orchestra played "Silent Night" to close the celebration and Ray did not appear.

I longed for his presence behind me and the feel of his breath on my hair. Somehow this night felt worse than the day I left him, maybe because this time he had rejected me. I tried to tell myself to be patient, rationalizing that he'd received an important call or was following up a lead on Tim's death or Erica's escape, but even as I did, nagging doubts said, "he thinks you hid Erica and her merry robber band," and, "he thinks you know something about Tim's death," or worse, "he thinks you killed Tim." And for some unfathomable reason, I felt guilty, guilty, guilty, even though I was innocent. I blinked back my tears.

A hand grabbed my arm. Relieved, I turned.

My disappointment must have shown on my face, because Cory snapped his head back in surprise. "Did I do something wrong?"

"No, I thought you were Ray."

"I haven't seen him." Cory scanned the crowd. "I was on the other side until I saw you. Did he say he was going to meet you here?"

I shook my head.

Cory knew about our standing date. I didn't have to tell him I was devastated. "Jo, you know he's investigating a murder and a robbery, and he's on the lookout for Erica. I don't think he's ever been this busy before."

True. I didn't remember anyone ever being murdered in our village, the town encompassing it, the nearby townships, nor even in Ray's larger territory beyond. Only the nearby cities had that kind of action. All our deaths had been accidental, if drinking and driving still fell in the accident category. And armed robbery? Well, no, I didn't remember anything like that either. Usually it was a bike "borrowed" from one kid's backyard and found in another's or a television that jogged down the street on its own. Ray spent most of his time on domestic disputes, motor vehicle issues, and drugs. Drugs pervaded every corner of the world, even our picture postcard village.

Cory was right. The investigation neared the close of the first forty-eight hours, and, as far as I knew, Ray didn't have a clue as to who did it. Everyone knew the first two days were the crucial period in any murder investigation. I gave myself a mental kick in the pants.

"You're right. I'm being self-centered and selfish. He's doing his job, and helping me in the process, I'm sure."

The crowd began to leave. Cory seemed to be exchanging looks with one of the Dickens cast, a tall, fortyish man with graying hair and a flowing moustache, before he turned back to me. "Did you drive the Porsche?"

"No. I walked."

Cory glanced at the man again, who appeared to be waiting for him as the rest of the cast dispersed. "Do you want me to walk you home?"

"No, thanks. You go ahead with your plans."

Cory smiled in relief. "Okay. I'll see you Tuesday." He sauntered across the park and spoke briefly with the Dickens man. The two of them took off down the sidewalk.

I realized I was alone in the park with the brightly lit Christmas tree.

Alone and incredibly sad.

EIGHT

I WALKED HOME, WAVING to the occasional neighbor's car as it passed. Walter rolled by in his patrol car and waved as well, most likely on the prowl for hooligan teenagers who had attended the tree lighting ceremony without their parents. I think most of the families had rushed home to bed, given it was a school night. I took my time, becoming more determined with each step.

I had to talk to Ray, not just about the Vegas misunderstanding or Erica's whereabouts or even Tim's death. I had to talk to him about our marriage, however painful the conversation might be. Why hadn't he said anything during the last three years about the fact we were still married? Was he as ambivalent about our divorce as I was? Did he find it as difficult as I did to admit failure? Was he holding out the same hope we would still live happily ever after? Or had he moved on to the arms of Catherine Thomas, while waiting for me to act responsibly and file the papers? After all, I had handed the papers to him, not the other way around. But he had signed them, although he'd never once said he didn't want to be married to me anymore, just that he wanted a baby. Our baby, the mix of his chemistry and mine. The mix I feared the most. Ray just didn't understand what it was like to feel responsible for someone who struggled as much as my sister, or how difficult it was to share her pain.

A fresh set of car tracks greeted me in the driveway. I froze, checking my windows for lights or a flip of a curtain and fearing Erica had come home to roost with her sociopath in tow. Nothing caught my eye, so I proceeded onto the front steps and turned the key in the lock. My home was silent and dark, as it is every night. I checked under the beds and in the closets anyway. I often did now that I lived alone. Someone must have used my driveway as a turnaround, because I saw no sign of a visitor.

My thoughts churned as I removed my contacts and left them to soak. Had Erica really robbed a convenience store at gunpoint? Would she be put in prison? Or permanently relocated to a prison-like mental facility? That might relieve my financial burden but not my familial burden. And I would miss her. I'd been pretty much her mother since she was seven and I was twelve. She still had days when she acted like she did before the onslaught of her illness. Erica wasn't so bad to live with on her good days. It was the bad days that made me feel like I had failed her as a surrogate mother, quelling any scrap of desire to attempt motherhood.

My doorbell rang, startling me as I was slipping my nightshirt over my head. I didn't get many callers, especially this time of night. It had to be Erica. Would she be beaten and broken again this time?

It was Ray. I regretted wearing my ratty thermal nightshirt now. My high beams flicked on in response to the cold draft of air flowing into the house behind him. Goose bumps raised the hairs on my unshaven legs as I crossed my arms over my chest and waited for him to speak.

He was not in uniform, but in jeans that hugged his sexy butt and muscular thighs. God, I used to love just following the man through the grocery store, taking in that view. He shrugged his leather jacket off and tossed it onto the back of my wingback chair before dropping onto the couch. "We need to talk."

"Yes." I curled up on the chair across from him, pulling my nightshirt over my knees and down to my ankles for both warmth and protection.

"A corner store on the outskirts of the city was robbed around five. According to reports, the store has videotape of two suspects. Same camouflage outfits. But this time the store manager said both robbers spoke and one was a woman. The store's parking lot camera was broken so I don't know if these two were riding in a Lincoln with someone else or not, but it looks like the same two as the 7-Eleven robbery.

"This store's out of my jurisdiction. The state police have been called in. If it's Erica, she's in serious trouble.

"One last time—do you know where she is?"

"No."

"All right." He looked down at his hands, which were clasped in front of him almost in a prayer position. "Second thing we need to talk about—" His gaze darted to the right and he raised his eyebrows. "Is that a mouse?"

In a flash, I was standing on top of the chair seat. "Where?"

He looked me up and down, then stared pointedly at my legs. I glanced down and realized I had raised the hem of my nightshirt reflexively from my calves to above my knees, trying to keep the little bugger from climbing my clothing.

"You know how I feel about mice. They're little and hairy and dirty and sneaky and... and... have beady eyes. Where is it? Get rid of it! *Get rid of it*!"

"All right. Settle down. It's in the corner, hiding. It's more afraid of you than you are of it." He looked me up and down again. "In theory, anyway." He headed for the kitchen.

I saw the tiny gray breathing ball crouched in the corner of the living room, hiding in the shadows inches from the edge of the lamp light. Its whiskers twitched and it appeared to be chewing on an elbow macaroni, probably from Erica's feeding frenzy earlier today. She probably left the door open while she carried in the groceries, leaving a trail of bread crumbs, no doubt. Let's just bring all the vermin in through my doors. "Uh, you're going to leave me here alone with it?" My voice squeaked.

"I'll be right back. I'm going to get a container or a bag to trap it in. You can come with me if you want."

Ray disappeared through the door as I assessed the possibility of jumping from the chair to the couch, which was closer to the kitchen. I didn't think I could bridge the gap between the chair and the couch without falling into the great divide and leaving me open to a mouse attack. I kept my eye on the little bugger instead. He rose up on his hind legs and... defied me.

"Ray!"

"I'm right here." He had my green plastic Rubbermaid pitcher and its lid in his hand. He slowly crept up on the mouse. When it spied him coming and started to dart out of the corner, Ray blocked its exit on both sides and scooped the little devil right into the container, slapping the lid on tight. "Got it."

I clapped wildly. "My hero."

He swooped the container under my chin. "Want to see it up close?"

I jogged in place on the chair. "No! Put it outside."

Ray carried the container out the front door. Minutes later he reappeared in my living room with the empty container. "I'll wash this out for you."

My lip curled in reflex. "Throw it away, please. The trash can's on the side of the house."

He disappeared through the door again and returned empty handed. "You know what they say: if you see one, you have ten more."

"Don't remind me. I'm buying traps first thing in the morning. Or maybe a hungry cat."

He smiled. "Let's not go overboard. You're allergic to cats." He walked over to my chair to help me down.

I placed my hand in his and moved the arch of my foot to the edge of the seat, promptly losing my balance and lurching forward right into his chest, his arms closing around me. I found myself nose to nose with him, his breath smelling of garlic masked by peppermints.

His smile faded. We stared into each other's eyes. I felt his breath on my lips. I closed my eyes, feeling safe and warm—maybe a little too warm in the nether regions.

I recalled his breath on those areas. I wiggled.

He loosened his grasp. I slid down his body, feeling all the buttons and bumps, and smacked my heels on the wooden floor. All my memories of the way we were went right back into their mental drawers.

Ray stepped back. "Do you have any coffee? I'll make it for myself if you do."

"Yes." I led the way into the kitchen, feeling all tingly and confused. If only it didn't feel so much like home every time we were together. If only he wasn't the only man I'd ever really been attracted to, let alone slept with. If only I didn't feel so inexplicably bound to him even after three years of trying to stop missing him and failing miserably.

I opened the cupboard door and set my coffeemaker on the counter. Then I found the bag of filters and a tin of Maxwell House. Ray took them from my hands.

I moved over a few feet to lean against the counter. "So what was the second thing you wanted to talk to me about?"

"Do you have a receipt for the pizza you purchased Friday night?"

"A receipt?" Why would Ray want a receipt? Because he doesn't believe you, stupid.

I choked my response out around the lump in my throat. "Let me look in my purse."

I grabbed the purse off the counter and dug through it. Credit cards were a way of life for me now. But I didn't always keep the food receipts. I could feel Ray's gaze on me as he waited with his arms folded. I started to sweat as I scanned each piece of paper without success.

It was the last receipt I unfolded. "Here it is." I waved it triumphantly.

Ray accepted it, looked it over, and shoved it into his pocket. "Thanks. I also need a list of all your customers." He opened the filter bag and stuck his hand inside, withdrawing a yellowed paper disk. "How old are these?"

"I have no idea. It'll work."

He grimaced and stuffed the filter in the coffee machine.

"The list should include customers who made appointments or called by phone, not just paying customers. Go back a year at least."

"Okay. I can put it together from my calendar and computer records. I'll do it tomorrow."

Ray lifted the plastic lid off the coffee can and stood staring into the can for so long I feared the coffee might somehow have gotten moldy. "What?"

He reached into the can and pulled a bunch of bills out. A bunch of crisp new bills that still smelled of ink. I couldn't tell for sure without my contacts, but they looked like hundred dollar bills. Bills I'd never seen before.

"What's this doing here?"

At first I thought it was Erica's money from the 7-Eleven, but how many new hundreds would a 7-Eleven have in the drawer in the middle of the night? None.

"I'm not sure."

He fanned the stash. "There's two thousand dollars here, Jolene. When we were married, you were a fanatic about keeping money in the bank to earn interest. I didn't realize your business was such a cash cow that you'd changed your philosophy."

My business was the cow that ate the cash. "It has its moments."

Ray set the coffee can and the money on my kitchen counter. "What's going on, Jolene?"

I didn't know and I didn't want to admit I didn't know. I feared it tied to Erica somehow and I needed to protect her. Ray took the law very seriously. I did, too, but Erica required allowances. Until I knew for sure who the money really belonged to, I'd pretend it was mine.

"It's just money, Ray." I straightened up off the counter. "Maybe you should go now. That coffee's too old to drink anyway."

I walked into the living room and picked up his jacket. I held it out to him when he followed me into the room. "I'll have my customer list ready for you tomorrow."

Ray didn't accept his jacket. He folded his arms and glared at me instead. Great, he was going to be obstinate. I could be obstinate too. We still had that in common. I shook the jacket at him. "Please."

He continued to glare. I walked to the front door and opened it, immediately regretting my action as the icy wind bit at my bare legs.

He followed me over and closed the door, trapping me between it and his outstretched arms. He leaned down to lock eyes with me. "I want to know where the money came from, Jolene. Tell me the real truth."

The last time I told him the real truth—that I didn't want a child—he said "fine." But it wasn't fine. I had counted on his promised support, and he withdrew it. I was still smarting from that betrayal. How could I trust him now when the stakes were so much higher and our relationship so much more tenuous? Not to mention, I didn't know where the money came from.

I smelled the garlic and mints again. Had he dined out this evening? Perhaps he took Catherine Thomas to the same restaurant where we ate on Saturday. If nothing, I was the master of distraction. "Like you told me about Catherine Thomas?"

His head snapped back like I'd landed a roundhouse punch. I knew it was all true. My heart broke in two.

He straightened and took his jacket from my hand. "Where did you hear about Catherine?"

"She introduced herself to me at the Coachman Inn on Sunday. She has a gorgeous diamond ring on her finger. Much nicer than the one you bought me."

His eyes closed for a second. "You picked your ring out."

And I wouldn't trade it for the Hope diamond, but I couldn't stop myself. I wanted to make him feel the pain I felt, even if I'd given away my rights three years ago. "I picked out one in keeping with your salary. I guess living in my house saves you a lot of money."

His hand clenched his jacket so tightly his knuckles turned white. "I'll be out of your house at the end of the week."

"Fine."

What was I saying? I didn't want the house. Worse, would he move in with Catherine?

Fix it. Say something to fix it.

I didn't get the chance. Ray yanked open the door, pinning me between it and the wall, and stormed out into the snowfall.

As his car screeched out of the driveway and roared off down the street, I congratulated myself on winning another loss.

Shivering uncontrollably, I headed into the bedroom and put on an old pair of sweatpants, my college sweatshirt, and my fluffy white slippers. Even they didn't cheer me up. Ray bought them for me.

I didn't know what to do about Ray, not that I ever did. He and I had struggled over control for years. This wasn't a new problem, just a new wrinkle in the old one. I couldn't let him shake me again. Besides, the two thousand dollars in cash was yodeling to me from the kitchen. I scuffed my way in there and stood looking at the money for all of two minutes. I had one option—to tear my house apart and find all the hidden treasures inside.

It took me two hours to do a thorough job. Erica had suffered from illegal drug addiction at one time, and she used to hide her stash in the most unusual places. I'd been taught by the best—Ray—how to find them. I only had a one-bedroom apartment to search now. I put my skills to good use and found a thousand dollars in my *When Harry Met Sally* videotape container in the living room, three thousand in an empty paint can in the basement, five thousand in a Kleenex box in my bedroom, two thousand folded inside a bath towel in the linen closet, and two thousand inside the hub cap of my car, which was parked outside in the driveway. After I discovered the money in the towel, it occurred to me these hiding places were beneath Erica's considerable talents.

My landlord, who lived upstairs, had the garage privileges, but I searched the one-car stall just in case. I didn't find any money, but I did find a sheath for a knife in the Miracle-Gro fertilizer box.

A sheath that could have easily housed the knife that had been sticking out of Tim Lapham's chest.

NINE

I TRIED NOT TO panic. I failed. I took the knife sheath into the house, placed it and the money in separate plastic baggies, set them on the coffee table, and dropped onto the couch to stare at them.

At first, I clung to the notion that the knife sheath was just a coincidence; something innocently mislaid long ago, something my landlord had misplaced. Too bad he was unavailable to ask, closeted in a hunting lodge somewhere near the Catskills with his old Army buddies, reminiscing about the good old days when America went to war for freedom, not oil.

The worst-case alternative—that it was the sheath from the murder weapon—sent shudders up and down my spine. Other thoughts—that Erica had joined forces with a murderer, an insane move even for her, or that I was being framed for the killing—terrified me. Who had access not only to my showroom but to my house? Who hated me enough to try to lay Tim's death at my doorstep? If I was being framed, then I had to believe the killer knew me. Why would a stranger go to so much trouble? And I'd so liked the idea of an out-of-towner. I'd always thought of my town and myself as safe. Now I knew nowhere was safe.

Should I tell Ray about the rest of the money and the sheath? Were they related or two separate issues? Were they even clues? All I knew for sure was neither one belonged to me. I didn't want to obstruct justice, but I didn't feel confident confiding in Ray anymore, either. I couldn't decide. I had two things to fear: an unknown trail of evidence and the big hound dog named Ray, who may have followed it to my door.

Calling Greg Doran and asking him what to do was an option, but not one I wished to pursue. As a lawyer, he'd no doubt recommend that I turn it all in to the police. I feared Ray might conclude that Erica and her merry band had stashed the money in my house or that I had obtained it illegally, perhaps from poor, dead Tim. I needed to find Erica and figure out what was going on, because it was possible her new friends had left me holding the bag.

But if they hadn't, I would have to face the fact that someone was framing me.

First things first. I decided to hide them where no one else would find them.

Afraid to let any of it out of my sight, I picked up the money and the sheath and carried them into my bedroom while I dressed. Then I carried them into the living room and put them on the floor while I shrugged on my coat and hat. Before I stepped out the door, I stuffed the baggies in my purse.

When I got in the car and turned the ignition key, I realized I had nowhere to go at two thirty in the morning. I backed out anyway and started driving up and down the quiet streets, hoping for inspiration and envying everyone else who lay sleeping at peace in their warm beds.

If I left the money in my apartment, Ray might come back with a search warrant. If I left it in my office, the same was true. If I took it to the house we once shared and hid it there, he'd probably sniff it out like a dog to a bone. If I gave it to Isabelle or Cory for safekeeping, I might be making them an accessory to an as-yet-unknown crime.

I came to a T in the road. I turned right and passed my bank. Depositing the money in my personal or business accounts would be suicide. Unfortunately, I didn't have a safe deposit box, and opening one now when all the eyes of the town seemed upon me wasn't prudent. Ray could get a search warrant for that, too. Too bad Wachobe didn't merit a bus or train station with storage lockers. The nearest ones were thirty minutes away. I couldn't take the chance. With my luck, I'd be pulled over for erratic driving.

At the next T, I turned left onto Main Street, which was still and silent, past closing hour at the bars and too early for deliveries. About the right time to leave a body in a Ferrari, I supposed.

Alone on the roads, I felt more nervous and exposed than when surrounded by strangers. My gaze flickered from the windshield to the rearview mirror to the side mirrors to the road and sidewalks again. I could smell my perspiration, but felt chilled inside and out. Tears warmed the corners of my eyes. I pulled to the side of the road as my vision blurred. I had nowhere to go and no place to hide this money.

While I swiped at my tears, I realized I'd stopped in front of the park near the town Christmas tree—where Ray had stood me up on Sunday. More tears threatened.

The tree glowed in the night like a fiery beacon and lit up the whole park. Sparkles of light glistened on the fake packages under the tree and the surrounding snow. The longer I looked at it, the more blinding it became.

Then the lights went out. I could barely make out the outline of the tree against the moonlit lake.

Power failure? But the street lamps were still lit. Then I remembered.

For two entire meetings, the merchants association had discussed the benefits of leaving the lights on twenty-four hours a day versus doing our part to conserve energy and shutting them off at three a.m. We opted to conserve.

A hiding place popped into my head. The tree. It sat on crates covered by a red tarpaulin and surrounded by fake packages in gold and silver, red and green, all of it wired down to prevent it from taking flight into the lake with a big gust of wind. As in prior years, the display would remain here until a week after New Year's Day. It just might work.

I checked the street. Still vacant. I checked the sidewalks. Vacant, too.

I started the Porsche and crept down the street, checking constantly for signs of life. I turned into the drive for my shop and parked in the shadows behind the building, easing myself out of the car with my purse in hand.

I slinked down the narrow alley that ran behind the shops facing Main Street. I could hear the lake lapping against the shoreline but as much as I strained, I heard nothing else.

I reached the end of the alley and stood at the edge of the park. I scanned it and the road and saw no sign of movement. I listened and still heard only the sound of the waves. Main Street was devoid of cars.

Now thankful that the rest of the town slept, I tiptoed through the shadows and scrambled up the stairs of the gazebo. I dropped to my knees at the base of the Christmas display. The fake presents were solid boxes made of some sort of plastic. They didn't budge when I tried to lift them.

I slid closer, squeezed my hand between the presents, and stuck my hand under the tree skirt. I felt the wooden crate the tree stand rested on, looking for a gap. When I found one big enough, I took the baggie of money out of my purse and slid it through the hole.

Something tiny and fast and mouse-like ran out from under the tree skirt and across the park. I stifled a scream. No way would I stick my hand in again. Dropping the skirt into place once again, I took one last look at the park and the road and headed to my car on winged feet.

I carefully drove home, feeling pleased with myself.

The feeling died the moment I saw Ray's car sitting in the driveway. He sat on the front porch in my wicker rocking chair, and an aura of unhappiness hung over him. That was fine, because I sure wasn't happy to see him again so soon, especially since I still had the knife sheath in my purse.

I parked behind his car and took up a position at the base of the front steps. "You're up early." It was only a quarter to six now.

His face was a thundercloud. "I couldn't sleep. I wanted to talk to you."

"What about?"

He rubbed the full day's growth of whiskers on his chin. "I wanted to talk to you about us. But now, I'd rather talk about what the hell you're doing wandering the streets at this time of the morning dressed like a second-story man."

I looked down at myself. My black jeans, black turtleneck, black coat, and black knit hat told the tale. I hadn't even realized that I'd dressed for sneaking around in the shadows. Could I have no secrets from this man? "I couldn't sleep either. I went for a drive."

Ray rose to his feet. "Can I make some coffee?"

I should have seen that one coming. He planned to ask about the bills again. "Sure." I unlocked the door and tried not to race him across the floor to the kitchen. While I stopped to take my coat off and throw it over the kitchen chair, Ray continued straight to the coffee can and opened it.

"Where's the money, Jolene?"

"It's not there?" I peered into the can, feigning surprise. "Maybe Erica was here again." I felt guilty smearing her character when it wasn't true, but it had been true often enough in the past.

Ray set the can on the counter without a sound. "You're lying, Jolene. What did you do with the money?"

Not only is the man a great detective, he knows me too well. Too bad I wasn't blessed with a face that could bluff. Once again, I would need a distraction. "Ray, you can't keep coming over here and insulting me. I won't stand for it." I crossed my arms and glared at him.

He turned to study me from head to toe. "Then you'd better improve your behavior."

"What's that supposed to mean?"

"I spoke to the chair of the zoning board. He said Tim talked to you about relocating your store and you flew off the handle. He said Tim found your reaction so disturbing that he recommended backing off on asking you to relocate."

Tim didn't tell me that. He had left me with the impression that he would vote against me to move my shop off Main Street. Perfect. Now even I was convinced that I had a motive for killing him.

I swallowed. "I told you. We discussed the merits of their recommendation. I was pointing, Tim was pointing, and I bumped him. We did not argue. Tim was only feeling me out on the issue, not forcing it. I did not threaten or kill Tim Lapham."

Ray locked gazes with me. "Did Tim give you any money at any time?"

That took me by surprise. "No. Why? Is there money missing?"

His eyes narrowed. "Jolene, I have an open murder case and an open robbery case, both of which seem to tie to you. I need answers, honest answers. And I need them now."

"I can't help you, Ray."

"Can't or won't?" He folded his arms across his chest in a parody of me.

I raised my chin and refused to break eye contact first.

He lowered his arms and leaned down until I could feel his breath on my face. This time it smelled like coffee. Clearly, he'd already had some. I tried not to blink, but his sheer proximity made it impossible.

He pronounced his words slowly. "Do I not drop everything and come when you call for help with your sister? Do I not care for your family home? Do I not trap mice for you?"

I wasn't sure where he was going with this, but I feared I wouldn't like it. "You do, Ray."

"So why won't you help me do my job?"

"I am. I'm going to make the list of my customers this morning. Right away." I backed up a few steps. "I'll go now."

He straightened to his full intimidating height. He didn't scare me. "But you won't tell me the truth about what happened to the money?"

I remained silent. My good angel and my bad angel started a knock-down, drag-out fight inside my head that they didn't have time to finish before Ray spoke again.

"Okay, Jolene. Let me tell you how things are going to go from now on. You're not going to call me anymore if you need help. You're not going to expect me to help you. I'm going to move out of your house, and I'm going to do my job, even if it means your sister or you end up in serious trouble, including jail time. Do you understand me, Jolene?"

"Yes." My response was barely a whisper.

"You can fax me the list at the station." Ray turned on his heel and strode into the living room with me jogging at his heels, knowing I had lost something very important today.

As he whipped open the front door, I said, "Do you hate me, Ray?"

He paused for a moment in the doorway but didn't turn to face me.

"The opposite of love is not hate, Jolene. The opposite of love is indifference."

As his car disappeared from my sight, I still hadn't figured out for sure what he was trying to tell me.

TEN

I UNLOCKED THE DOOR to Asdale Auto Imports around eight a.m., turned off the alarm, and took a quick tour of the showroom to ensure I didn't have any new, unexpected arrivals—and I wasn't thinking cars. I found nothing to cause me or anyone else more grief.

As I headed toward the door to the shop, I saw a gray Camry pull up next to the curb in front of the shop. Cory hopped out with a newspaper tucked in his armpit and leaned inside the car to say something to the driver, the man from last night's Dickens cast. Apparently, Cory had more fun last night than I did.

I approached the showroom window and, after watching the car pull away from the curb, knocked on it. Cory jumped six inches into the air and spun around to gape at me. I waggled my fingers and he gave me a sheepish grin in response before coming inside.

"You guys hit it off last night, eh?"

Cory flashed his pearly whites. "Yes, we did. We're seeing each other again tonight."

"So this might have long-term relationship potential?"

"I hope so. He lives about an hour away, not too far to see each other regularly."

I hoped it would work out for Cory. A "happy-ever-after" ending would be nice for someone. Ray and I certainly hadn't managed to achieve it.

I headed toward my office. "I have to make a list of all of our customers for Ray. Can you look it over when I'm done to make sure I didn't miss any maintenance-only customers?"

"Sure, Jo."

As I logged into my computer, I heard Cory call my name. "Can you come here a minute?"

I found him standing in the doorway to the garage. "What is it?"

He moved to the side so I could see. Or rather not see. The DeLorean, owned by Mr. Oliver of Oliver and Associates, Attorneys at Law, no longer sat in the garage. My mouth dropped open as I turned to look at Cory.

"I'll call nine-one-one." He turned on his heel and headed for the showroom phone.

I walked the perimeter of the garage, staring at the oil spots on the cement floor and wondering what to say to Mr. Oliver. He loved his car. He'd entrusted it to us, and we'd lost it. Once again, my shop had been visited in the middle of the night by someone who knew my alarm code. I gave myself a mental slap in the head for not changing it immediately after the first invasion. Apparently I was destined to repeat my mistakes.

Cory and I sat in my office to wait for the police. I crossed my fingers Ray would come, leaving me some reason to hope he still cared for me, but this time Deputy Sheriff Steven "Gumby" Fellows arrived on the scene. Gumby was the one man I knew who was taller than Ray and twice as slick. He was the first man to ask me out after Ray and I split. I declined him then, and I cringed now as he stooped to give me a kiss on the cheek.

"Jolene, you're as gorgeous as ever."

I waved him off. "I lost a car, Gumby. Can you find my car?"

He pulled out his notepad. "Give me the details."

I pulled up Mr. Oliver's file on the computer and read his address and registration number to Gumby, who duly noted them. Then he followed Cory into the garage to take a look at the crime scene. When they reappeared five minutes later, Gumby shook his head. "I called for a fingerprint technician. Same guy who was here Saturday. He's coming, but he thinks it's a waste of time."

Secretly, I agreed. "How hard can it be to find a DeLorean on the road?"

Gumby scratched his chest. "Well, if a pro took it, next to impossible. They drive it inside the back of a semi, and it's in New York City or even California in a couple hours, being loaded onto a freighter."

Now I was definitely back to thinking Wachobe had been invaded by out-of-towners, thieving, murdering professionals. "You're not making me feel any better."

"Sorry, Jolene, but the truth is, it's probably long gone."

I picked up the phone and dialed with a feeling of dread. Mr. Oliver was armed and dangerous, like any lawyer with a temper. He could sue me and I'd lose everything. My business, my family home, my car, my meager savings, my reputation, my life. Well, maybe not my life exactly. I'd still be alive, adrift on the lake without a paddle. Nevertheless, I'd be in better shape than poor Tim Lapham. I needed to suck it up and take it like, well, a man.

Mr. Oliver expected the unexpected. That's why he was a good lawyer. But that temper. I could hear it sizzling in every word he spat out, including his final parting shot "Miss Asdale, I hope you're insured."

I riffled through my files with a sick feeling. Nope, I wasn't insured. My bill was due last Friday and it still sat unpaid in my drawer. Maybe I had a thirty-day grace period, but it was definitely too late to get the payment postmarked prior to the theft, even if I had the money to pay the bill.

Which I didn't.

My fingers inched toward the phone again, itching to call Ray. He was a better detective than Gumby. He could find my car. He'd sniff it out like a bloodhound. Of course, right now he was busy tracking a murderer and my sister, the robber.

Besides, he wasn't mine to call on anymore, especially after his statement this morning. He'd made it very clear that I was on my own.

I liked to think I could handle it.

ELEVEN

WACHOBE HAD STOPPED LOOKING like a picture postcard town to me and more like a total den of depravity, infiltrated by a killer and a car thief I preferred to think of as one or more unidentified out-of-towners gone wild. All I could do was put a stop to my slow spiral into personal and business hell, starting with the simple things first.

I dug through the files in my desk and located the manual for the alarm system, never opened before this day. I thumbed through it to the page about changing alarm codes, then to the page about customized numbers for each user. I read both pages once. Twice. A third time. I whimpered. Although I'd been around mechanics my whole life, I understood mechanical things only in theory, not practice.

Cory had sat through Gumby's questions and was headed out the door when I grabbed him by the arm and shoved the manual into his hands. "We're changing the alarm code as soon as you tell me how to do it."

He held the manual in front of his face before peeking over it at mine. That twinkle in his eye rekindled my fury with my own ineptitude. But minutes later, we had each entered a new individual code in the system.

I locked the front door behind Cory and watched as his navy BMW eased into traffic and disappeared.

My cell phone rang and for one wild moment, I hoped it would be Ray.

It was Brennan Rowe. My heart beat accelerated. I'd forgotten all about his car, a sure sign I'd lost my mind yet again, a concern not to be taken lightly.

"Miss Asdale, any word yet?"

"No, sir, but I'm on it." I snapped my phone shut and raced into my office to bring up the auction house's website on screen. Relieved to find the bidding still unscheduled, I began the arduous task of rebuilding my appointment calendar in order to create the customer list Ray had requested.

Three hours later I had compiled a decent list. Frankly, I was wondering why I didn't sell more cars and make more money. I certainly talked to enough people in a year, although many were maintenance-only customers.

Then I realized I never should have let Cory leave the shop, because I needed him to look the list over before I gave it to Ray. I dialed his home and cell phone numbers but got only his voicemail in response. I left him messages.

Once I resigned myself to not hearing from Cory anytime soon, I drove to the bank, where I drained my personal account down to two hundred and fifty dollars. With the payment in hand for my insurance bill, I drove to the tiny white Cape Cod on Edwards

Street that housed my insurance agent's office. I was surprised to find Becky's AWOL friend Sally Winslow sitting behind the desk, her black hair shiny as piano keys. Blatant misuse of Miss Clairol.

After we greeted one another and exchanged pleasantries about today's weather, I got right down to business. "Here's my insurance premium payment. It's four days late."

"No problem." Sally took the money and the statement from my hand. "You have a grace period."

"Great. Is Bernie in?" I glanced around the office at the gray walls and maroon furniture as though expecting to find him hiding behind the potted ficus in the corner of the room.

Sally fixed her disapproving eye on his empty desk, strewn with papers and Dunkin' Donuts napkins. "No."

"I had a break-in at the garage this morning and one of my customer's cars was stolen. I'd like to file a claim."

"You're having quite the week, aren't you?" Sally spun in her chair and pulled a form from the file cabinet. "I can't believe we've had a murder and now a car theft in our town. We're doing everything we can to bring more tourists into town, but we seem to be attracting the wrong kind of people, too."

I'd been wondering if she might refer to Tim's death, especially given her long friendship with Becky.

Sally continued, "It must have been quite a shock for you, learning about Tim's death after your date with him Friday night."

My chest tightened. "Tim and I didn't have a date Friday night."

Sally studied my face for a moment then dropped her gaze to the paper on the desk. "I must have misunderstood."

She began reading questions from the claim form. I answered all her questions, all the while wondering where she got the idea Tim and I had a date. When she asked me to sign the claim form and told me Bernie would be in touch, I decided to ask her.

Sally busied herself with shuffling papers around her desk and refused to look at me. "Oh, you know, some of the girls got together and were talking. I should have known better than to believe them, let alone repeat what they said. I'm sorry, Jolene."

I knew Chrissy Martin, Celeste's sister, was one of Sally's friends. The gossip gene ran rampant in that family like mental illness did in mine. I tried not to make too much of it, but Ray's request for my pizza receipt seemed to substantiate that someone believed Tim and I had a date Friday night. Of course, now I couldn't even ask Ray who that might be since he was angry that I hadn't explained the money he found.

I had a hard time focusing on the rest of my conversation with Sally, because my fears overcame me. My imagination had no trouble generating the image of Ray putting me in jail. I tried to convince myself that notion was ridiculous, in particular because I was innocent, but my head started to throb with tension. My mouth felt dry. I craved the sleep I'd lost over the last few days. I couldn't figure out the answers to all my own questions, let alone anyone else's.

On my way back to the office, I moved on to the question of whether Bernie would be in touch with the forty-five thousand dollars Mr. Oliver's car was worth on the open market. Even if he was, I somehow doubted Mr. Oliver would just accept his money and walk away gracefully. My business would take another knock with this fiasco. If I didn't get arrested for murder, I could still go bankrupt. It was always nice to have options.

My cell phone rang as I pulled into the parking lot behind the boutique. Once again, it wasn't Ray. I'd spent three years trying to avoid the man. Would all my remaining days be spent wondering if he might ever speak to me again? And they say women are fickle.

"I got your message, Jo. I stopped by the office and read the customer list. It looked complete to me, but how come you underlined Brennan Rowe and Mr. Hughes' names?" Cory sucked in enough air to make the phone line hiss with static.

I hadn't realized I'd underlined anything, but they were my two leading local suspects for the murder. Mr. Hughes was angry about the zoning board decision. He was wealthy and clever enough to mastermind Tim's murder and arrogant enough to appear in my showroom to see for himself that the job had been done. Brennan Rowe flew just under the radar in town most of the time. Could he have bribed or blackmailed Tim into voting in his favor? "Just a slip of the pen. Where are you?"

"At the gym, working out. Want to come over?"

"Ha, ha, ha." Cory knew exercise and I did not go hand-in-hand. I was willing to walk, but rarely willing to work up a sweat. The last time I sweated was—oops, this was no time to be thinking about fun times with Ray.

I entered my office and plugged in my fax machine. Once it warmed up, emitting a burnt odor from long disuse, I faxed my list to Ray's attention at the Sheriff's Department and resisted the urge to call and verify its receipt. Then I sat with the list in my hand, wondering if this list of a hundred or so names was the only lead in the investigation into Tim's death. If so, I knew these people better than Ray, or at least, I thought I did. They were my customers. I could make a few phone calls and ask some questions. It would beat sitting around waiting for the next body to appear or the next car to disappear—or worse, for Ray to come slap the cuffs on me. And I knew just who to call first.

I dialed the number and spoke to his secretary, who put me through to the big man himself seconds later.

"Miss Asdale, what can I do for you?"

"I'm calling to apologize for Saturday, Mr. Hughes. We're still not sure what happened here, but I'm sorry you were involved."

"I wasn't involved, Miss Asdale, nor do I intend to be."

That statement shut me down for a minute, but I rallied. "The victim, Tim Lapham, was the town treasurer, and he served on the zoning board, too. Were you acquainted with Tim?"

The line was silent and I wondered if Mr. Hughes had hung up. Then he spoke. "We met when I approached the board about a zoning change and building permit for a grocery store in Wachobe. They turned me down."

"How disappointing."

"Not at all, Miss Asdale. Merely one more challenge to overcome. Challenges are what make life interesting, wouldn't you agree?"

Not today, but I wasn't about to admit it. "Of course. How are you planning to overcome this one, if you don't mind my asking?"

"Not at all. With Mr. Lapham's death, the votes will change on the zoning board. All I have to do is request another hearing and vote." He sounded rather pleased.

I swallowed the bile rising in my throat. "I wasn't aware the individual votes were made public."

"They're not, Miss Asdale."

Once again, he stopped me cold. I wondered if his words held a hidden message or if he was so confident, he didn't concern himself with subterfuge. I pressed on. "Did anyone know about your ten o'clock appointment here to see the Ferrari?"

"What an odd question, but I'll answer it. Just my wife. I told her where I was going when I left the house."

"Yes, of course. Well, again, I apologize. I won't keep you."

"Actually, I'm delighted you phoned me today. I've been thinking about calling you. I've decided on a car."

My heart filled with joy. A man of the world like Mr. Hughes wouldn't let a dead body dissuade him from purchasing a stylish red Ferrari. "Yes?"

"I understand a 1957 Mercedes-Benz 300SL roadster is coming up for auction. It's tan with a green interior. I'd like you to bid on it for me." He reeled off the name of the auction house and a vehicle identification number which matched the one written on my hot pink Post It note.

"Ahh…" Now I really was at a loss. He wanted the same car as Brennan Rowe, who I represented on the QT.

"I'm willing to pay you a ten thousand dollar finder's fee."

Twice what Brennan Rowe had offered to pay me. Oh, this couldn't be happening. "I'm sorry, Mr. Hughes, I can't bid on that car for you. I'm already representing someone else interested in the roadster."

"Oh, well then, may the best man win." Dial tone filled the line.

I didn't really care for his parting shot. Did he mean the best man between him and Brennan Rowe or the best man, meaning I as a woman would never win? Either way, I'd had enough of the two of them.

I locked the shop and walked the two blocks to the town offices, intent on speaking with Henry Hart, the town supervisor. I didn't have an appointment, but Henry liked me. Henry could give me the real scoop on the zoning board's decision.

The town office sat on the corner of North Street and Lincoln Boulevard. It was an expansive forty-thousand-square-foot, two-story brick building that also housed the parks and recreation department, including an indoor water park. The lobby felt warm and humid and smelled of chlorine when I entered. Both the lobby and the pool were empty at this hour of the day, since school was in session.

I asked for Henry at the desk. He appeared moments later, his hand swallowing mine as he greeted me with a broad smile on his florid face. His silver hair looked stylish with his light blue dress shirt and slightly darker tie. He'd be the consummate politician except for one little habit: he scratched his crotch while he talked, every once in a while. I don't know if it was jock itch or if he was checking to make sure his equipment hadn't been stolen, but I'm sure it was keeping him from moving up in local government. As town supervisor, he didn't make many speeches or glad hand too many people. At least I didn't see him grab his crotch until after I'd shaken his hand today.

"Come on in and sit down. How's your sister?" Henry always asked about Erica because Erica was the spitting image of Mom, whom he used to date in high school. Sometimes I thought if he wasn't too old and already married, he might like to make a play for Erica.

"She's doing all right. She's still in and out of the psych center."

I didn't bother to mention today was an unauthorized "out" day.

I followed him into his office. It was adorned with softball trophies and pictures of each year's Memorial Day parade—Henry and his wife riding in the lead car, of course.

He nodded with a grave expression. "I pray for her every night."

"Thank you." I shifted in my chair. "I wanted to ask you about Mr. Hughes and Brennan Rowe. I understand they're fighting over the same plot of land, and it's coming up for a revote with the zoning board. Could Tim have been ... swayed by either of them?"

Henry had been a politician long enough to know he was being asked about bribes. "Of course not. Tim was by-the-book."

He tipped his head as he gazed at me. "I heard you and Tim had an argument yourselves about the zoning board's suggestion that you relocate Asdale Auto Imports. I heard you got physical with him."

I felt myself stiffen and tried not to sound defensive. "It was not an argument. I was pointing at the street, he was pointing, and I bumped him. That's all. It was all very innocent, not at all physical."

"I see." He didn't sound like he saw at all though. "You need to be careful about making any accusations, Jolene. You're in a precarious position right now."

"I don't understand."

Henry's averted gaze disturbed me, but his words struck fear. "The zoning board thinks your cars are an eyesore and wants your shop relocated. Mr. Hughes thinks your property would be a prime location for his daughter's flower shop. The majority of the board seems to agree."

"But … don't I have any say in this?"

Henry shrugged. "You'd have to go to one of the zoning meetings to say your piece."

I didn't want to go to one of their meetings. I was too afraid of what they'd have to say. In my mind, I pictured myself with my arms folded across my chest and my heels dug into the ground by the end of the meeting, saying, "You can't make me move."

I decided to change the subject. "What did you think when you heard Tim had been killed?"

Henry fiddled with the letter opener on his desk. "I didn't know what to think. He was fine man. A hard worker. I thought he was honest."

He sounded like he might have recently changed his mind on that last point. What happened to "by-the-book"? Had that just been a knee-jerk politician's response? "But you don't think he was honest anymore?"

"I didn't say that, Jolene." Henry rose to his feet and held out his hand. "I have to run to a meeting."

I shook his hand and left the building.

But as I walked past his window, I looked back inside to see him still sitting at his desk, looking as confused and scared as I felt.

TWELVE

HENRY'S WORDS ECHOED IN my head as I walked back to the shop to retrieve my car and drive home. Just days ago I thought I was on the road to becoming a successful businessperson in Wachobe, maybe even a respected one, something my dad failed to achieve. Now I was skidding into a crash and burn with my business undermined and my personal reputation in question. Was someone trying to ruin me or was it all just an unlucky twist of fate?

I remembered to purchase a package of mouse traps on the way home. At least I could eliminate one of my concerns. If I actually snagged one of the varmints, I would just have to step up, or maybe suit up, to empty the trap. With one of Cory's mechanic outfits, my rubber gardening boots, some welding gloves, and a beekeeper's hat, I might feel confident enough to scoop up one tiny dead mouse with an iron shovel, as long as its handle was at least four feet long. There, I had a plan, and it didn't include Ray.

In my kitchen I tore open the package and removed the traps. After chunking up some cheese and smearing it with peanut butter, I set the traps in the corners of my kitchen, living room, and hallway and headed for my bedroom to tuck one under my four-poster bed. The sight of my bed stopped me dead in the doorway.

The intricately hand-embroidered quilt of morning glories lay crumpled at the foot of the bed. The blue thermal blanket and white sheets with crocheted edges were balled in the center of it, and the pillows both bore the indentations of the heads that had laid there last. It took me only a few seconds to find two long blond hairs on one side of the bed, and a dark short one on the other, similar to the hair on Sam Green's head, based on the picture I'd seen. Apparently, my bed had been a stop on Erica's passion trail.

Four towels lay damp and discarded on the tile floor of my bathroom. Only the heady aroma of lavender suggested Erica had supplied her own toiletries. I sank onto the side of the bathtub and wondered how much my landlord would charge me to change the locks. He prided himself on the historical value of this 1870s colonial, including the original locks. A deadbolt from Ace Hardware probably wouldn't sit well with him, but, right now, I was ready to install two on each entrance. Erica had the uncanny ability to do the absolute wrong thing at the wrong time and the fact that she was now doing it on my mattress revolted me.

I rose wearily, slid the mouse trap under the bed, and set to work stripping the sheets, careful not to touch anything but their corners. Perhaps I could set a trap for Erica, too. But first, I'd try leaving a sticky note on each door to the apartment, worded to convey my maternal disappointment in her behavior and threatening a move to a maximum security mental facility in another county once I got the net over her again.

It might work. After all, she must gain comfort from my proximity. Why else would she keep coming back here again and again?

By nine o'clock the next morning I was dressed for Tim's funeral and waiting for Cory. My pantsuit, a gray double-breasted number, was lighter in color and weight than I wanted for this somber occasion. But it was clean, unlike my black suit, still covered in slush from the day I discovered Tim's body. Plus the gray blended with my only pressed blouse, a black one.

I had a plan for the day. At Tim's funeral, I would learn more about his family and friends. If I eavesdropped on enough conversations, maybe I would get a clue as to why someone might have wanted to kill him. If I were really lucky, maybe I'd uncover a killer in their midst.

Life should be so simple.

If not, I would hunt down my sister before she caused any more trouble. I knew which bars she liked to frequent and where her few friends lived. If she were in town, I could find her.

Of course, lately my plans had a way of going awry. I hoped today would be the exception.

My jaw dropped when I opened the door for Cory. He had really outdone himself this time. He wore a black suit, a white shirt with gray cravat, a black Dickens cape that fell to his calves with a shorter collar-like cape around the shoulders, and a black felt top hat, all appropriate if he was an undertaker leading a funeral procession with a casket on a wagon pulled by horses wearing feathered funeral headdresses to a burial plot on a hill outside Devonshire.

Which he was not.

I stepped aside to let him enter. "Didn't your mother teach you it's not polite to outdo your date?"

"You're not my date. You're my boss, my boring uptight boss, based on that ensemble." He cocked his head to one side. "I don't know, it might even say 'lesbian.'"

"I'll put my mother's pearls on. They say 'Barbara Bush.'"

"And here I thought you were for Hillary." Cory flicked his cape out behind him and perched on the edge of the ottoman to wait.

When we left the house, I put up my sticky notes but didn't bother to lock my door. Why kid myself? Locks weren't keeping anybody out of my life these days, even dead guys. Cory read the notes over my shoulder but didn't ask any questions.

The lobby of the funeral home smelled like Pledge with a hint of eau d'embalmment clinging to the sails of the model yachts featured on the tables in the entryway. It also brought back painful memories of my mother's and father's deaths. My mother had been laid out here. I still remembered her fire-engine-red lipstick and the delicate baby's breath my dad had asked Mr. Young to put in her hair. It made her look more like a bride than a poor sad woman who'd taken her own life. Maybe that was why Dad requested it. I didn't know. He chose the cremation route for himself.

Mr. Young dipped his silver head of hair deferentially as he greeted us and directed us to the viewing room on the left. He still had a tan worthy of the height of summer, and I wondered if he'd die of skin cancer after all his time on the water. "When you've had a chance to pay your respects, please move across the hall where we will hold the service."

"Why isn't the service at Tim's church?" I whispered to Cory, trying to respect the hushed atmosphere. "He and Becky belonged to the same church. They still sat in the same pew every Sunday, as far as I knew."

"I don't know." Cory swept his hat off, followed by his cape which he swirled in the air once and draped over his forearm while holding the hat in his left hand. He reminded me of Zorro somehow, clearly not the image he hoped to evoke. I kept the thought to myself out of respect for his art—and his feelings, too.

We took a moment to pay our respects to Tim, then moved into the other room where Becky sat between her children in the front row of folding chairs. Little Emma's braids hopped up and down on her back as she swung her legs to and fro. Mark's knee bobbed up and down like a jackhammer. Only Becky was motionless. An elderly man and woman flanked Emma. I assumed they were Becky's parents.

The service was conducted by a minister I had never seen before, who had a voice loud enough to shatter eardrums. He introduced himself and said he was from the city. Clearly, he thought he was preaching in a cavernous church, not this puny parlor. The mourners included two elderly ladies, Sheriff Burnbaum and his overweight wife, Martha, a couple women I thought might be teachers at Tim's children's school, Sally Winslow, Chrissy Martin, her sister Celeste, and my insurance agent Bernie. The ten others who sat together might have been Tim's staff. A handful of males sat alone, and, as a last-minute rustle at the back of the room announced, Ray was in attendance.

He glanced my way but didn't acknowledge me as he slipped into the last row. His gaze darted about the room, no doubt assessing the group assembled. My eyes watered. I faced the front of the room, determined not to let on that his indifference bothered me. Still, I wondered if he thought it was a modest turnout, too.

I couldn't believe the members of the town board, namely Henry Hart, and the zoning board had not attended at least to honor Tim's years of service to the town. And what about his fellow parishioners? Tim was a dedicated churchgoer. How come none of them showed up? And where was his precious bowling team that he'd helped win the first place trophy seven years in a row? Or a few token members of his high school class? Surely all of them hadn't moved out of town for bigger and better things.

The Reverend kept the service mercifully short and to the point. No one offered a eulogy. No one shed a tear, either, not even Tim's children.

At the close of the service, Becky and her family rose and created a receiving line in the lobby. The other rows emptied from the front to the back of the room, leaving Cory and me to bring up the rear of the line. Ray had disappeared before the service ended, most likely to answer a call. I was relieved not to have to face him today, unable to provide the answers he wanted nor summon the bravery to seek the answers I desired.

Bernie stopped next to my elbow and leaned in over his beer belly to have a word. "Call me later. We need to talk about your claim."

This statement did not bode well, but Bernie moved on with the tide of mourners before I could question him.

I took the opportunity to study the group again. Could one of these people be the killer?

I ruled out the two old ladies, Becky and her family, Walter and his wife, Cory and Ray, all for obvious reasons, which left me with an insurance agent, three women who couldn't stand to break a nail, and a bunch of people I didn't recognize. Maybe now would be a good time to sneak a peek at the guest registry.

"Cory, I'm going to the ladies' room. I'll be right back."

Two of the unidentified guests were just signing the book as I approached, so I decided to slip into the restroom first. Inside, Celeste and her sister Chrissy were talking. Their voices dropped to whispers. They turned their backs to me as I entered.

The whispers died out. I heard someone leave.

When I emerged from my stall, Celeste was repairing her war paint in the mirror. "Hi, Jolene. I like your suit."

She sold it to me six months ago. "Thanks."

"That's not the blouse I sold you to go with it, is it?" She capped her lipstick and dropped it inside her clutch.

I busied myself at the sink and pretended not to hear her over the water. "Nice service. I was surprised it wasn't at Tim's church, though."

"He'd been all but excommunicated anyway." Celeste used her fingertip to dab at a spot of excess lipstick.

"What are you talking about?"

Celeste turned to face me with a half-smile. "Don't you know?"

The look on my face must have answered her question because she continued, "During the sermon a couple weeks ago, our pastor said he didn't think gays should be allowed to marry or have legal rights to benefits and wanted the congregation's support by mounting a letter-writing campaign to our state senators. Tim stood up and disagreed with him."

"Wow." I was impressed. Tim had seemed pretty meek and mild for such a bold move. He was, however, very fair-minded and honest. "And people are holding it against him?"

"Let's just say no one likes the way he treated Becky, and his actions added fuel to the fire. You can understand that, can't you?"

Not really. I avoided Celeste's eyes and looked at her chin, then down to her neck. She had on a gorgeous white gold and pearl necklace. I checked her wrist and ears and found the matching pieces. They looked identical to the set Isabelle wore to lunch on Sunday. Where did an unmarried retail store manager like Celeste get that kind of money? Maybe I needed to seriously consider changing my line of work. Maybe catering to the expensive sports car tastes of, well, let's face it, mainly men wasn't going to make me a successful woman after all.

"That's a beautiful necklace, Celeste. And the matching pieces, too."

She ran her fingertips over the necklace, all the while grinning like the Cheshire cat. "Thank you. They were gifts."

I almost had the nerve up to ask from whom when little Emma skipped into the room, passing between us and entering a stall. Celeste picked up her clutch and disappeared out the door.

I waited for Emma to reappear. As she washed her hands, I said, "I'm sorry about your daddy, honey. He was a very nice man. I'll miss him."

She picked up a paper towel and dried her hands. "He was going to take us to the zoo for the Santa breakfast. Mommy said she'd take us now."

Ah, the young never lose their focus. "I hope you have a good time."

I held the door open for her and followed her into the lobby where Bill Young was just handing Becky the guest book. Apparently, the receiving line had moved faster than I expected. Only Becky's family remained in the room.

Cory appeared at my elbow with my coat. "Brennan Rowe asked if the auction was scheduled yet. I told him you were on it but nothing had happened yet."

"He called your cell phone?" The man must be FBI.

Cory held my coat. "No. He was here. Didn't you see him?"

I shrugged my coat on and turned to face Cory. "I've never actually met him. We've done all our business by phone and mail, and I don't travel in his social circle." Not that I have a social circle. "Which one was he?"

"The good looking one in the blue suit."

"I saw five of those. Can you narrow it down?"

"Not really, Jo. He didn't have a rose between his teeth or anything."

Interesting. Rowe knew Tim well enough to attend the funeral. Or was he just guilty about Tim's death? Could Rowe have been involved?"

"How do you know Rowe, Cory?"

"He works out at the gym sometimes, and he brought his car in for service once or twice." Cory swept his cape over his shoulders and tied it. "It's snowing heavily. I'll bring the car around." He stopped on his way out to bend chivalrously over Becky's hand and whisper something that made her smile before donning his top hat and disappearing out the door.

I approached Becky to say my good-byes just as Bill Young tipped his head over her in that sympathetic way funeral directors do. "Would you like to take the flower arrangements home with you? If not, I'll take them to a nursing home."

Becky furrowed her brow. Her mother patted her on the arm. "We'll take a few flowers to press in a Bible for the children." She followed Bill into the other room with her husband and grandchildren trailing, leaving me alone with Becky.

"Again, I'm so sorry about Tim. If there's anything I can do…" I wrapped my scarf around my neck, thinking my words sounded so empty.

Becky's eyes filled with tears. "Can you tell me where the money is?"

"What money?"

"Henry Hart stopped by yesterday. He said the town board is calling an emergency meeting for tonight. It seems over a hundred thousand dollars is missing from the books, and they think Tim is responsible." She hiccupped. "Do you think Tim is responsible?"

Henry Hart was not a man to point fingers without evidence. Funny he hadn't mentioned the money yesterday when we talked about Tim. Maybe he had caught the scent of impropriety and couldn't find the source, just like the rest of us. But apparently he did have doubts about Tim's honesty. I shook my head in bewilderment. "I don't know. It doesn't seem like the Tim I knew."

Becky swiped the tears from her cheeks. "It's not the one I knew, either. But maybe we never really knew him at all."

Becky's parents and children emerged from the other room, carrying a bouquet. Emma asked her grandmother about what would happen to the flowers when they were pressed in the Bible. Her grandmother did her best to tell her all about the ins and outs of dried flower preservation, bless her heart.

I waved to Becky and took my leave, wondering why her mother thought the child would want flowers to remember this day when her father was ripped from her for the last time. I certainly didn't appreciate having any trigger to recall the raw emotion of my parents' funerals. Having to drive by this funeral home and the cemetery on occasion was quite enough.

The heavy wet flakes of snow had already turned the funeral home's driveway to slush. When Cory pulled his car into the turnaround, I rushed out the double glass doors and hopped into the front seat, slamming the door to keep the flakes out.

"I can't believe all this snow so early in December. Where'd it come from so fast?" I brushed the snowflakes from my hair and fastened my seat belt.

The car shot forward and slid onto the main road, fishtailing. I grabbed the door handle. "Geez, Cory, where's the fire?" I turned my head to glare at him.

Only it wasn't Cory. It was a thin man with the largest hawk nose I'd ever seen, holding a switchblade in his right hand as he steered the car with his left.

I didn't know for sure, but I was willing to bet his friends, if he had any, called him "the Beak."

THIRTEEN

"Who are you? Where's Cory?"

In reply, the Beak ran a red light, causing a Mac Tool truck to slam on its brakes as it entered the intersection. The truck lurched side to side but came to a halt without impacting my passenger door. As I checked my seat belt, I congratulated myself on the forethought to use the restroom before leaving the funeral home.

"Where are you taking me?"

Given the slippery road conditions, the Beak now had his gloved hands in the ten and two o'clock positions with the knife pinched between his knuckles. "Shut up."

I picked up my purse and smacked him in the head with it. "Answer me!"

He took his foot off the gas and snatched my purse from my hand, scraping my coat sleeve with the knife blade in the process. My purse flew past my head and landed in the backseat. "Bitch."

I realized the error of my ways. My cell phone was in my purse. I should have dialed 911 instead of hitting him.

He spun the wheel. We made a hard right, grazing the snow bank on the street corner and rebounding into the oncoming lane where we came face-to-face with a Saab. Seconds before impact, the Beak veered right, but not before I saw the woman driver's mouth open to scream. I thought I saw a car seat in the back of her vehicle as we passed.

"Slow down! You're going to kill somebody."

He slowed down but only so he could bring the knife point to my neck. "*Shut up.*" He made a left, withdrawing the switchblade so he could grip the wheel with both hands again.

I looked out the window and tried to figure out where he was headed. From the direction he'd chosen, he seemed to be racing out of town. A few miles from the lake, the area turned to snow-covered fields and very few houses. I didn't want to go there with him.

Ray had enrolled me in a self-defense course for my birthday one year when I'd asked for a new vacuum cleaner. He told me it never hurt to be prepared. The class instructor said never let an assailant take you somewhere else because somewhere else would always be worse than fighting where you are now. Fewer witnesses. Less chance of help. And he did recommend putting up a fight. When I told Ray what the instructor had said, Ray agreed, reiterating that the bad guys never want a fight. They hoped for complete submission. Well, this bozo was trying to peck the wrong chick.

When the Beak braked ever so slightly for a right turn, I braced myself. My left hand pushed the release button on my seat belt as my right hand opened the car door. I tucked my legs, scrunched my neck, led with my shoulder and rolled out, hitting the slush. I felt the pavement against my butt and thighs. My left elbow snagged on the seat belt and caught in the partially closed door. The car dragged me down the road for the length of a football field. My butt and thighs started to burn. My arm felt like it would pull right out of its socket. I started screaming. Horns blared. I heard other people screaming. I bounced over the pavement, slush flowing up and over my face like the wake from a motorboat, choking and blinding me. Another football field went by and I feared I would die. My head slammed against a boulder of ice. I felt myself losing consciousness. Brakes screeched. I lurched forward. My head met an immovable object. I saw stars. I felt a hand on mine. The Beak unhooked my hand from the clutches of the seat belt and pushed it out of the car. I heard the roar of an engine, more brakes screeching, then nothing more.

—

I came to briefly in the emergency room, my body one throbbing nerve of pain. A man held a flashlight to my eyes and asked me questions, too many questions. I closed my eyes and shut him out.

For a while I heard voices, felt hands on my body, and couldn't hold onto a thought for more than a second. I heard Cory, Isabelle, and Ray, my mom and dad, too. Even Erica. And the pain. A couple times I thought I saw the light. I ran toward it. Anything to ease the pain.

Next time I woke, I was looking at the floor through a hole in a gurney. I heard a plink every few seconds as the intern picked the pebbles from my thigh with tweezers and tossed them in a stainless steel bowl. I know this because she told me before I passed out for a second time.

When I opened my eyes again, I could see the moon outside the window. Ray sat in a chair next to my bed, watching me without expression. He wore his uniform. He always looked nice in his uniform. I love a man in uniform. I love you, Ray. Oops, did I say that out loud? My eyes closed again.

I tried to sleep but it seemed like every five minutes a nurse woke me up to ask my name. At one point, I offered to write it down for her since obviously her memory wasn't worth beans. She had a thing about thermometers too.

I felt the sun on my face. My right arm felt like it was being squeezed, tight. Too tight. My eyes flew open. A red-headed nurse, more sunburst orange actually, smiled at me. "Good morning." She put the stethoscope to the hollow of my arm and released some of the pressure from the cuff. "Your blood pressure is good. Can you open your mouth for me?"

I opened my jaw, and she slid a thermometer inside. "Hold it under your tongue. Lips closed." I nodded obediently. All the fight was gone out of me anyway, and from the agony just breathing caused, I doubted it was ever coming back.

I noticed my left wrist was wrapped in one of those stretchy brown bandages. My whole left arm was in a light blue sling pulled tight to my chest, which felt bandaged as well.

"Okay." She slipped the thermometer out of my mouth. "What's your name?"

Again? "Jolene Asdale." My throat was dry. I croaked the words.

"Good. Would you like some water?"

"Yes." I sucked greedily from the straw while she held it with cheerfulness frozen on her face. When I had my fill, she set it on the rolling tray table beside the bed.

"I'll call the doctor and your husband." She turned to leave.

"Wait. What happened to me?" I didn't miss her reference to Ray as my husband. All my senses had returned full force. I smelled disinfectant, which made me nauseous. I heard carts rolling in the hallway and knocks on other patients' doors, along with the loudspeaker requesting Dr. Warner to report to Emergency. I saw the sun and wondered what day it was. And felt my headache.

I reached up and my fingers touched the bandage on the side of my head. "What's this?"

She kept moving toward the door. "I'll let them fill you in. They'll be right here."

I watched the hand on the clock move. One tick. Two ticks. Ten ticks. I felt around the sheet for the call button. I couldn't find it. I hurt myself trying. My left leg burned. I realized it was bandaged, too. Tears threatened.

Sixteen ticks later, Ray walked in. He had on street clothes. Before I could speak, the doctor appeared in the doorway behind him. "There she is." The doctor strode into the room and unwrapped his stethoscope from his neck to listen to my chest. He had huge sweat marks under the armpits of his blue scrubs. I wondered why he didn't have a white jacket on to cover them up. "Feeling better?"

Better was such a relative term. "Safer."

He nodded. "You are safely out of danger, but you had quite a time for yourself. You arrived here yesterday with a severe road rash on your left buttocks and thigh, a broken rib, a dislocated shoulder, a sprained wrist, a three-inch gash in the side of your head, some facial lacerations, and a mild concussion. You've been in and out of consciousness for the last twenty-four hours."

I reached for my water and he put the Styrofoam cup in my hand. "So today is Wednesday?"

"Yes. Good."

I wished everyone would stop saying "good" like I was a dog performing on command.

"Can I go home soon?"

The doctor breathed heavily out his nose, making the gray hairs in his nostrils dance. "Well, you've passed the twenty-four-hour mark for a concussion, but I'd still like someone to keep an eye on you for another day or so. The worst of the pain is over now that we have your shoulder back in place and you're all stitched and bandaged up. You might need some Tylenol 3 to take the edge off. If you'd be more comfortable at home and you have someone to watch over you, maybe we can release you later today."

I nodded and kept my eyes studiously off Ray's face. Who would that be?

The doctor promised to check on me again in a couple hours and left whistling "Oh Susannah." Ray pulled up a gray molded plastic chair next to the bed and rested his forearms on the mattress.

"What do you remember?"

I closed my eyes. "I remember—"

I sat bolt upright in the bed. Or at least I tried to. The pain in my rib cage made me change my mind a quarter of the way up. "Where's Cory?"

"He's at home, although he was here last night for observation. He got knocked unconscious by Fitzgerald Simpson when he failed to give him the right answers."

I flopped back onto my pillow. "The Beak."

"Right. The one who abducted you in Cory's BMW, I assumed."

Abducted? Hmmm, let Ray think that. I didn't want to admit I clambered inside the car without looking at its driver, idiot that I was. "Yes."

"And then what happened?"

I gave Ray the recap, surprised how much detail I could recall. Right up until the moment I opened the car door to exit the moving vehicle. "I don't know what happened after that."

"Simpson dragged you next to the car for a quarter mile. The man in the car behind you said your head hit the passenger door when Simpson braked and the door flew open. The man called an ambulance for you. Simpson took off in Cory's car, which the State Police later recovered at a gas station, with your purse. You're lucky you weren't more seriously injured. When I got to the scene, you were lying in the gutter like roadkill. The State Police recovered a sheath for a knife, the same brand as the one found in Tim Lapham's chest. It was lying on the floor of the car along with the contents of your purse. They figure Simpson left it behind by accident."

A wave of nausea washed through me. "A knife sheath?"

"Yep. The State Police are running the fingerprints on it now. It looks like Simpson may have been involved in Tim's death."

I didn't bother to ask Ray if he meant the sheath or the baggie I had stuck it in. I knew the state police would be clever enough to check both for fingerprints. How long would it take them to realize the fingerprints on the baggie were mine? I was about to become a prime suspect in Tim's death.

I crossed my fingers, hoping Erica's prints were not on the sheath and changed the subject. Ray would come back to it in time, I had no doubt.

"What did the Beak ask Cory?"

"He asked him where the envelopes are. The ones from inside the Ferrari hubcaps."

"What envelopes?"

Ray pressed his palms together and pointed the tips of his fingers at me. "That was Cory's answer too. Simpson didn't care for that answer."

"I have absolutely no idea what he's talking about."

Ray leaned back and folded his arms across his chest. "Neither did Cory. I did a little checking with the Phoenix Police Department. Seems the guy you bought the Ferrari off has ties to high stakes gambling. Rumor has it some records of unpaid debts have gone missing from his care. Maybe records he kept in his vehicle that weren't removed by his chauffeur prior to the sale. Maybe he sent Simpson to find them. I'd only be guessing."

I had watched Ray's lips move as he spoke all these incredible words, but I still didn't think I'd heard him correctly. "How'd you find all that out?"

"Phoenix has an undercover officer close to busting the guy. Seems the chauffeur is a talkative fellow."

"So what do we do now? We don't have his records."

"We're keeping an eye on Cory, and we'll keep an eye on you, too. Maybe Simpson is on his way back home. We haven't been able to find him here." Ray unfolded his arms and flexed his fingers. "Believe me, I looked."

Reassuring to know, but not reassuring enough. The Beak might pop up again, and I was in no condition to put up a fight this time. "What about Erica? Did you find her?"

"Not a trace, but we haven't had any more robberies, either. They may have taken the money and run."

I remembered the smell of lavender in my tub and doubted it. I could make a few phone calls, but I really needed to drive around to visit some of her old haunts. My right arm and leg still worked, so it might be possible in a day or two, if I could go home.

I looked over Ray's navy sweater and jeans and noticed his green parka in the corner. "Aren't you working today?"

"I am working. I just interviewed a victim. You."

Then where was his uniform? I decided to change the topic. I didn't want to chase him off. His presence meant security and reassurance. I didn't want him anywhere else but with me, today, tomorrow, and forever, even though I wasn't ready to admit it to him. "Becky Lapham said something at the funeral about money missing from the town treasury. Did you hear about that?"

"I did, a two hundred thousand dollar discrepancy in income. They hired an independent auditor a few months ago to look over the books." Ray leaned over me. "You don't suppose Tim was storing any of it in coffee cans around town, do you?"

I hoped not, but someone had entered my home sometime and placed the money there. My bet was still on Erica's band of merry men, however. "Tim always picked me up and dropped me off at the door, thank you."

"I don't suppose you were using the cash in your coffee can to bribe him to swing the zoning board in your favor, were you?"

My hearing must have been damaged by the impact with the car door. "Surely you jest."

Ray settled back in his chair. "Just looking at all the possibilities."

"It's innocent until proven guilty, remember?"

"Only in a court of law, darlin'."

I didn't have the strength to argue. I couldn't prove his accusations false—about Erica, Tim, or me. In fact, I had more questions than he did. I knew the knife sheath had been in my garage first. "I'm going to take a nap, okay?"

"Sure." Ray slid his chair away from the bed, making a noise worse than fingernails on a blackboard. "I'll join you." He kicked his feet up onto the end of the bed, folded his arms and closed his eyes. Seconds later, he was snoring.

Now that was an annoying habit of his I remembered well. He could stay awake forever and fall asleep in a moment. And he frequently snored, which meant I tried to fall asleep before him every night. Otherwise, I would lie awake for hours listening to him, trying to nudge him awake, all the while feeling guilty for depriving him of his much-needed sleep. This time the events of the prior days precluded his ability to rob me of my rest. Within minutes, I slept, too.

Two hours later my eyes opened with the unnerving realization that three days had passed since I checked on the auction for Brennan Rowe. What if I missed bidding on the car?

Ray was gone, but his parka remained. He must be off in search of coffee or food. I grabbed the phone next to the bed and listened for a dial tone. Nothing. I tried to sit up. My rib and thigh resisted. I used the bed control to raise myself to a sitting position and flung the sheets off. Then I inched my legs toward the edge. A nasty pinching in my nether regions let me know I was hooked to a catheter. I inched my legs back and rolled on my side, attempting to locate the call button.

"Darlin', that's quite a view."

I flopped onto my back and glared at Ray, who now stood in the doorway holding an extra large steaming cup of coffee in his hand. I held out my hand. "Can I borrow your cell phone?"

"You're not allowed to use a cell phone in the hospital. They mess with the machinery. You don't want to send the old guy on the heart monitor next door to the hereafter earlier than scheduled, do you?" Ray settled into his chair.

"I need to call Cory. I have a car I'm supposed to bid on."

"The roadster?"

My eyes nearly popped out of my head. "How'd you know?"

"Cory told me. He was worried you weren't going to be well enough to handle the bidding. He checked online. The auction is Monday."

"That's a relief."

Ray took a sip of his coffee. "You may not see it that way later."

I pointed to the sheet and blanket at the end of my bed. Ray stood to draw them up over me. "What's that supposed to mean?"

"You're bidding for Brennan Rowe. I heard Hughes wants the car, too. He's planning to outbid you."

I could kiss my fee goodbye. To my knowledge, Rowe hadn't achieved Hughes' multi-millionaire status yet. "Why does he want that car? I could get him any other car."

Ray shook his head. "It's not the car. It's Brennan Rowe. Hughes hates him. Seems Rowe applied pressure to the zoning board and they refused to allow Hughes to build his grocery store here in town. Rowe wants the site for an office building. Hughes wants revenge."

So Mr. Hughes was the vengeful sort, but was he also vengeful and determined enough to kill Tim Lapham? As a participant in the shocking discovery of the body, he might then be overlooked as a suspect. That way he could get the property for the grocery store and my property for his daughter's flower shop. And to think I used to like this man. Not anymore. Had this killer already returned to the scene of the crime?

I opened my mouth to share this notion with Ray, but the doctor walked in before I had the chance.

"I'm going to remove your catheter now. The nurse will be in to check your dressings and help you to the bathroom. If all goes well and you have a bowel movement after lunch, we'll be able to release you this afternoon."

How kindergarten. I tried to sit up but he pushed me back. "You're going to have to relax for me. Excuse us for a minute." He swirled the curtain around the bed, shutting out Ray.

He pulled the sheet down and I averted my eyes, trying to focus on anything but his task. "I need to make a phone call to find someone to stay with me."

Ray's voice drifted over the curtain. "Who ya gonna call?"

"Isa BELLE."

The doctor held up the tip of the catheter. "Good."

I winced.

"Actually, Mrs. Parker, your husband already completed all the paperwork so he can take you home this afternoon and keep an eye on you. Does that sound like a plan?" The doctor whisked the curtain open as he smiled at me.

A plan? It sounded more like Custer's last stand.

FOURTEEN

THE HOSPITAL GAVE ME a pair of scrubs which a nurse helped me slide into. They also gave me a pair of scrub slippers, which only touched the ground for the six steps I shuffled from the wheelchair to Ray's open car door. Ray put his green parka around my shoulders and toughed the cold with only his navy crew neck sweater, the sweater I gave him for Christmas five years ago. It had worn better than our marriage.

I had decided not to take a stand against having Ray drive me home. Then I saw the familiar pansies painted on the mailbox and the 1920s yellow-sided colonial standing neatly in a row with the rest of its neighbors like soldiers lined up for inspection.

"Where are you taking me?" As soon as the words left my mouth, a vision of the Beak entered my head. Déjà vu.

"Home." Ray made the final turn into his driveway—my driveway—our driveway?

"I want to go to my apartment."

Ray stopped the car next to the back door and shut off the ignition. "You can't. It's being fingerprinted."

I gasped. "What for?"

Ray turned toward me and rested his arm on the steering wheel. "I went there to look for Simpson. The place was trashed. Obviously someone had been looking for something. I don't suppose you have any idea what that might be?"

It had to be the money. Good thing I'd put it under the Christmas tree. "Not really."

Ray frowned. "It was such a mess I couldn't even find a clean outfit for you to wear home from the hospital. Isabelle and Jack offered to clean it up for you tomorrow when the technicians are done. She came by to see you yesterday, but you were still pretty out of it. She'll call you later."

Ray settled me on the sofa in the living room. The two steps up from the driveway to the back door to the kitchen had been killers. I laid my head back on the sofa pillow and noticed cobwebs on the wrought-iron light sconces. Nice to know he still needed my cleaning talents, if not me.

I glanced around the room. He'd changed nothing since I moved out. We'd painted the walls in this room pale yellow, bought a huge navy throw rug to cover part of the wooden floor, purchased this red sofa and two coordinating navy, red, and yellow plaid chairs, refinished some worn oak coffee and lamp tables we found in an antique shop, and dotted the room with wrought-iron accent pieces. I was somewhat alarmed to feel so at home here.

"Can I get you anything? Pepsi? Cheetos? Chubby Hubby ice cream?"

My favorites. Nice to know he remembered.

"Not yet, thanks. I'm going to close my eyes for a second."

Ray checked his watch. "You can close them for up to an hour. Then I'm going to wake you just to make sure I can."

Turned out he didn't have to. The phone rang instead, right on the end table next to my head, shattering my sleep cloud and drumming me into consciousness. As my eyelids peeled open, I saw Ray pick up the receiver. He said "hello" twice then he hung up. He shrugged at me. "Must be a wrong number."

The phone number here was unlisted so we never got prank or threatening calls—issues for a law enforcement officer.

I shifted to the right on the couch. Ray sat on the edge next to me and laid his hand on my forehead, then my cheek. "Feeling all right?"

His hand felt warm and set off sparks in other areas of my body. "Yes." I pulled away. "Fever's not a concern, is it?"

"Infection is. Your thigh was ripped up pretty good and you have stitches in your head." He rose to his feet. The sudden release of his weight off the couch pushed the leather against my thigh, causing a twinge of pain. "Just be a good patient, will you? I'm going to make us clam chowder and grilled cheese sandwiches for dinner."

I had to use the bathroom. I found the least painful way to get off the couch was to roll on my side, fall on my knees to the plush rug below, and stand with my right leg first. Thank God Ray didn't see me. I hated being so pathetic.

A quick perusal of the bathroom cabinets didn't turn up any evidence of Catherine Thomas' presence in this house. No extra toothbrush, deodorant, or even condoms to be seen. Maybe I'd have the strength to tackle the issue of marriage—our old one and his planned new one—with Ray tomorrow. When I finished in the bath, the phone rang again.

Ray called to me from the kitchen. "Will you get it? It might be Isabelle."

I answered.

"Are you all right? I've been worried sick since I saw you on the news."

It wasn't Isabelle. I moved as far across the room from the kitchen as the phone cord would reach. Why didn't we ever spring for a cordless?

"Where are you?" I fought to keep my voice at a whisper.

"I'm two blocks over. Get rid of Ray. We need to talk."

Trust my sister to ask for the impossible. "Did you rob the 7-Eleven? Did you leave fifteen thousand dollars at my house? Did you then trash my house when you couldn't find it again?"

I heard Erica cup her hand over the phone and yell to someone "She's on drugs. We'll have to come back."

I resisted the impulse to yell, choosing a low snarl instead. "Erica, I'm completely with the program. You have a lot of things to explain."

"Then get rid of Ray. I'll be right there."

"Alone?" I couldn't deal with another sociopath today. A bipolar disorder would be more than enough, thank you.

"Sure, whatever. Just lose Ray."

Ray chose that moment to appear, carrying a tray with our dinner on it and placing it on the used cherry dining table we'd bought from my aunt's estate. I dropped the receiver back in the cradle.

"Was that Isabelle?"

"No" —I crossed my fingers, hating to lie— "a survey. Wanted to know what radio station we listen to."

"What did you tell them? The classic rock station?" Ray started to unload the tray on the dining room table.

"I told them"—I crossed my fingers again like it really erased my sin—"I don't participate in surveys." I watched as he set the hot bowl of soup directly on the polished cherry surface of the table. That was going to cause a ring. I let it slide and carefully lowered my sore backside onto the Chippendale side chair. At least it was cushioned.

After my last few bites of grilled cheese, I let the bomb drop. "Ray, when I was in the bathroom, I realized I got my period. Can you go buy me some Kotex after dinner?"

His spoon stopped halfway to his mouth and his gaze met mine. "Can't you just use Kleenex or a paper towel, or something?"

"Only temporarily. I'm not even wearing underwear, you know. You're going to have to buy me some of the panties that hang in the aisle with the boxed hosiery, okay?"

He put his spoon down, clearly not hungry anymore. "Okay."

When I finished my dinner, I wrote down what brand and absorbency I wanted, plus my panty size. "And get the pads with wings, okay?"

He squinted at me as though he didn't think he'd heard me correctly.

I tapped the paper with the pen. "It's got to be this brand or I'll be leaking all over the couch." I named three stores, only one of which carried exactly what I'd asked for. I named them in the least likely order of finding the items in order to buy Erica and me at least half an hour.

Ray braced his shoulders like he was entering the battlefield and accepted the list, making me swear to lock all the doors behind him.

Five minutes later I opened the back door in response to Erica's knock. She stepped into the kitchen and threw her arms around me, squeezing tight. I screamed.

"Huh, sorry. I'm just so glad you're all right. The news said some bird watcher tried to drag you to death behind a stolen car. They have an APB out on him." Erica made quote marks with her fingers.

"Yeah, well, they have one out on you, too." I grabbed her arm and swung her into a kitchen chair, then stood over her to assess her current state.

She had on blue jeans with holes in the knees, fleece-lined clogs, a red sweater, and a navy pea coat. At least she was wearing her own clothes. Her blond ringlets fell to her waist and were clean. She smelled like lavender. No surprises there. Her hands looked dry and chapped.

She rubbed her arm and gave me a dirty look. "Why? I didn't do anything. I've been at Turning Stone Casino. We won six hundred dollars, and we only started with fifty."

"Where'd you get the fifty? The 7-Eleven?"

"What's with you and the 7-Eleven, anyway? You got stock in the place?" Erica stood, brushed past me, and helped herself to a cup of coffee from the coffeemaker on the counter. She opened the refrigerator and poured milk into it.

"Two convenience stores have been robbed since you and Sam Green went AWOL. You're suspects. You have done that type of thing before, remember?"

"Oh, I get it, blame the crazies. Well, we didn't do it. Sam's cousin took us to the casino. We checked into a room and we didn't check out until today. Satisfied?" Erica dropped into her chair and raised her eyebrows at me.

"What about the fifteen thousand dollars?" I explained about finding all the different hiding places in my apartment.

"Not mine. I would have hidden it better." She saluted me with her coffee cup in emphasis.

True, so true. "What about Sam and the rest of your friends?"

Erica shook her head. "They were only in the kitchen."

Now I had no clue as to who hid the money all over my apartment. "So you left the psych center just to go to the casino?" I tried to sit, then changed my mind and leaned my right hip against the counter instead.

"No, I left to talk to you about what the man said. I tried to call you, but you didn't answer. Then you didn't show up at the psych center. I waited for hours for you to show. Tommye kept telling me you were coming, but I didn't believe her. Sam said he'd call his cousin to take me to you. You weren't home." She let out an exasperated huff.

"I showed. You were gone."

"Whatever. I tried your house again on Sunday. You don't work on Sundays, but you weren't home. I gave up and we went to the casino."

For anyone else, that would be twisted logic, but not Erica. "So what did the voices tell you?"

"Not voices. I heard a man in the hall at the psych center. He said, 'God damn Jolene Asdale. She'll pay for this.'" Erica looked at me as if to say "see, now aren't you impressed?"

"What else did he say?"

"Nothin'."

"What did he look like?"

Erica rolled her eyes again. "I didn't see him, Jolene. I heard him." She flipped her ringlets over her shoulder. "Mom said you need to watch your back."

I stopped short of asking her what Dad thought. She'd been off her meds for almost a week. I couldn't believe anything she said. Erica still had conversations with Mom every day. I'm not sure if they occurred telepathically or if she mouthed the words for both of them, but she insisted Mom talked to her. I'd given up trying to dissuade her of this notion long ago.

"All right, well, I appreciate the warning, but now it's time for you to go back to the psych center. Ray can drive you."

"I can't go back. I haven't gotten your Christmas present yet. Mom gave me a great idea. Sam said he could hook me up and he did."

The phone rang twice and stopped. Then it rang two more times a couple seconds later. Erica leapt to her feet. "Ray's coming down the street. Gotta go."

I couldn't move fast enough to catch her before she got out the door. "No, wait, I don't need a Christmas present. Erica, you ... you ..." I watched her struggle through the two feet of snow in Ray's back yard. She fell on her knees twice. A silver car pulled up at the curb on the road behind ours. The door flew upward.

I let out a shriek. "Erica, you give me back that car right now!"

"I just need it a few more days to get your present." She waved with a broad smile and jumped inside the car, pulling the door down behind her. The DeLorean left a strip of rubber as it pulled away.

"SHIT!"

I'd have to put twenty dollars in the can for that one, but it was worth it to release the tension inside my head.

If I sent Ray after the car, he'd bust Erica for car theft. If I didn't send him after her, I'd be complicit in car theft and insurance fraud, at the very least. Who would be crazy enough to drive that car around in broad daylight, anyway? But that was a rhetorical question.

As I stood fuming in the doorway, I realized I never asked her about the knife sheath. It wasn't really necessary. I knew she hadn't killed anyone or been a party to killing anyone, just as sure as I knew I hadn't.

But she had confirmed my worst fears—the money and the sheath must have been hidden in my house to set me up as a thief and a killer.

I slammed the door, eased onto a kitchen chair and put my head between my knees.

Two minutes later Ray walked in. "Whose footprints are those outside? Did someone try to get in the house?"

I held out my hand for the two bags. "I don't think so. I didn't catch anybody."

Ray took off to follow the footprints. I felt bad for letting him go on another wild goose chase. Then I looked in the bags and realized he'd bought the wrong brand of sanitary napkins and the right size underwear—if I were a little girl. He did throw in a package of crew socks that would fit me, though.

When he entered the kitchen a few minutes later, his pant legs were soaked. "Whoever it was, they're gone."

I pulled on a pair of the socks. "Could have been Boy Scouts selling Christmas wreaths." Of course, it wasn't. It was my sister—the car thief.

Ray slid his parka off and eyed the bags on the table. "Don't you need to put that stuff on?"

"Actually, it was a false alarm, a little leftover blood from the catheter, I think. Sorry." I stood and hobbled into the living room, lowering myself on the couch in a seated position. My thigh throbbed a little bit, but not too bad.

Ray followed me with a mug of coffee in hand. It had hearts on it and a little Boynton critter holding a balloon with "Love you" written on it. Ray collected mugs and I didn't recall ever running that one through the dishwasher while we were married. Maybe now would be a good time to ask him about Catherine Thomas.

He took a sip and gazed at me. I still couldn't read his expression.

"So what progress have you made in the investigation of Tim's death?" Okay, I was a coward when it came to talking feelings, especially with Ray.

"The brand of knife used in the killing is sold at several local sporting goods stores including The Bass Pro-Shop. We asked the stores in a fifty-mile radius to check their records. They gave us a list of names from credit purchases but no one popped out at us when we checked the list. It may have been a cash purchase or a purchase from the Adirondacks or Daytona, who knows? No fingerprints, naturally. The state police didn't lift any off the sheath they found on the floor of your car, either."

I had the foresight when removing the sheath from the Miracle-Gro box to grasp it with a tissue, but lost it when I opened the baggie with my bare hands to drop it inside. I wondered why Ray hadn't mentioned matching the prints on the plastic bag. Maybe the sheath had fallen out of it— if so, a lucky break for me. It was, however, unfortunate that the sheath didn't have any fingerprints. It wouldn't help identify the killer, unless, of course I admitted to finding it in the Miracle-Gro box. Then it would add to the evidence piling against me. I decided to change the topic.

"Who saw Tim alive last?"

Ray grimaced. "Besides the killer? His landlady heard his door slam around six o'clock the Friday night he was killed. She said he had a way of bounding down the porch steps. She's pretty sure it was him."

"No leads from his co-workers or his bowling team?"

"They all describe him the same way as you." Ray took another sip. "Forensics found a few carpet fibers on his pant legs. A common rose-colored residential brand and a common gray carpet used in automobiles. Some human hairs in shades of brown and gray that we would need weeks to match to a DNA sample of a suspect, if we had one. At this time, I have no leads at all."

I shifted toward Ray, trying to take the weight off my left thigh. "At Tim's funeral, Celeste told me Tim had stood up in their church and disagreed with the pastor about gay rights. Do you know anything about that?"

"I heard the day it happened. He may have had some supporters, but they didn't choose to stand with him."

I rested my head against the back of the couch, feeling drained. "Do you think that's a motive for murder?"

"If we lived in a town where the KKK was active, I'd say maybe. But the issues aren't even a referendum on a ballot this year, so I doubt it. It did make him persona non grata with the conservatives in town, though. He might have lost his position on the zoning board and his treasurer's office in the next election."

"What about Mr. Hughes? He's angry about the zoning board vote. He as much as admitted to me that he knew Tim cast the deciding vote against him."

Ray leaned forward in his chair. "When did you talk to him?"

"Monday."

Ray stared into his coffee cup. "I'll check it out, but I think Hughes can find another plot of land. He's being stubborn; that's all. He's used to getting his own way. Besides, I like to think people don't kill each other over zoning board issues."

He didn't look up as he said this, but the implication that I remained on the suspect list for the same reason as Mr. Hughes hung in the air between us. My master of distraction instincts kicked in. I didn't want to discuss this with him. I didn't have any better answers for him now than before.

"Any chance the Beak killed Tim? Maybe Tim saw him in my shop, taking the hubcaps off the Ferrari and tried to stop him?" I wouldn't mind putting the Beak away forever. It would be a service to society.

"I don't figure him for the killer. I don't think Simpson had access to your alarm code, and Tim's body was moved to your showroom. Even if Simpson cracked your code, why would he kill Tim and then move him, only to draw attention to himself?"

"But what about Tim's trip to Vegas? Do you think he's on the list of people who owe money?"

Ray tipped his head back and drained his coffee mug. "It might account for why the money is missing from the town books. I already called the Vegas cops to see if they could uncover any more information about Tim's stay there."

I hated to believe Tim was less than honest—he'd be another man I misjudged. The first, of course, was Ray, who I could always rely on, even after I left him and ran over his toes. Shame on me.

Then a more frightening notion popped into my head. "If the Beak could somehow get in my showroom, do you think he would plant the body to frighten me into returning the lists? Especially if Tim's name was on it? Maybe he's trying to kill me now, because he thinks I've read the list."

Ray set his coffee mug down and reached for my hand. "I spoke to the Arizona cops. A man identified with one of Simpson's known aliases flew into town Wednesday, so it looks like he won't be bothering you again. They're going to try to apprehend him."

Good to know. My eyes started to sting and burn. I needed more sleep. Maybe a new idea would come to me in the morning.

I thought about the soft bed we used to share on the second floor. No way could I make the stairs and I didn't want Ray to get the wrong idea. Hell, I might even get the wrong idea myself, if I wasn't in agony from simply breathing. "Can you get me a pillow and blanket? I'm ready to call it a night, right here on the couch, if that's okay."

Ray took the stairs with enviable ease and reappeared with my requests. I lay down on the pillow and he covered me with the blanket, tucking it under my sides until I felt like I was in a cocoon.

"Thank you, Ray. You missed your calling. You'd make a great nurse. But I thought you weren't going to take care of me anymore," I murmured drowsily.

He knelt beside me and gave me his most charming lazy grin, the lines in the corners of his eyes deepening and showing his age. A few gray hairs at his temples that hadn't been there three years ago winked in the lamp light. The dark circles under his eyes seemed permanent.

"You had to get yourself kidnapped and assaulted. I'm required by law to investigate."

I met his gaze and held it. "You're not required by law to take me home and care for me."

He leaned his head over mine. I felt the warmth of his coffee-scented breath on my cheeks. "Old habits are hard to break." He kissed me on the forehead, his lips warm and moist enough to create a feeling of evaporation once he lifted them. I felt loved for all of two seconds. Then Ray stood and set his hands on his hips.

"But I'll break myself of you soon enough, don't you worry, darlin'."

FIFTEEN

When I opened my eyes the next morning, Ray was sitting in his favorite armchair, sipping coffee and watching me. If he hadn't worn a fresh red chambray shirt and a different pair of jeans, I'd have thought he sat there all night. I sensed he wasn't happy.

A glass of juice waited for me on the coffee table. I picked it up, ignoring the ring it left, and sipped.

Ray cleared his throat. "Isabelle and Jack cannot clean your apartment today. Cassidy has had the stomach flu since dinnertime last night. That's why Isabelle never got around to calling you. Jack started with it a few hours ago. Isabelle's got her hands full."

Ugh. I'd have to thank her for keeping the germs confined to quarters. That would be all I needed on top of a broken rib. "I'm feeling much better anyway. I haven't needed any Tylenol. Maybe I can tackle it."

Ray pinched his lips together so they flat lined. It was a new look for him, and I didn't know quite what to make of it. I was relieved when he opened his mouth instead, but only for a second.

"It occurred to me after you fell asleep last night that you haven't asked me about your sister. She's now been missing for almost a week. Your lack of concern tells me you know where she is."

The orange juice stuck in my throat. I started to cough, spewing drops of it on my blanket and the coffee table. My ribs protested with sharp pains as I fought to get under control. "Not so. I do not know where she is."

"But you're no longer worried about her."

I reached for a tissue from the box nearby and blew the remnants of the orange juice out of my nose, which now stung and burned.

"Jolene, your sister remains a suspect in a robbery investigation. You're obligated by law not to conceal her. Think about that while I make your breakfast."

Ray stalked into the kitchen, the stick up his butt ruining the view of his backside I used to enjoy so well. If he was this upset about Erica, just wait until he found out the truth about the money and the knife sheath.

The phone rang. I grabbed for it. Ray and I said "Hello" at the same time, blasting each other's eardrums.

"Ray? It's Catherine."

I gently set the receiver back in the cradle and listened to the murmur of Ray's words as he talked to his fiancée. When that became too painful, I gazed around the living room and remembered: the conch shell from our honeymoon in Martha's Vineyard, the sideboard we refinished together after we found it in an antique store one lazy Sunday afternoon, the wrought-iron chandelier with real candles that we only lit on Christmas Eve, and the cream-colored afghan his Aunt Dorothy crocheted for us as a wedding present. In truth, I remembered where we got every item in the room, as well as what occasioned the purchase. We'd spent a lot of time making this house our home, pleasurable time. Now, it brought me only pain.

When I no longer heard murmuring, I lifted the receiver and dialed. Time to call in the cavalry.

—

If Ray was surprised to find Cory on his doorstep at nine a.m., he caught on quick. He put his green parka on my shoulders and pushed me out the door. It bothered me a little that he didn't even ask me where I was going.

"Thank you for putting me in the middle of a very awkward situation." Cory deftly glided his BMW over the snow-covered roads.

"I'm sorry. He got a call from Catherine Thomas this morning and it rattled me. I had to get out of the house."

"He didn't tell you?" Dismay was written all over Cory's face.

"Tell me what?"

"I have it on good authority from the guys at the gym that he's moving out of your house today. A couple of them work for the Sheriff's department. Ray's making his new home somewhere east of here." Cory took his eyes off the road to search my face. "I'm sorry to be the one to tell you."

I leaned back against the headrest and closed my eyes. My throat tightened. Catherine Thomas lived east of here. I'd missed my chance to reconcile with Ray. A single tear jumped free from the pool in my eyes and dove down my cheek. Its traitorous friends soon followed.

Cory handed me a wad of tissues from a box tucked in his dash and drove me home in silence.

Since I was all cried out when we entered my apartment using my spare key, the sight of my belongings strewn and, in some cases, broken all over the floor didn't even faze me. Bending over to try to pick them up did. I decided to take a shower to see if the hot water would loosen me up a bit. It took me a while to unwrap and rewrap my ribs and change the dressing on my thigh. Cory tackled the obvious tasks of replacing cushions, refolding the linens, and remaking the bed in the meantime.

Four hours later everything was either back in its place or swept up and tossed in the garbage. The only good news was the untouched mousetraps. Maybe this time Mickey had been the lone marauder bent on cheesy mac.

Cory ran out to buy us submarines for a late lunch, and I gingerly lowered my backside onto my desk chair to call and retrieve the messages of the shop answering machine.

Beep. "Jolene, this is Bernie. We need to talk about your claim. Call me. Bye."

Beep. "Jolene, this is Bernie again. We need ... What? What are you flapping your arms at me for? ... No, I didn't see the news ... Oh, geez, Jolene, I'm real sorry. Sally says you were kidnapped and dragged behind a car last night by a hawk or somethin'. I'll—" Beep.

I rolled my eyes.

"Hey, this here's Matt Travis. I'm looking for a 1978 candy apple red Jaguar XJ6L with a camel interior for my wife, Estelle. I'd like to have it in time to put it under the Christmas tree. Any chance you all could find one for me? She used to have one when we got married, and I'm trying to rekindle the romance, if ya know what I mean? My number is …"

I grabbed a pen and scribbled Matt's down number.

Beep. "This is Cindy in Accounts Receivable at Vernon's Auto Parts. You have a bill for four hundred sixty-seven dollars and eighty-two cents that is over ninety days past due. If you pay it now, we won't have to send you to our collections agency. Please call me." Cindy reeled off her number.

The other five collections calls went on my list, too. December was a bad month for auto sales, and my cash flow had dwindled to the point where each bill I received almost brought me to tears.

I was surprised Brennan Rowe hadn't left me a message. He'd been quite a pest until now. I said as much to Cory when he returned with the food.

"Oh, he knew you were in the hospital. He's called me every day to make sure you'd be up and around by Monday."

How chivalrous of him to be concerned for my health.

I filled Cory in on the rest of the messages. "So, the Jag is worth about four thousand. If we broker the deal, we make a few hundred at best. What am I going to tell all these bloodsuckers?" I gestured to the list.

Cory replied around a mouthful of submarine. "Too bad we don't know the whereabouts of the three hundred thousand dollars missing from the town coffers."

"Where'd you hear about that?"

"The gym."

"That figure is bigger than Ray's."

A smug expression settled on Cory's face. "I got a lot of things bigger than Ray's, Jo."

I wasn't going there.

After we finished eating, Cory picked up the garbage and carried it into the kitchen.

I gave him his marching orders when he reappeared. "We're going to have to start calling our customers about their overdue bills. I want to be clear of debt by year end."

"Okay, you rest. I'll go into the office and start calling."

I stretched out on my couch. "Ask them to pay by credit card. We'll get the money faster."

As soon as the door closed behind him, I struggled to my feet. I couldn't rest. I had to find my sister and a killer before Ray asked me how my fingerprints got on the baggie holding the knife sheath. Was he deliberately not mentioning it and waiting for me to trip up? He'd been so free with information yesterday, except for that. Was that part of his good cop routine, waiting for me to confess?

I thought about the fifteen thousand dollars sitting under the Christmas tree in the park. If it wasn't Erica's, could it be Tim's? When and why would Tim have snuck into my house to store it there? Or had the killer placed it in my home to frame me? If so, he'd done a good job. Even Ray suspected me.

But why frame me? Did Mr. Hughes want my property that badly? Ray said Mr. Hughes liked to get his own way. Just how far would he go to get it? By eliminating Tim, he could get the property for his grocery store *and* a better shot at turning my sports car boutique into his daughter's florist shop. But I couldn't think of any other wrong I'd ever done Mr. Hughes that would provoke such wrath against me. I'd sold him only the best cars, just like all my other customers.

My phone rang. It was Isabelle, full of questions about the events of the last few days. When she satisfied her curiosity, I got to ask a few questions, too. "How is everyone?"

"Cassidy is dancing *The Nutcracker* and Jack is still whining. Why are men such wimps when it comes to illness?"

"They're just big babies. You know that. I have a question for you."

"Shoot. CASSIDY, GET OFF THE COFFEE TABLE. YOU'RE GOING TO FALL. Sorry, go ahead."

With the blast from Isabelle's built-in fog horn, I almost forgot what I wanted to ask. "Oh, yeah. The jewelry set you wore to lunch the other day, the one with the pearls?"

"Yes?"

"Celeste has a set like it. Did she buy it at your store?"

"Jolene, it wasn't an exclusive. A lot of jewelry stores sold it."

"What's it worth?"

"Wholesale or retail?"

"Retail."

"Hold on." Isabelle dropped the phone and I heard footsteps then nothing. Minutes later I heard footsteps again. She must have climbed the stairs to ask Jack. "Around seventy-five hundred. Jack says we did have two sets and the second one sold a few years ago. He'll look up who bought it when he gets back to work. It might not be until the day after tomorrow, though. He's feeling so poorly, you know."

I knew sarcasm when I heard it. "Okay. Give me a call then."

Seventy-five hundred. A lot of money for a retail store manager. Knowing Celeste, she got the jewelry from a man with money. Could that man have been Tim Lapham? Could the money not have been his to spend?

My doorbell rang.

Ray stood in the doorway, in uniform and angry. Very angry. I could tell from the red flush on his neck and the way he clenched and unclenched his fingers. He pushed past me and I closed the door.

"I'm going to ask you one last time, Jolene. Where's Erica?"

"I don't know, Ray. Really, I don't."

"The convenience store on Hogan was robbed this evening at five o'clock. Two men in camouflage entered the store and pulled a gun on the owner. The owner tried to get his gun from under the counter and the gunman fired on him." Ray leaned down so we were eye to eye. His hands cupped my uninjured shoulder and squeezed. "He's in critical condition, Jolene. I want to know everything you know abut Erica's whereabouts and I want to know right now."

I made a feeble attempt to protest his conclusions, since he'd cleared the long jump to reach them. "You can't be sure it was Erica. You can't even be sure it was the same men. They haven't struck before in the daylight."

Ray released me, straightened and folded his arms. "It's dark at five, Jolene. But it may not have been the same men. A witness said they peeled out of the parking lot in a funny-looking silver car."

"Funny peculiar or funny ha ha?"

"What? Wait a minute…" I saw the realization dawn in Ray's eyes. "Gumby told me about the DeLorean stolen from your garage. Are you telling me Erica is robbing convenience stores disguised as Marty McFly?"

"I'm telling you she came to your house yesterday to see me. She left in the DeLorean."

"Is that why you sent me on the wild goose chase?" Ray spat out the words. I had to brush a fleck of spittle from my check before answering.

"This is what I know. Erica claims she heard a man outside her room say 'God damn Jolene Asdale. She'll pay for this.' She left the psych center with Sam and went to my house to warn me. Sam's cousin picked them up. I wasn't home so they went to the casino. She came back yesterday to see me and took off again. She said they were at the casino the whole time and didn't rob any stores."

"Does she know the identity of the man she claims to have heard?"

"No. She didn't even see him."

The dismissive expression on Ray's face told me he filed her claim under more lunacy. I took offense. It was one thing for me to doubt or criticize Erica but a whole different thing when he did.

Ray continued his interrogation. "Did she name Sam's cousin?"

"No."

"Why are you letting her run around without a leash?"

"She swore she hadn't robbed any stores, and she had an alibi. Besides, I wasn't in any condition to tackle her, Ray. I tried to get her to stay with me and go back to the psych center with you. She said she needed to get me a Christmas present first. Something

Mom told her to get." As I finished my sentence, I realized I was the one who ought to be locked up.

"She doesn't have any money. Maybe you gave her the idea for robbing this store. Great. Just great, Jolene." He yanked my front door open and stepped onto the porch. "Stay here. If she shows up again or calls you, you get a grip on her and keep hold until I get back."

I wished I had a direct line to Mom like Erica. Maybe she'd fill me in on whatever the hell was going on. Since I didn't, I tried the next best thing. I phoned Tommye.

SIXTEEN

Tommye answered the phone at the nurse's desk, and she didn't know the name of Sam Green's cousin. She didn't even seem sure of her own, making me wonder what the current crisis at the psych center was. She wasn't too keen on telling me how to reach my darling sister's new boyfriend's parents, either.

"Now, Wheels, you know I can't give out personal information about the patients or medical information."

Ray could get the nephew's name quickly enough by himself, but I felt the need to redeem myself in his eyes. If I could give it to him first, maybe he'd think less harshly of me. "I think they may have shot someone dead last night."

"It's that boy. Your sister would never harm anyone except herself."

I heard papers rustling.

"Wheels, I can't tell you Sam's parents' home phone number is—" Her voice dropped to a whisper. She read off the number to me. “Get our baby girl back in here. She’s not fit to be wandering the streets alone.”

If only Erica were alone. I thanked Tommye and tried the number she gave me. On the seventh ring, a man snarled something into the receiver.

“Mr. Green?”

“Yes. What do you want?”

I didn’t even bother to explain who I was. He didn’t sound interested. “I need the name of your nephew. Apparently he’s the one who picked your son up from the psych center.”

“Little shit. It’s my wife’s nephew. When I get my hands on him, I’m going to kick his ass.”

“Yes sir. I need his name.”

“Theo Tibble, Theodore Tibble. Who’s asking anyway? Are you from the sheriff’s department?”

I set the receiver in its cradle without a sound and waited a minute for Mr. Green to realize I’d hung up on him. Then I picked up the phone again and dialed Ray’s cell.

“I don’t suppose Green told you what this kid looks like?”

“No.” And I didn’t plan on calling him back to find out.

“All right. I’ll see if he has a record and put an APB out on him, too. If we find him, maybe we’ll find Erica too.” Ray’s radio squawked. I couldn’t make out the words. He disconnected.

I just hoped if and when they found Erica, they wouldn’t have grounds for her arrest.

—

After a near sleepless night, I awoke and took inventory of my body. My shoulder still hurt if I tried to raise my elbow, my rib ached with every breath, my road rash felt itchy, but my headache was gone. Progress.

I wanted to go to the shop and process all the credit card payments to clear up my accounts receivable. The sooner the money hit my bank account the better. Cory didn't answer his home phone or his cell phone, which meant I would have to drive myself.

I put on my old gray sweats, the only loose pants I had, along with my old ski jacket with the grease stain on the front. The whole ensemble made me look like a poster child for the homeless. I hoped my neighbors wouldn't spot me.

It was snowing again. I had to place each foot carefully. I was sick to death of this stuff already, and winter hadn't even officially begun. I slipped twice, but almost made it to my car without being seen.

"Jolene Asdale, is that you?"

I lifted my head to see my neighbor, Mr. Murphy, approaching at full steam. He was a sprightly old guy with two tufts of hair sticking out just above his ears, which have the biggest lobes I've ever seen. His mother must have dragged him around by them as a child because they hung clear down to his jaw, which was always flapping, usually to complain about where I placed my trash cans.

"Jolene, I heard you were on the news. Some pelican fellow tried to abduct you at gunpoint? Is that right?"

Close enough. You'd think people would get the story right, but they never do. If I corrected him, he'd flub it some other way the next time he repeated it. Like all gossips, his interest lay in the titillation, not the truth.

"Yes, but I'm okay now. I have some work to do at the office." I tried to get around him to my car. He blocked me with ease.

"I heard you were leaving Tim Lapham's funeral at the time. Strange happenings with that boy. Did you hear about the four hundred thousand missing from the town treasury? It's got his name written all over it." Mr. Murphy shook his head as if this news saddened him. The truth was it probably made his day. Not too much excitement in our town most of the time. This last week was the equivalent of an oil strike.

"Yes, I heard about that, too."

He bobbed his head in agreement. "And leaving two young ones behind. So sad. Sally Winslow over to the church said Tim left them well-off though. A million-dollar life insurance policy. That sum ought to tide them over."

I stopped with my hand on the door handle. "You don't say."

"Sally Winslow said so. She works over to Bernie's insurance office. She ought to know."

"Yes, she ought to." I yanked the car door open and gently lowered myself inside. Sally also ought to keep those kinds of things confidential instead of blabbing the information all over town.

Mr. Murphy leaned into the open door. "I hear you misplaced a car. Someone stole it right out of your garage, ain't that right? No one's going to want to trust you with their vehicle no more, if you can't guarantee its safe return, now are they?" He rapped the palm of his hand on the roof of my car and closed the door in my face.

I backed out and childishly refused to return his wave.

So Tim had a million-dollar life insurance policy. I wondered if Becky was the beneficiary or if the children were. Becky didn't seem like a cold-blooded killer, but Tim had left her. Maybe a desire for vengeance and the allure of the cash pushed her over the edge. Somehow I doubted it. Still, it bore closer examination. Ray had probably already looked into it, not that he was in any mood to share more information with me. I could always ask Bernie about the insurance policy when I returned his phone call.

Walter was writing a ticket for an expired meter in front of my shop as I approached. Good old Walter was like the post office: neither sleet nor snow nor rain would deter him from his appointed rounds. He tucked the ticket under the Dodge's windshield and moved to the next car. His shoulder slumped inward, giving him a dejected look. He didn't appear to notice me as I pulled into a spot behind where he stood.

"Hi, Walter!"

He looked up, clearly startled. "Hi, Jolene. I heard about the abduction. How are you? You look … different."

"I'm stiff and sore. I look like a bag lady. Don't sugarcoat it." I walked over next to him.

He took a step away, tilting his ticket book so I couldn't see it.

Excuse me. I hadn't realized tickets were so confidential. "How are things at your house?"

"Hectic as always. You know how it is with teenagers."

His laughter seemed forced. He waved and continued down the road. Most of the parking spaces were occupied, but I didn't see him find another victim to ticket. I wondered why he appeared to be less than his usual jovial self. Maybe the weather had gotten him down, too.

Two members of the Dickens cast greeted me as I unlocked the front door to the showroom. After returning their cheerful good mornings and admiring their costumes, I locked the door tight behind me and scouted the entire building.

The Ferrari still occupied the showroom—without any passengers, live or dead. The garage remained empty. I'd half hoped to see the sheen of the DeLorean's stainless steel bodywork waiting for me. Guess Erica still needed it. For what, only God and Mom knew.

I found the results of Cory's collection calls on my desk and ran the twenty-eight credit card payments through the authorization machine. They would add a little more than nine thousand to my business checking account. My creditors would get their payments in the mail this week. One less thing to worry about.

I decided to call Brennan Rowe. He'd certainly called me enough, and I might be able to learn more about the Rowe and Hughes feud. I flipped through my Rolodex and dialed.

"Brennan Rowe."

"Mr. Rowe, this is Jolene Asdale. I wanted to let you know that the auction is scheduled for Monday. Bidding begins at ten a.m. Are you still willing to bid as high as seven hundred and fifty thousand?"

"Yes, but not one penny more."

"I feel obligated to inform you that I've been advised of another serious bidder who may be willing to go higher."

"Hughes." It was a statement, not a question. "He's mad I'm going to get zoning board approval to build on his lot."

"So I've heard. He's also mad Tim Lapham voted against him."

Now it was Brennan Rowe's turn not to reply. I forged ahead. "I heard a rumor some folks think Mr. Hughes might have wreaked his revenge on Tim Lapham."

"I'm surprised, Miss Asdale."

"Surprised at the rumor?"

"No. Surprised you'd repeat it. You have a reputation in this town as a sensible, level-headed businesswoman. That's why I came to you. You won't disappoint me, will you?"

I twisted the phone cord between my fingers, feeling chastised and guilty. "I'll do my best, Mr. Rowe. But if Mr. Hughes bids higher than your final offer, there's not much I can do."

"Then may the best man win."

That damn saying again. I planned on the best woman winning.

Rowe hadn't seemed inclined to comment on Tim's vote. Had he paid him for it? Was that the fifteen thousand dollars hidden in my apartment? Why hide it there? And why set me up to take the fall if Rowe killed Tim to cover up their actions? Rowe needed me out of jail in order for me to bid on the car—unless he really didn't want the car. That didn't make any sense, but then, not much had lately.

I locked the front door behind me and spotted Celeste turning the key in the lock at Talbots across the street. I glanced down at the ugly sweatpants I'd put on again this morning with my equally ugly ski jacket. A new dress coat might be in order and maybe a loose pair of dress slacks. I had to win an auction on Monday, and it always helped to look as well as feel like a successful businesswoman when taking on the men.

When Celeste's eyes roamed over me a few minutes later, I regretted providing her with so much ammunition to launch an attack on my person. But, for once, she had other things on her mind.

"Jolene Asdale, I heard all about that pecker face who tried to kidnap you. Are you all right?"

"I'll heal, but my clothes were ruined when he dragged me with the car. I need a new coat and maybe a loose pair of slacks. My leg got ripped up pretty good."

"I have just the thing." Celeste beckoned. I followed her across the floor to the most beautiful winter white wool coat I'd ever seen. "Try on this coat and this pink scarf. Pink works with your coloring."

When I looked in the mirror, I had to admit it all worked. But a quick glance at the price tags made me hesitate.

Celeste slid the coat off my shoulders and headed toward the register with it. "Don't worry, Jolene. I'm going to give you my employee discount. Consider it a reward for bravery."

I decided to wear my new clothes out of the store and asked Celeste to ring up a pair of dress pants for tomorrow.

At the register, Celeste reached behind her on the counter and picked up a fluffy turquoise angora-like sweater.

I waved my hand. "Oh, no, not for me."

She held it up by the shoulders. "I was thinking about Erica for Christmas. She'd look fabulous in it."

Trust Celeste to know her clothes. Erica would love it, and I hadn't picked anything out for her yet.

Celeste rang everything up and held out my shopping bag. I reached for it. She pulled it away at the last minute. "I heard Ray moved out of your home yesterday."

I resisted the urge to lunge for the bag, run out the door, and drive over there to check. Instead, I shrugged.

"It's funny. I always thought the two of you would get back together. That's why I never made a play for him myself."

Was I supposed to thank her? I settled for a non-committal smile and a change of subject. "You mentioned Tim's disagreement with the pastor at your church. How bad was it?"

Celeste set the bag on the counter. "Tim and the minister had words after the sermon. It wasn't pretty."

"Do you agree with the minister?"

"No, I don't, but in this town, it doesn't pay to be open with your opinions. I guess Tim found that out."

I cocked my head to the side and stared at Celeste. "Are you saying Tim was killed because of his beliefs?"

Celeste waved her hand dismissively. "No, oh no, not at all. I'd be more inclined to think it had something to do with the half million missing from the town coffers."

I picked up my bag. "Every time I hear the number it's grown. Where are these numbers coming from?"

"The town's independent auditors are looking over five years of financial statements." Celeste leaned over the counter. "The rumors are flying."

I hated to encourage her, but knew she'd have the information I wanted. "Did you hear anything about Tim's life insurance?"

"He left a million to the children, split fifty-fifty, in a trust fund. Becky will have to submit receipts for the children's expenses to the bank in charge of administering the trust and she will be reimbursed. At least their college funds are guaranteed."

"So Tim didn't leave Becky any money directly?"

"No. They had their wills changed after their divorce. Greg Doran handled it."

I thanked Celeste for her help and headed back to my car, thinking about our conversation. It didn't sound like Becky had a motive for murder, but the missing money sure pointed to Tim's knowledge of, or involvement in, something unseemly.

Now if I could only figure what.

SEVENTEEN

I POINTED MY CAR in the direction of home and for some reason it chose to transport me not to my apartment but to the home Ray and I once shared. I pulled up in front of the house and looked for signs of life. Nothing.

My key still worked in the lock. No surprises there. I stood in the middle of the living room and looked around. The pillow and blanket I'd used two days ago were folded and stacked on the corner of the couch. But some things were missing.

The big open spot in the living room shouted "Ray's favorite armchair and ottoman." The empty hooks on the coat rack said "Ray's jackets." I climbed the stairs to the second floor, ignoring the discomfort from my scabbed thigh. The hangers and bureau drawers were empty. I checked the drawer Ray usually locked his service revolver in. Only a hint of leather and gun oil remained, along with the key to the drawer which he had always hidden before. The spicy scent of Ray's aftershave lingered in the bathroom, but his razor and toiletries were gone. In the kitchen, a big gap on the counter told me Ray had taken the coffeemaker. I'd bought it for his birthday last year.

He'd left behind all the things we had inherited from my father or purchased together as a couple, which meant he'd left almost everything. I didn't want any of it, either. I just wanted Ray, but this move had an aura of finality to it. My realization had come way too late.

The doorbell rang. I ignored it. Probably nosy neighbors come to get the scoop.

I heard a key in the lock. The door creaked open.

I walked into the living room and came face to face with Catherine Thomas. She let out a yelp of surprise when she spotted me. I was glad to have my new clothes on because she looked like a true business professional: black pantsuit, boots, and wool coat much like the one I used to have. Her hair fell in glorious waves to her shoulders. I had to give her credit—she was a knockout. "Jolene, hi, I, uh, I thought no one was here. I didn't see any cars in the driveway."

"I parked in the street." I took a few more steps toward her. "Ray's not here. Were you meeting him?" If so, I planned to run out the door.

"Sort of. He told me to stop by and pick up my bike from the garage. I had a waffle iron in the kitchen that belongs to me, too."

"Oh, well, I guess you guys are going to need that." Pictures of the two of them sharing breakfast and the Sunday comics filled my head. Ray and I used to do that. A lump formed in my throat.

Catherine tipped her head to the side. "What do you mean?"

I forced the words through my lips. "Ray moved in with you, didn't he?"

An emotion I couldn't pinpoint floated through her eyes. "He moved in with one of the guys from the sheriff's office temporarily."

I wanted to do the happy dance, but I sat gingerly on the sofa instead, an immense sense of relief flowing through me. "Really? But you have a ring."

She crossed the room and took the chair across from me. "It's just a ring. It doesn't mean anything." She looked at it as if for the first time. "I thought it might someday, but now I know it won't."

"I don't understand. Ray gave it to you, didn't he?"

Catherine blushed a becoming shade of pink. "He asked me what I wanted for my birthday, and I told him the truth. A diamond ring."

"And he gave you this ring?" I pointed to her finger.

"Yes, but he didn't say the magic words that usually accompany a ring the way I hoped he would. Instead—" Catherine twisted the diamond ring around her finger. "Well, you know the Meat Loaf song? You know the one, 'Two Out of Three Ain't Bad'?"

I knew it. The chorus was about wanting and needing, but not loving a person. The track was on one of Ray's favorite Meat Loaf albums. "Yes."

"It was playing on the stereo when he gave me the ring, like a subliminal message." Catherine slid the ring from her finger and pinched it between her thumb and pointer finger. "Ray doesn't say too much, but I'm pretty sure the only girl he's ever going to love is you."

I resisted the urge to clap my hands in glee.

"He told me when we met that his divorce wasn't finalized, but he planned to take care of it. I knew that day in the Coachman Inn he hadn't. He would have had to tell you about me, and you had no idea who I was. I'd had the ring for two months. He never even asked if he could move in with me now."

She laid it on the coffee table and stood. "I'm going to take my stuff and go. Maybe you can return this to him when he gets here. I don't want to embarrass myself further by crying in front of him." Her voice broke. "Because I do love him, but I don't want to be his backup plan."

She stumbled out the door, crying.

I felt guilty, as though I had ruined her dreams and broken her heart.

But Ray had taken up with her, not me. Of course, maybe if I'd never left him, he never would have taken up with her in the first place. Maybe if I'd wanted, needed, and loved him the way he wanted and needed to be loved, none of this would ever have happened.

I wasn't too keen on being the one to tell him his relationship with Catherine was over. She'd abdicated responsibility rather quickly and if I'd been less in shock myself, I would have refused to do the deed. If Ray truly loved her, I'd break his heart a second time.

I eyed the diamond ring on the coffee table. If I just left it there he'd get the message, wouldn't he? He would call her and she would tell him, right?

The front door swung open before I had a chance to bolt. Ray stepped inside and took off his deputy sheriff's hat. "What are you doing here?"

I moved between him and the ring. "I heard from Celeste that you moved in with one of your friends. I came over to verify for myself."

He dropped his hat on the chair and put his hands on his hips. "I told you I would move out. The house is yours, not mine. You can move back in or sell it, whatever you decide."

I summoned all my courage and swallowed all my pride. "I wanted to tell you how…" What should I say? How sorry I am that I left you? How much I love you? I fumbled for the right words.

Ray's head tipped to the side. I could tell he'd caught sight of the ring on the table. "What did you say to Catherine?"

"Nothing. She came to pick up her bike and waffle iron."

He strode across the room and snatched the ring from the table. "And left her ring by accident?"

"Not exactly."

"Then, tell me, Jolene, what *exactly* did happen."

Ray's neck had that telltale red flush. He was pissed and apparently pissed at me. I took offense and let it all spill out unedited. "Apparently, you gave her a ring. She expected you to ask her to marry you. You didn't. She introduced herself to me last week at the Coachman and realized I had no idea who she was. She surmised you never spoke to me about finalizing the divorce the way you promised her. She decided today she didn't have a future with you because you didn't even ask to move in with her." Okay, so the coward in me left out the part about how she figured he still loved me. I didn't want to be too sure of myself.

"I didn't promise her." Ray pushed the ring into his pant's pocket. "Is that all she said?"

I tried to read the tone of his voice to see if he was asking if he had a chance to make up with her, but I couldn't. I was going to have to lay it all on the line. "No, she said she realized you were always going to love me and she didn't want to be your backup plan."

A nerve in Ray's cheek twitched—something I'd never seen before. Did he care for Catherine? Was she wrong?

"Thank you." He pulled a ring of keys from his jacket pocket and detached the one for my house. He held it out to me. "I think that's it."

If I took the key, we would be through. "Tell me, Ray, is she right? Do you still love me?"

Ray's arm dropped to his side. "Jolene, you left me and then you pretty much ignored me for the last three years, unless you needed me to help with Erica. I was *your* backup plan and I'm tired of it. I don't want to wait around for you anymore."

My heart skipped with joy at the thought he'd been waiting around—until Catherine's face popped into my mind. "I would hardly call almost a year-long affair with Catherine waiting around."

"Thank you. I feel guilty enough about how I treated her. Tell me, Jolene, do you ever feel guilty about how you treated me?" His gaze zoomed in on my face. I had to look away.

I did feel guilty. I should have stayed to work it out with him instead of packing and running away. But it wasn't entirely my fault.

I met his gaze. "What about the way you treated me, Ray? What about all the pressure to have a baby with you, a baby you knew I didn't want to have?"

His eyes glazed over. "I was wrong, Jolene. Wrong to pressure you, wrong to think we would have been happier with a baby, and maybe even wrong to marry you in the first place."

His words drove a knife into my heart. My eyes filled with tears. I wiped them with the tail of my new pink scarf. "What are you saying, Ray? That you never loved me? That all ten years of our marriage were a mistake?"

"I don't know. I married you thinking I could change you. I was wrong. It was wrong."

The tears flowed down my face now. I felt like I was drowning. I needed to sit down. I fumbled for a chair, but Ray pulled me in his arms first.

He pressed his lips to mine, sending a shock wave through my body. I resisted, flattening my hands against his chest and pushing. He refused to budge.

Instead, he cemented his body to mine. His tongue teased my lips apart. Our tongues entwined.

I slid my hands up his chest and curved them around his neck and into his hair. I grew faint from lack of air, but I didn't want to break off the kiss. Ray didn't show any signs of stopping.

Not that I wanted him to.

His lips moved to my ear.

His breath tickled it.

I tensed in anticipation, waiting for the familiar bite on my earlobe, knowing where it might lead and more than willing to be led. This man was the only one I ever truly wanted.

He whispered, "One last chance, darlin'. Tell me the truth about the money."

My back stiffened. How cop-like to attack the witness in a weak moment. But then, Ray's job always was his first priority. Just once, though, I would have liked to have been placed ahead of his job.

I shoved him away, my face flushed with anger. "We were talking about our marriage, Ray."

He folded his arms across his chest, clearly back in control. Had he felt nothing just now? Was it all just an improvised interrogation technique? I tried to compose myself, not wanting to let him see that he still had the power to break my heart.

"I want to talk about the convenience store robberies, Jolene. The witnesses to the last robbery where the clerk was shot and killed said the getaway car was funny ha ha, like a clown car, and didn't have plates."

"A Mini Cooper? Someone robbed a store driving a Mini Cooper?"

"That was my first thought, too. A Mini fits their description of a small car with two doors, but I can't find a Mini registered to anyone within a hundred miles. Do you know anyone who owns one around here, maybe a collector?"

"No one in particular, but I remember seeing one on the list of customers I compiled for you. I'll have to go back to the office and go through the records again."

Ray nodded. "I think you were right about this robbery. It's a copycat. But I think you were wrong about Erica. Sam's cousin Theodore drives a late model dark-colored Lincoln."

All the air rushed out of me like a punctured tire. "Oh." I still didn't want to believe it, but I'd been so wrong about so many things.

"I've got an APB out on Theodore Tibble. He shouldn't be too hard to find now that we have a plate number." Ray picked up my hand and held it. "I think the fifteen thousand you found in your apartment is evidence of Erica's involvement."

A warning bell went off in my head. "How do you know I found fifteen thousand?"

Ray's grip tightened on my hand. "I saw you in the park that night, putting the money under the town Christmas tree. I have the money in the evidence lockup."

I whipped my hand away, rose to my feet, and glared at him. "You followed me? Then you had the nerve to come to my house and question me as though you didn't know what was going on?"

Ray looked up at me, rubbing his palm over his chin and making a scratching sound on his five o'clock shadow. "You weren't exactly being honest with me, either."

"Is there anything else you're not telling me?"

He stood, towering over me. "I could ask you the same. Where did the money come from?"

"I don't know."

Ray snorted. "You expect me to believe that?"

We used to trust each other, but apparently we'd lost that, too. I didn't even bother trying to convince him that this time I'd told him the real truth.

"So Erica has been your number-one suspect all along. Tell me, do you think she killed Tim Lapham, too?" I held my breath.

"She's riding with a sociopath in a DeLorean stolen from your garage. Did you know Sam Green wasn't in the psych center the night Tim was killed?"

I held up my hand as if to say "Stop." It was too much for me to process all at once, but I knew Erica was not involved in murder.

His radio squawked his car number and a code. He raised it to his lips and acknowledged the call. "I have to go, Jolene."

He laid his key to our home on the table.

"Ray, we're not finished talking."

"I think we are. I need to do my job. And I will—whatever it takes." Without a backward glance, he turned and walked out the door.

That was not the man I married.

EIGHTEEN

My first loyalty was to Erica. First, last, and always. Like a mother to her child. She needed my protection. Ray didn't. I would prove Ray wrong. But I would have to call Tommye again to find out why Sam Green wasn't in the psych center the night Tim was killed.

I dialed the number from my cell phone in the Porsche.

"Sam signed himself into the psych center so he could leave at any time. His parents picked him up to go to his brother Alex's eighteenth birthday party. Big to-do." Tommye sounded as tired as I felt. "Sam had been behaving himself pretty well in here, so the doctors thought it would be good to have him try a short stint of family life again. I guess he got a taste for freedom instead."

And the opportunity to arrange his escape, no doubt. "What's his home address?" I could use the reverse phone directory to figure it out, but having Tommye tell me would be a lot faster. She must have realized the same because this time she didn't even protest.

"Sixteen Vineyard Street."

I thanked her and headed my car in that direction. I wanted to see for myself where Sam grew up and what cars were parked in his driveway. I couldn't be lucky enough to find a late-model Lincoln or a DeLorean there, but I hoped.

Ten minutes later I sat across the street from what would have been considered a mansion in the 1830s and still said "wealthy" today. Heavy on the brick and turrets, it towered above the road and cast a shadow over the entire manicured lawn, enhancing my feeling of dread. The only car in the driveway was a white BMW. I thought about ringing the doorbell and introducing myself to Sam's parents, but after recalling his father's attitude the other night, their welcome seemed remote. I figured them for the kind of parents who blamed everything on their child's friends and never on their child. I had to ask myself if the same was true of me when it came to Erica. I liked to think it wasn't.

I'd hoped to come away from Sam's home feeling more confident in Erica's innocence, but one thing stood in my way. When I pulled up, I noticed the sign in front of the mansion across the street from the Greens' house. It read "Offices of Timothy Lapham and Associates, Certified Public Accountants."

Tim Lapham must have known Sam Green. Only a two-lane side street separated Tim's office from Sam's home. If only I could locate Erica, maybe I could get some answers—even meet the elusive Mr. Green. All I knew about him was that he stabbed his mother in the hand over a pork chop and captured my sister's affections. He must have more to his story than that. I hoped it didn't include a chapter where he killed Tim and placed him in my Ferrari.

I eased the car into drive and headed for the office, bent on looking up the owner of the Mini Cooper and crossing my fingers it wasn't one of Sam Green's friends or neighbors.

It wasn't. According to our records, the sparkling silver metallic car belonged to a collector named Brennan Rowe.

—

I debated then called Ray. After I said Brennan Rowe's name, I thought he'd hung up on me because the line fell silent. But no, he was just as flabbergasted as I was.

He sighed. "I'm going to go to his house and knock on his door. If he calls you for some reason, say nothing. I don't want him to have a heads-up before I get a chance to question him."

"Okay. Will you call me and tell me what you learn?"

"No." He disconnected, leaving me kicking myself for even wasting the breath to ask.

When I arrived home, I was too exhausted and too stiff to look under the beds and in the closets like I usually did. I'd never found anyone there before. Why would this night be any different?

I soaked in the tub for an hour. Then I sat staring at the television set for two more. Who knew what show was on? Who cared? Ray didn't love me anymore. Worse, he thought my sister was a robber and that I might have killed Tim Lapham.

Or was I just being paranoid? Tim hadn't been wearing a coat when we found his body, which suggested he'd been killed indoors. Ray hadn't obtained any warrants to search my apartment for evidence like blood. Or had he come over here the day I was in the hospital to search, only to find the place trashed? Maybe he trashed it himself. I liked to think not, but he'd been manipulative this afternoon, a whole new facet to his personality. Of course, I'd never been implicated in any of his investigations before.

The money and the knife sheath must have been left by someone to frame me. I could think of no other reasonable explanation. According to Cory, Brennan Rowe had called and learned that I was in the hospital. Rowe would have known it was safe to visit my apartment. Could he have been the killer? Maybe he bribed Tim to vote in his favor, and then Tim changed his mind, forcing him to kill him in order to cover up the bribes. Or maybe he had been blackmailing Tim. But what would a nice guy like Tim be involved in? Gambling? Embezzlement? How would Rowe have known about either one? He was at the funeral service. Maybe he and Tim had been friends. I could always ask Rowe the next time we spoke. Hopefully it would be on Monday after the auction. He should be in a good mood when he won the car. Maybe he would let something about Tim slip. It was worth a try. Had he tried to frame me, knowing that his ties to Tim would be discovered in time?

If only Ray would tell me what he knew about Tim's death. He had to know much more than he had shared to date. Of course, I knew more than I shared to date, too. I still hadn't told him about the knife sheath. I couldn't, not until I knew it wouldn't convict me as Tim's murderer.

I rose and headed into my bedroom, shutting off the lights as I went. In the bathroom, I went through my nightly bedtime ritual, finding it difficult to raise my arm so I could remove my contacts. It was even harder to pull my nightshirt over my head.

On the way to bed, I tripped over something on the floor. It was a mousetrap, already activated but without a mouse inside.

The peanut butter and cheese on it was smeared but mostly intact. The little guy must have gone for it and been frightened away when the trap snapped. Great, I had lucky mice, fast on their feet.

I climbed slowly onto the bed and pulled up the covers, straining my ears for the sound of scurrying feet. My apartment was silent, dead silent. I reached over and turned off the lights.

But I didn't fall asleep. Visions of mice danced in my head. I pictured one running over my face, then one halfway inside my open mouth, tail wiggling, as I drifted off. Or was that my mouth? The lips were fire-engine red. Familiar lips. Familiar tail.

I heard a squeak. Not the squeak of a mouse. The squeak of a door opening, a closet door in my living room. Someone was in my apartment. I reached for the phone to dial 911. No dial tone.

I froze as I heard footsteps. Were they coming toward me or moving away? I opened my mouth to scream but nothing came out. My hands were shaking. I dropped the phone. It crashed onto the floor.

Now my intruder knew I was awake. I didn't hear any movement. I slid out of bed and got on my knees, trying to think of a weapon. I didn't have any nearby. My whole body trembled, covered in cold sweat.

I recalled my self-defense training. *Pretend you have a weapon.*

I tried to speak but only a croak came out. The words couldn't make it past the tightness in my throat. *Come on, Jolene.*

"I have … a gun … GET OUT! I HAVE A GUN!"

All was silent for a moment. Then I heard it. The sound of footsteps running away. The kitchen door banged. He was gone.

I crept out of bed and into the living room to find my purse. I dialed 911 on my cell phone and reported an intruder. Then I hid behind the sofa.

Walter arrived within minutes. I heard his sirens and saw the flashing lights through the front window. I clambered out from behind the sofa and met him at the front door.

This time he was armed and in his black uniform. I told him what happened. With his gun in hand and me within a yard of him, Walter looked behind and under every piece of furniture, in all my closets, behind the shower curtain, and even in the dryer.

I raised an eyebrow at that one.

"Some of these cat burglars are tiny guys and clever. Is anything missing?"

I'd looked every room over more thoroughly than Walter. "Not that I can see."

"My guess is you scared him off before he had a chance to grab anything."

I didn't really have anything of worth to grab except a twenty-seven inch television. Even my wallet held only maxed-out credit cards. "I'm not sure it's that simple. Ray told you about the money I found here, didn't he?"

Walter holstered his gun. "No."

"Oh. Well…" Now I didn't know what to share, so I used my distraction technique. "My phone was dead, Walter. I used my cell to call 911."

He rushed off to investigate. I followed and watched as he checked the cords and plugged them into the phone outlets again. He picked up the receiver and listened. "They work now."

"Do cat burglars usually unplug the phones?"

"No." He pointed to a chair. "Want to tell me about the money?"

Not really. I sat down with him anyway. I thought Ray's department worked more closely with Walter, but then Walter was only a glorified parking meter attendant. I didn't want to damage Ray's investigations any more than I already had with a slip of my lip. "I found some money in my coffee can and a couple other hiding spots. Ray has it now."

Walter shifted his weight and his leather holster creaked. "Where did it come from?"

"I don't know." I couldn't bear to rehash the last week, nor did I know if Ray would be angry with me if I did. "You better ask Ray about it."

"I will. I should call for a fingerprint technician."

The way Walter said it I knew it would be another waste of time and taxpayer money. "Don't bother. I'm sure this guy was smart enough to wear gloves."

Walter nodded. "Let me check to make sure your locks aren't damaged."

I waited for him to return to the living room.

"No sign of forced entry. Guy must be a real pro. Although those skeleton locks are easy to pick. You might want to consider a deadbolt." Walter sat across from me again. "So you don't really have a gun?"

"No, not even pepper spray."

"I'm not sure Ray would approve of pretending that you do. It worked this time, but next time, the guy might have a gun and fire in self-defense toward the sound of your voice."

That was a pretty picture. Walter needed some work on his crime victim reassurance skills.

Walter continued, "Do you want me to call anyone? Ray maybe?"

"No thanks, Walter." Ray had been too manipulative yesterday, and even though he'd cared for me after I body-surfed behind a car, I wanted to hold onto what little pride I had left.

"Well, if you're sure. I'll swing by every hour just in case. Leave your living room and kitchen lights on. That should keep him away."

I walked Walter to the door. "Thanks for coming so quickly. I was never so happy to see you."

"I was just three blocks away on another robbery call. The intruder was already gone when I got there." Walter stopped in the doorway. "In fact, this may have been the same guy."

I doubted it.

After Walter's squad car pulled out of the driveway, I curled up on the couch under the afghan Ray's Aunt Dorothy made us. I'd brought it home with me so it wouldn't be lonely in our empty old house. I knew I wouldn't be sleeping anymore tonight, but maybe I could stop shivering.

Then it hit me. Had the killer returned to make sure the evidence was still planted in my apartment or, worse, to plant more evidence?

I stumbled off the couch at that terrifying thought and started searching. After two hours, I hadn't found anything suspicious. Of course, the only evidence left to plant was trace evidence, like blood. Stuff I wouldn't be able to see with my naked eye.

Stuff that would guarantee an airtight case against me.

NINETEEN

THE NEXT MORNING I showered with the sunrise and took off for the diner on Main Street, fleeing my apartment and my fears. I sat there for two hours, dawdling over my breakfast and reading the Sunday newspaper from cover to cover. I might even have dozed off for a second or two. My waitress was ticked, until she spotted the twenty dollar tip I left her.

Then I went to sit in the shop. Somehow the place where I'd found a dead man seemed safer than my home where I'd surprised a live one. In the wee hours of the morning, I'd almost managed to convince myself that if my intruder wanted to kill me, he would have done so last night. Of course, the killer's weapon of choice, as well as the Beak's, had been a knife, which required close proximity. Guns trump knives. Maybe that was why I was still alive.

Or maybe the killer had no need to eliminate me, since Ray and the court system would have me locked up soon enough, based on the evidence. The thought terrified me. Prison was the one place I never wanted to go, and if I was in there, Erica would be running around unsupervised. Given enough time, she'd probably end up in the cell next to me.

This time the master of distraction needed a distraction. Otherwise, I would drive myself crazy thinking about all the possibilities.

I fired up the computer and searched the Internet for a candy apple red Jaguar that might fit Matt Travis' requirements for his wife's Christmas present. I located one in Albany. I called and spoke to the owner, who had a pretty impressive paper trail. Good quality automobiles are all about paper trails: purchase documents, maintenance records, and so on. I hung up positive that I'd found the right one. It gave me some hope.

I rose to put on my coat. I would go home and sleep in the daylight.

Then I heard a scratching noise. I froze. The sound seemed to be coming from the garage bays. My hand hovered over the phone receiver. Should I dial 911? If it was only a mouse—the garage did have its share of infestations—I'd look like an idiot. If it was a killer, I wanted Ray or even Walter. I swallowed the lump in my throat and rose to my feet to investigate with nine and one already dialed into my cell phone.

As I stepped into the bays, the side door slammed closed. One garage door began to roll up its tracks, squeaking in protest. When it reached the top, the stainless steel DeLorean glided inside. The driver's door opened and Bob Cratchit stepped out. The passenger door clicked open and rose, and his wife appeared. I took a closer look under the red plaid and black velvet bonnet.

"Erica!"

"Hey, Jolene. How do we look?" She twirled and her full skirt billowed around her ankles. "We dressed for the celebration today.

It's only two weeks until Christmas." She stopped twirling and leaned toward me. "Your present's all set. I can't wait for you to see it." She clapped her hands and raced around the front end of the car, grabbed the driver's arm and pulled him toward me.

"This is Sam. Sam, this is Jolene."

Sam was good-looking, for the devil. He had wide shoulders, a small waist, brown hair that curled around his face, expressive brown eyes, and the unlined skin of a man in his twenties. It was clear she'd fallen for a younger man. At the moment, his eyes expressed happiness at being in Erica's company. God help her if she ever served him a pork chop as his mother did.

He held out his hand. "Nice to meet you, Jolene. Erica talks about you all the time." He gestured to the DeLorean. "And thanks for letting us borrow the car. It was way cool."

I scowled at Erica. She shrugged. She didn't even have the sense to look apologetic.

"Yeah, well, I'm glad you're both here. I have to ask you a few important questions."

Sam frowned and pulled out a pocket watch. I wondered where they'd found such authentic costumes. I should call the town to see if they'd had a theft from the costume closet. "We have to meet my cousin in ten minutes. He's over at the Rotary Club hanging with Father Christmas."

"Are they friends?" If so, I was going to have to talk to Henry Hart about the town's hiring policies.

"Not really. Theo's got a thing for candy canes and the girl working with the Father."

I wanted to pull out my phone and dial Ray, but I knew they'd bolt if I did. "Sam, did you know Tim Lapham?"

His eyebrows shot up in what appeared to be genuine surprise. "Not really. He had his office in the house across the street from my parents. He waved to me every once in a while; that's all."

"Do you know who hid fifteen thousand dollars in my apartment?"

This time he laughed. "No. If I had access to that kind of cash, Erica and I would have gone to the Caribbean, not the casino."

I didn't want to mention the knife sheath so I chose the next best question. "Do you have any idea who would have wanted to kill Tim Lapham?"

Sam's expression sobered. "No. He seemed like a nice enough guy. He did my dad's books. My dad was happy with him, and my dad isn't usually happy with anybody." His chin dropped to his chest.

Erica sidled close and hugged him. "Sam's dad sent Sam to the psych center. He never even came to visit."

I tried to nod in a sympathetic way, confident Sam's parents had another side to the story. "Can you prove your whereabouts for the last week?"

Sam's head snapped up. "You can ask Erica and my cousin, Theo."

I winced. "Does Theo own a late-model Lincoln? A dark-colored one?"

"Yeah." Suspicion narrowed Sam's eyes. "Why?"

If I explained, Sam would know they were suspects in the convenience store robberies. They could disappear, and Ray would have an open case on the books forever. "Just curious. Someone saw a late-model Lincoln stop for two people a street away from the psych center."

Erica bit her lip. I knew I'd surmised correctly.

"Any chance either of you were in my apartment last night?"

They said "no" in unison, then looked at each other and smiled that sickly sweet smile new lovers have.

"Why do you ask, Jo?" Erica's blue eyes seemed to hold honest interest.

"I thought maybe you stopped by; that's all."

I felt more confident in their innocence. I decided I needed to get Ray over here so they could convince him as well. My fingers twitched on the phone in my hand. Erica spotted the movement and started tugging Sam toward the still open garage door. "We gotta go."

I summoned my best parental voice. "Erica, you have to go back to the psych center. You both do. You were never officially released."

"Not today. I'm going to party. Merry Christmas." She waved and the two of them ran out the back.

I dialed Ray.

He growled my name when he answered. "Brennan Rowe wasn't home. I didn't find Theo Tibble or Erica yet."

"Fine. Don't hang up. Erica and Sam Green were just here."

I ran out of the garage to the showroom window and looked out onto the sidewalk. With two weeks until Christmas, it was packed with antique store combers, doily shoppers, and Dickens cast members. A woman passed by the window and blocked my view for a moment with the huge bag of toys in her arms. "She's headed…" I saw one outfit that looked like Erica's, then another, and another. All the men appeared identical. It was the Thomas

Crown affair without the bowler hats. "She's gone. They said they were going to meet his cousin Theo at the Rotary Club, though."

"I'm on my way."

I hit the end button and headed into the garage again to lower the overhead door and inspect the DeLorean. Surprisingly, it did not have any Slurpee stains. As a matter of fact, it was spotless. Too spotless, like someone had cleaned it to hide the evidence.

Evidence of what, I couldn't say for sure.

TWENTY

At five minutes to ten on Monday morning, I sat at my desk in the shop, focused on winning an auction and refusing to allow any other thoughts to intrude.

Like the thought that I had spent all of yesterday alone at home, waiting for Ray to call and ask me about my Saturday night intruder. I couldn't believe word hadn't reached him about it. Had we come to the point in our relationship where he was indifferent? That was the word he'd used to describe the opposite of love. Ray never even bothered to call me and let me know if he found Erica and Sam Saturday night. Was that his way of answering my question? Didn't he care enough about me to keep me informed anymore? I had watched the news but didn't see anything reported.

I also didn't want to think about Mr. Oliver's reaction to receiving a call from Gumby that his DeLorean had been "borrowed" by the sister of the person he entrusted it to for safekeeping. The car only had fifty new miles on it. Whatever they had done with it, they hadn't gone far.

No, this morning I wouldn't even think about Brennan Rowe. This morning all I could think about was the prize: the title to a 1957 Mercedes-Benz 300SL roadster and the broker's fee of five thousand dollars that would make me feel like my business was back on track to success.

I had left my arm sling at home and removed the bandage from my wrist, leaving only the one around my rib cage in place. It had a rather nice slimming effect, like Control Top panty hose and I planned to milk it. But otherwise, I wanted to be in fighting form, and the bandages just reminded me I'd been in a weakened state.

The auction representative issued his last instructions to me. "Miss Asdale, when the bidding begins, I will repeat the current bid and you will state the amount of your bid to me. Please think of yourself as being here in the auction room with us, and only state bid amounts, no superfluous words or conversation. The bidding will move quickly. I don't want you to miss your opportunity to participate or have any confusion at this end as to your current bid. Is that clear?"

"Yes." I knew my maximum bid would be six hundred and eighty-two thousand, because Brennan Rowe had authorized me to spend not one penny more than seven hundred and fifty thousand dollars, and this auction house charged ten percent of the sale to the participant, a bidder's premium. Ten percent on top of a six hundred eighty-two thousand dollar bid would take me to exactly the seven hundred and fifty thousand he was willing to pay, and he would reward me with the additional five-thousand dollar finder's fee I so desperately needed.

"Excellent. The roadster is the fifth car on the block this morning."

Perhaps I should consider putting the Ferrari on the block at the auction house. Would I have to disclose that its last passenger rode it on the stairway to heaven?

"Okay, Miss Asdale, we're on. The bidding opens at ... five hundred thousand. It's five fifty, six, six fifty, six fifty-five, six sixty, six sixty-five ... Six sixty-five going once—"

Could I be so lucky? "Six seventy."

"Six seventy. Six seventy. Six seventy ... Going once. Going twice. Six seventy-five."

With the bidder's premium, I was coming dangerously close to my cutoff. "Six seventy-seven."

"Six seventy-seven. Six seventy-seven. Six seventy-seven ... Going once—Six eighty."

Too close, too close. I closed my eyes. "Six eighty-two."

"Six eighty-two. Six eighty-two. Six eighty-two ... Going once, going twice—"

I heard a rustle and opened my eyes. A man in jeans, a blue Oxford, and a Stetson appeared in my office door. I jumped to my feet in surprise.

"Six eighty-five, Miss Asdale." I could hear the excitement in the auctioneer's voice.

"What?"

"Six eighty-five is the current bid, Miss Asdale. Going once. Do you wish to increase your bid?"

The man held out a large envelope to me. I caught the words "Stanley Oliver and Associates, Attorneys at Law" in the corner. I dropped back into my seat.

"Going twice. Miss Asdale?"

The words came out of my mouth in reflex. "Six eighty-seven."

The man laid the envelope on my desk. "Have a nice day." He tipped his Stetson and disappeared.

"Six eighty-seven. Six eighty-seven. Six eighty-seven ... Going once. Going twice. Six eighty-eight."

I didn't stop to think. I was too dazed. "Six ninety."

"Six ninety. Six ninety. Six ninety ... Going once ... going twice ... last call ... SOLD. Congratulations, Miss Asdale, you're the new owner of a 1957 Mercedes-Benz 300SL roadster for six hundred and ninety thousand. Stay on the line and we'll finalize the deal."

I put my face in my hands and tried to keep from weeping, not tears of joy but tears of frustration. Including the bidder's premium, I had really just paid seven hundred and fifty-nine thousand dollars for this vehicle, nine thousand more than authorized and four thousand more than my finder's fee. Even if I forfeited my fee, I was still over the amount Brennan Rowe would pay.

When I hung up from the auction house, I slit open the envelope Tex left on my desk and perused its contents. Mr. Oliver planned to sue me for breach of contract and damages in excess of ten thousand dollars. Maybe I could take it out of Erica's trust fund.

Too bad she didn't have one. I was her trust fund, and my coffers were almost empty.

I lowered my head into my hands and rested them on the desk. I should not have expected the auction to go well for me. Nothing else had this month. I took a deep breath, stood, pushed in my desk chair and locked up the shop. I needed relief.

As I drove my Porsche out of the town limits and headed toward the county road, I considered simply continuing westward, to California, perhaps. I could get a job as a movie extra and blend forever into the background. Being in the forefront of the action was too draining.

But I couldn't leave Erica. She needed me and I loved her. And I couldn't leave Ray again, at least not until the fat lady sang, if she ever would. So I did the next best thing. I turned onto the county road and hit the gas.

At a hundred and ten, I began to feel better. Everything in my mind blurred and the yellow line disappeared. At a hundred and fifteen, I felt the adrenaline rush. At a hundred and twenty, I knew Cory needed to adjust the alignment. The steering wheel jerked and vibrated, bringing me back to reality. I eased my foot off the pedal. I brought the car to a halt at the side of the road and wept.

I wept for my mother, who left me to face life alone. For my father, who didn't quite know how to fill her shoes and his own simultaneously. For me, the failure as a surrogate mother and wife.

And finally, for my business, which looked like it would be finished before it ever really had time to get off the ground. At least the zoning board would be pleased.

I gave myself all of five minutes for my pity party. Then, never one to concede to defeat without a fight, I dried my tears and started to plan as I drove home.

I'd check on Isabelle's family's health and prompt her again about Celeste's jewelry. Then I'd call Greg Doran. Might as well let him know I was being sued over what amounted to fifty additional miles on the DeLorean. It wasn't like Mr. Oliver's prize breeder had been impregnated by a mutt. It was fifty lousy miles that he didn't get to drive himself. I'd have Cory check the car over thoroughly tomorrow, but I was sure that's all it amounted to, certainly not worth ten thousand dollars. And I'd call Cory today to let him know he needed to check out the candy apple red Jaguar in Albany tomorrow. The few hundred I could make off that deal would help.

Brennan Rowe made my list of people to call. I would call him and offer him the car for seven hundred and fifty-five thousand, foregoing my finder's fee. If he didn't take it, I would offer it to Mr. Hughes. I couldn't stand the man now, but I needed the money. If neither one of them wanted it at that price, I'd lower it. I would have to see if I could increase my business line of credit to cover the difference. I didn't think the bank would raise it far enough for me to afford to drive the thing around myself, and I couldn't afford to have such an expensive car sit in the showroom waiting to be noticed.

I didn't know what more I could do about finding Erica. She clearly wasn't hanging out with her old friends in her old haunts. As for the Beak and the killer, I now feared one or both of them wanted to find me. But that didn't mean I would stop asking questions. I'd just keep moving fast and look over my shoulder.

I peeked in all the closets and under the bed when I got home, even though it was daylight. Bending down to see under the bed made my stitches pull and ache.

Isabelle didn't answer her home phone but her cell phone only had to ring once. We verified that we and our loved ones were still healthy. I didn't tell her about my home invasion. She wouldn't ask if she could move in with me; she'd insist. And her family needed her more.

Instead, I filled her in on Erica's latest adventures.

"So what's Sam like? Does the madness make his eyes glitter?"

"He's charming and cute. But Ray always says it's the quiet, polite ones that are the most dangerous. They lull you into a false sense of security, then spring on you when you least expect it, like Hannibal Lecter."

"Do you think Erica is in any danger?"

I recalled the affection on Sam's face when he looked at Erica. "Not for the moment anyway. Did you ever find out about Celeste's necklace?"

"Let me call Jack now and remind him. He did go into work this morning. I'll call you right back."

I phoned Greg Doran in the meantime. He was in conference, according to his secretary. She asked me to drop off the letter from Mr. Oliver so he could review it and get back to me. This would cost me more money. I refrained from adding up all my new debts.

My cell rang. "Jack checked the records. Remember what I said about those pieces? They sold in a lot of stores, not just ours."

"So Jack doesn't know who bought his second set?"

"Well, no. He does have a record of the sale."

"Who bought it?"

"I don't want you to get excited or read anything into this."

"Who bought it?"

"Your dad."

TWENTY-ONE

I GOT IN THE car and drove straight to Talbots. Celeste had the day off. I continued on to my old house, my dad's old house, where I rummaged through the few remnants of his life he'd kept in a box in the attic. The pictures of my parents' wedding and the notes my mother had written him while he served in the Army in Vietnam sent me into tears again and I needed more than five minutes to recover. But when I'd touched every last document in the box, I found no evidence of another woman in his life besides Mom, Erica, and me.

After consideration, I decided driving to Celeste's home and confronting her wasn't such a bad idea.

Celeste preyed on men. She used her feminine wiles to get them to pay for her food and entertainment, a well-known fact in our town. The jewelry was something new, though, and I didn't care for the thought that she'd taken advantage of my sixty-plus father. The thought of them together revolted me.

I pulled onto Celeste's street and remembered she lived two doors down from Walter Burnbaum, who was shoveling the sidewalk in front of his house. He also appeared to be either singing or talking to himself, since his lips were moving and no one else was in sight.

As I stepped from the Porsche, he stopped to move a sandwich board announcing his home had been renovated by The Dream Team, two other guys I went to high school with. They did siding, tiling, and flooring, improving the aesthetic appearance of the older homes in our town. They did good work, too. My father used them to put cedar shingles on the exterior of our shop five years ago. It wasn't obvious to me which service they had provided Walter.

Walter spotted me and waved, his lips no longer moving. I gave a feeble wave in return, thinking he could come over and save Celeste if things got out of hand during my little visit.

Celeste had on a leotard when she answered the doorbell, looking damp and out of breath. I could hear Kathy Smith chanting away on the television. Apparently, Celeste didn't know one of the advantages of belonging to a gym was the ability to meet men. Or maybe she'd run through all of them at the gym already.

"Jolene, what are you doing here?" She sounded more surprised than annoyed.

"I need to talk to you."

She didn't open the door. In fact, she pushed it closed ever so slightly. It took me a second to realize she might still believe I had something to do with Tim Lapham's death. After all, who in their right mind would let a suspected murderer into their house without hesitation?

"Walter's in front of his house. He waved to me a minute ago." I pointed to him. Celeste leaned out to verify.

Walter looked up and waved again. I couldn't have timed it better. At least Celeste could take comfort now in the knowledge that Walter knew I'd entered her house.

She stepped aside to allow me to enter. I stepped into the tiny foyer, then the living room beside it. The walls were painted a golden color and she had green and gold furniture, gold carpeting, gilt framed mirrors, and cherry accent pieces. It looked professionally decorated, but maybe Celeste had as good taste in home décor as she had in clothes.

She darted around me in the living room and hit the power button on the television, silencing Kathy mid-sentence. She gestured to the armchair beside me. "Sit down. Tell me what's going on."

I perched on the edge of the brocade chair. Celeste settled on the matching couch. I got to the point. "Last time I saw you, you were wearing a pearl necklace set that I recognized. Did my father give it to you?"

Her jaw dropped. She recovered quickly, flicking carpet fiber from her leotard as she smiled at me. "Why would you ask me that?"

"Because I want to know. Please answer my question."

Celeste frowned. "All right, but I don't know what good it will serve." She folded her hands in her lap. "Yes, your father gave it to me. He and I dated for a few months the year before he died."

I started to ask how come I never knew, but realized no one must have wanted me to know, including my father. That hurt worse than anything. I thought he and I were the best of friends. My face must have told the story.

Celeste pursed her lips. "Don't look at me that way. It wasn't like that. Your father was lonely. We kept bumping into each other in Starbucks and he got up the nerve to ask me out. He liked to go out to dinner. He didn't like to eat alone. And he was a nice-looking man."

"What about the necklace?"

"He gave it to me for my birthday. I told him it was too much but he insisted."

"When did you stop dating?"

"After the first time Erica tried to take her life. He needed to focus on her. I understood. It wasn't like our relationship had much of a future." Celeste glanced into the mirror on the wall next to her. It reflected a good-looking thirty-seven-year-old woman and another deflated one in the chair across from her.

I couldn't think of anything to say. I stood. "Thanks for being honest. It just caught me off guard, that's all."

I headed for the door, but stopped when my hand met the cold metal handle on the screen door. I looked back at Celeste, who hadn't risen off the couch. She was staring at the carpet, looking a little dejected.

"One more question, Celeste."

She lifted her chin. "Yes?"

"Did my father ever give you the code for the alarm system at the shop?"

Her eyes expressed genuine surprise at the question. "No, Jolene. He never had any reason to."

—

I went home to lick my wounds, then decided to call Cory. He must have known about this sordid affair.

When he answered his cell, I could tell he was at the gym from his panting and the background music. I got right to my question.

"Man, I thought you were calling me about the auction. Do we have to talk about this?"

Yes, because I sure didn't want to be reminded of the auction. "Cory, why didn't you tell me about Dad and Celeste?"

"You were doing the books for the garage from home. We didn't know each other as well then. Besides, their relationship was so icky. I didn't want to go there."

"Did my father really like Celeste?"

"Jo, he was lonely. He needed somebody."

"Do you think Celeste was nice to him or was she taking advantage?" I could still go over to the shop and rip the necklace off her if I had to.

"For Celeste, she was being a peach."

Okay, I'd let it go. Water under the bridge and all that. My reputation might not withstand another fight with anybody right now anyway. "Geez, Cory, first you don't tell me about Ray and Catherine Thomas. Now I find out you didn't tell me about Dad and Celeste. Are you keeping any other secrets about the men in my life that I should know about?"

"I'm the only other man in your life. You know all my secrets."

"True." Or, at least, I thought so. Who could ever really be sure?

"Listen, I need you to go to Albany tomorrow. I found a candy apple red Jaguar there for Mr. Travis' wife. The owner swears it's in mint condition." They all swear that. Sometimes it even turns out to be true. I read the address to Cory a couple times until he knew he would remember.

"If it looks good, call me and I'll arrange for the hauler to pick it up." I had an exclusive deal with a long-distance hauler to transport my vehicles for five hundred dollars a trip, a low rate on the market. He traveled all over the country and needed as much advance notice as possible. Given that Christmas was now two weeks away, I crossed my fingers he'd be in the New York area soon.

"Will do, boss, will do. What happened with the roadster? Did you win the auction?"

"Yeah, I won." Why ruin his day by letting him know he might be out of a job at the end of the year? Of course, he might want to know in order not to overspend on Christmas. I'd suggest he return my present if that happened.

"Congratulations. I'll talk to you tomorrow."

I rounded out my day by calling a final nine deadbeats about their outstanding invoices. I managed to connect with all of them and obtain their credit card numbers. After processing their payments tomorrow at the office, I would be halfway to covering my loss on the roadster. Yippee!

I had one more important phone call to make.

"Miss Asdale, how are you this afternoon?"

Great, now the man recognized my number when I called. I could hear hammering in the background and assumed Brennan Rowe was on a construction site. "Good. We won the auction this morning. I have secured the title to the roadster."

"And what was the final price?"

"Seven hundred fifty-five thousand." I crossed my fingers.

"Miss Asdale, I thought I was quite clear. My max was seven hundred fifty and not a penny more."

"The bidding was intense. Five thousand more seemed reasonable." Nine actually, but who was counting?

"Well, I'm glad you think so, because the car is yours. I'm not paying for it."

"I'm sorry you feel that way."

"I was not pleased to be contacted by the sheriff's department yesterday, either, Miss Asdale. You apparently told them I have a Mini Cooper in my collection matching the description of one used in the latest robbery attempt on a convenience store where a man was shot. Whatever brought me to mind?"

"The sheriff's department asked me if I was aware of any Mini Coopers in this area. Yours was the only one in my service records."

"Well, apparently I'm now a suspect because my car is sitting in my garage, linking me to the crime."

"Oh. Actually I thought someone might have stolen it." Someone like my sister's friends, although Sam seemed to think the DeLorean was a loaner. Maybe a rich kid like him didn't realize the value of a collector's item. Maybe to him it was just another car in the Hertz fleet.

Brennan Rowe was silent. I knew he was still on the line. I could hear shouts mixed with the tapping in the background, but I couldn't make out the words. "It's funny you should mention that, Miss Asdale. I understand a vehicle disappeared from your garage during the past week. My car is here, but it seems to have been detailed recently.

I don't track the mileage on the car so I can't be certain, but I'm thinking it's been out on the town without me. Did it have a date with you?"

"Of course not."

"Well, your mechanic is the best and only—so far as I know—detailer in town. I'm just not sure how he would have gotten around my alarm system. I'm looking into the possibility that he has a friend at the alarm company who might have shared my personal information with him."

I bristled as though he had told me my child was stupid. "Your accusation does not even merit a response, Mr. Rowe."

"Your husband seemed to think it merited investigation, Miss Asdale. He said he'd look into it."

I couldn't believe Ray would think Cory was involved, but then Ray had looked twice at Erica and me, maybe even three times. It was his job to look at everyone without bias. Too bad he did his job so well.

"I noticed you at Tim Lapham's funeral, Mr. Rowe." A little white lie. "May I ask how the two of you were acquainted?"

"I had to answer your husband's questions, Miss Asdale. I don't have to answer yours." He hung up the phone without saying goodbye.

I immediately dialed Cory again. His voicemail kicked in. I asked him to call me as soon as he got the message.

Cory was a potential suspect if I considered the evidence. He knew the garage alarm code and Tim Lapham. He was the best and only detailer in town. He might have had an opportunity to kill Tim, but for the life of me, I couldn't think of a motive. Nor could I believe Cory capable of such an act. He was, after all, a puppy. A gentle, loving puppy.

My fingers itched to dial Ray and ask him if he was looking into Mr. Rowe's accusations, but was afraid that by doing so I would be adding credence to Rowe's theory. No, this time I would have to wait and have faith in my friend. And my husband.

TWENTY-TWO

THE DOORBELL RANG AS I raised my dinner—a tuna fish sandwich—to my lips. I set it down on the kitchen counter and raced across the floor to the front door, hoping Cory or Ray would be on the other side.

Instead, I found a huge Douglas fir tree. It took up the entire doorway and then some, and instantly filled my living room with a glorious evergreen scent, mixed with a hint of wet wood and mold. Beyond it, I heard a squeal as someone burned rubber. I hoped the tires didn't belong to any vehicle associated with me in any way, shape, or form.

"Move so I can bring it in."

I recognized the voice and stepped aside.

The tree scratched and snapped its way through the door. I slid the couch to one side and bit my tongue as the trunk of the tree left a two inch groove on my oak floor.

"Get the tree stand! This thing weighs a ton, ya know."

“Hold on.” I walked into the kitchen and hobbled down the stairs to the basement, rummaging through the plastic storage bins until I found the box with the green metal stand in it. Going up the stairs took a little longer. I couldn’t take them two at a time with my rib still mending and my thigh still sore. Still, the whole task took me no longer than three minutes.

Erica had dropped the tree against the front window and taken out my curtain rod in that short space of time. She was struggling to extricate my lace sheers from underneath the tree and succeeding only in stripping pine needles that scattered all over the floor. I righted the tree and she lifted the curtains. In minutes, we had the tree in the stand and the curtain and rod back in place.

“There. It’s a nice tree, isn’t it?” She gazed at it, seeming pretty proud of herself.

“It is. I’m surprised you remembered, what with you being so busy with Sam and all.” We had a family tradition of decorating our tree at night exactly two weeks before Christmas Day.

“If you wait any longer, the best trees are gone.” I know Erica thought that was why we did it now, but in my dimmest recollections, I thought my mother had started the tradition more because the pine needles would last until New Year’s Day but no longer.

Erica removed her coat. I realized she was still wearing the same outfit I’d first seen her in after she left the psych center. The ripped jeans now had a brown smear on them, the clogs, a dark stain, and the red sweater had a pull that ran the entire front and allowed Erica’s bra to show through, all signs her mental condition was unraveling as fast as her sweater. Erica was nothing if not fastidious when on her game.

“Are you feeling all right?”

"Never better. We went sledding today on the hill behind the high school. It was great. We can go later, if you want."

It was dark outside and the hill behind the school had no lights. Sledding there now would be a suicide run. "Why don't I make some hot chocolate?"

We always had hot chocolate when we decorated the tree. Usually we had Christmas cookies too, but I hadn't known she was coming. I slapped another tuna fish sandwich together and garnished it with Oreos—the kind with the green icing inside that said "Christmas."

Erica hauled the lights and ornament boxes out of the basement. I found a radio station playing carols. We spent two hours unwrapping bulbs and admiring them before finding the perfect branch to hang each of them, arguing over whether or not all the largest bulbs really had to be at the base of the tree. We compromised and spread them around.

As we worked, Erica stopped periodically and peered out the window. At first, I thought she was looking for Sam, but when I asked about him, she said he was spending the night with his cousin. I crossed my fingers the convenience stores in the area would be safe.

When she checked the view for the fifth time, I realized she was exhibiting signs of paranoia. "What are you looking for?"

"Someone's following me."

"Who?"

"I don't know. I think it's a man. He hides whenever I look, but I feel his eyes."

"Do you feel them now?"

"No." But her glance darted toward the window.

I pulled her over to the couch and sat with my arms around her. "You're safe here."

"I know." She snuggled closer and sighed. "How come you never talk about Mom?"

She caught me off guard. "What do you mean? We talk about Mom all the time." I refrained from reminding her that she shared their almost daily conversations with me as if they were real.

"You never talk about the day she died."

I pulled her closer, drawing comfort in her proximity and warmth. "It was the worst day of my life, Erica. I don't remember much." It had been Christmas Eve. It was the only Christmas I don't remember, perhaps because I spent the next three days in the psychiatric ward of the hospital.

"I do remember looking for Mom, hearing the car running, opening the door, smelling exhaust, being afraid, and not feeling much after that until Dad came to get me from the mental ward for her funeral." When he put his arms around me and carried me out the door, I remembered being blinded by the sunlight glaring off the fresh snow. And my mother's face as she lay in the casket with her wreath of baby's breath and her lips that unnatural shade of fire-engine red. That was about all I remembered, but some days, it was all I could bear.

No one, let alone a twelve-year-old, should ever have to deal with suicide or its aftermath. But, more importantly, no twelve-year-old should ever be left in the driver's seat for another child's life, especially one like Erica. I did my best, but plugging away all those years had taken its toll. It was another reason I couldn't bring myself to have a child.

"I'm sorry. Mom's sorry, too."

"Is she?" The words popped out, bitter and full of pain.

Erica pulled back and gazed at my face. "Of course. She just couldn't stay with us anymore. She had to go. Sometimes people have to go."

"She chose to go. She didn't have to."

"Are you still mad at her?" Erica stroked my hair.

I felt like the child for a change. "I don't understand why she didn't love me—and you—best. She only thought about herself, not us, not Dad. When you're a mother, you're supposed to do what's best for your child. How could leaving us be best?"

"That's easy." Erica crept back under my arm to cuddle, and I took charge again. "She knew Daddy was best for you and you were best for me."

I couldn't speak for the next few minutes because of the huge lump in my throat. Erica didn't seem to require any conversation. In fact, for a time, I thought she'd dozed off. Then she started in with the tough questions again.

"What happened with you and Ray? You guys were so perfect together, starting in high school."

"You heard us arguing about having a child. I couldn't take it anymore." At the time, it seemed the healthiest thing to do was to leave.

Erica grinned. "I tried to help with that, you know. I replaced your birth control pills with some of my medication and poked holes in your condoms." Erica actually sounded proud of herself.

"You did that? I thought Ray did it. I accused him of doing it." He'd never responded to those accusations, of course. He'd just looked at me like I had two heads. I guess I owed him an apology. Erica certainly owed me one.

"I know." Erica stood and stretched her arms toward the ceiling, her back bowing into a graceful C shape. "He yelled at me."

"He did?"

"Yeah. But he said we'd keep it between us."

And so they did, until now. "What else did you two keep just between you?"

"Not much."

I wanted to ask Erica more questions, like if she knew about Dad and Celeste, but the phone rang.

Ray's weary tones flowed over the wires. "I have Sam Green and Theodore Tibble in custody. I've questioned Green. I can't place him at either of the convenience stores. I can't place Tibble there either. Supposedly, several hundred people can verify their whereabouts that evening—Green's brother's birthday party at the golf club. But I can identify Tibble's car based on the video. I'm holding him and I'm returning Green to the state psych center, probably tomorrow morning. They won't tell me where Erica is."

"She's here."

Ray heaved a sigh that made the line crackle. "Do you think you can manage to get her back to the psych center? I can question her there later, if I need to."

"Yes." I might have to handcuff her to me, though.

"All right, then. Good night."

I turned to Erica as I replaced the receiver. "Ray has Sam and Theo in custody. He's questioned them about the convenience store robberies. He knows Theo's car was used in the robberies. What do you know about that?"

Erica began to twirl her hair, a sure sign she knew something.

"What's Ray going to do to Sam?"

"He's taking him back to the psych center while he checks out his story. Again, what do you know?"

"Not much."

"Tell me. Now."

"Theo needs money. But he was with Sam at Sam's brother's birthday party the night of the first robbery."

"Sam had him in sight the whole time?"

Erica frowned. "I don't know. I'm sure they didn't go to the bathroom together."

"What about the second robbery?"

"I don't know where Theo was that night. Sam and I were at the casino alone."

"Do you think it's possible Theo was involved in the robberies?"

Erica avoided my eyes. "I can't say."

I interpreted her response to be a definite maybe. "I need sleep now, Erica. Let's go to bed."

She sprang to her feet. "You can't sleep now. You have to take me to the psych center."

If I hadn't been sitting down, I would have fallen over. "Just like that? No arguments?"

"Nope. I want to go back." Erica grinned.

"Because Sam's going to be there?"

She waggled her head from side to side. "Maybe."

"He's a sociopath."

"I know, but I love him. We're going to get married."

I opened my mouth to argue, then snapped it shut. I'm not crazy. If Erica was willing to go back to the psych center, then I'd be a fool not to take her. At least she'd be in the right spot. But I might try to talk to Mom myself later to see if she could intervene in the marriage plans.

—

After I tucked Erica into her bed at the psych center, I tiptoed down the hall and whispered in Tommye's ear that perhaps Samuel Green might be better suited to a room on another floor than the tower. Any other floor.

She couldn't have agreed with me more.

TWENTY-THREE

TUESDAY MORNING THE SUN didn't come up, or at least, that's the way it felt. The good news was my leg and rib didn't bother me as much anymore, and I was able to wear my black wool dress pants without any discomfort. I teamed them with an evergreen sweater in an effort to cheer myself up and get into the Christmas spirit. I still felt like something was going to go wrong.

The sky remained gray, gloomy, and threatening as I drove to the shop. The only call I expected to receive today would be from Cory, regarding the candy apple red Jaguar. I planned to call Mr. Hughes and try to sell him the roadster for seven hundred and fifty-nine thousand. I'd saved the call for today since my karma had been way out of whack yesterday. No use taking unnecessary chances.

I turned the security system off and took a tour of the shop. Nothing seemed amiss, although it occurred to me that I should call Mr. Oliver and ask him to get the DeLorean out of my garage once Cory had a chance to look it over and document its condition.

I thought about charging Mr. Oliver storage fees until he did, but aggravating the man probably wouldn't be the best approach to resolving our differences in my favor. No, this situation would take some finesse. I would drive Mr. Oliver's letter detailing his demands over to Greg Doran later today and let him work his magic.

At ten-thirty I dialed Mr. Hughes' office. His secretary greeted me as though she'd been expecting my call and put me through to him without a wait.

"Mr. Hughes, I purchased the 1957 Mercedes-Benz 300SL roadster at auction yesterday and am pleased to be able to offer it to you for seven hundred and sixty-two thousand dollars." I threw in a cushion for negotiation but secretly hoped he would take it at any price.

"You only paid seven hundred and fifty-nine for it, Miss Asdale. If I'd wanted to pay seven hundred and sixty-two for it, I would have continued bidding yesterday."

At least my gasp was silent, as were my screams. I scrambled for a response. "I didn't realize you were bidding, Mr. Hughes. I'm surprised you let a woman get the best of you."

He chuckled. "Miss Asdale, you are now the proud owner of a roadster you can't afford. It looks to me as though you're putting yourself out of business. If you'd be at all interested in selling your garage, my oldest daughter wants to open a flower shop. Your location would be ideal for her."

I slammed the receiver into the cradle without even saying goodbye. The man was trying to ruin me, no doubt about it. But had he hired someone to kill Tim and get the ball rolling?

When my cell phone vibrated in my pocket, I jumped six inches off my chair. I checked the incoming number and answered.

"Cory, how does the Jaguar look?"

"Amazingly enough, it is truly pristine. The seller will take four thousand. He's got some Christmas gifts to buy, too. Want me to close the deal?"

"Yes. I'll call Dudley and ask him to pick it up asap."

"Done. I'll see you around four."

I walked my fingers through my Rolodex to find our car transporter's number, then dialed. Dudley answered on the ninth ring. He sounded half awake.

"The phone rang nine times, Dudley. What took you so long to answer? Are you in the rig?"

"I am. I must have dozed off, because I only heard it ring three times before I answered. I think you saved my life."

And I was going to ask this man to transport valuable property for me. Well, I couldn't afford anyone else right now. "I have a Jaguar in Albany I need picked up and delivered here before Christmas. Can you do it?"

I heard Dudley hack and spit and pictured a stream of tobacco juice hitting the pavement, or worse, the windshield of the car next to him on the road. Dudley had a one-tin-a-day chewing tobacco habit that had turned his gums white with pre-cancerous tissue. Yet he chewed on. "Let's see. I'm in Ohio now, then I'm headed to St. Louis, then D.C., then Boston. Yeah, I could pick it up on the twentieth on the way to Boston and have it to Wachobe by the twenty-third. How's that?"

"I think as long as it's under the tree Christmas morning, my customer will be happy."

"Okay, I'll put it on the schedule." Dudley had all the latest technology including a laptop he kept humming twenty-four hours a day so he could get weather updates and talk to his family. "Remind me to swing by and give you the paperwork from the Ferrari when I get into town."

"What paperwork?" I paid Dudley in cash. He couldn't have another unpaid invoice for me.

"The two envelopes from the wheel. I tapped the hubcap when I was loading her, and it popped off. The envelopes fell out. I threw them in my glove box and forgot to give them to you when I dropped her off."

"Two envelopes?" Could they be the missing gambling records?

"Yeah. They're yours, aren't they?"

I'd known Dudley for three years now. He was an honest man. I decided to tell him the truth. "Sort of. They belong to the previous owner. He sent a thug to look for them. I think the envelopes contain lists of gambling debts, debtors really, illegal gambling debtors."

"Shooey. I thought it was a funny place to store paperwork."

"Dudley, can you do me a favor when you stop for the night and fax them to the sheriff's department? Fax a copy to me, too, please." I wanted to get a look at the names on that list. I reeled off Ray's fax number as well as my own. "You can drop the originals off when you get here." As an afterthought, I added, "Don't mention them to anybody, though. They've caused enough trouble already." I rubbed my rib cage reflexively.

"I can fax them to you the next time I pull over. I told you I'm state of the art, baby, state of the art."

"When will that be?"

"Oh, I'm goin' to have to take a leak soon enough. I had three cups of coffee this morning."

And still he was asleep at the wheel. Go figure. "Okay, I'll sit tight. Thanks."

My next call was to Ray, who was pleased to learn the gambling lists had been located. He said he would fax them on to the Vegas and Arizona police departments. I didn't bother to tell him I was getting my own copy. Instead, I asked him for an update on Theodore Tibble.

"I'm going to have to cut him loose within twenty-four hours. I just left the golf club. The Greens had over three hundred guests that night in the main ballroom and the smaller ballroom had a company Christmas party with over a hundred. The parking attendants said they didn't collect Tibble's car for him until two in the morning but they can't guarantee it didn't go in and out after he handed them the keys around eight-thirty. They only remember him because he was way underdressed for the club."

"Lucky for you he's a slob. Any progress with Tim's murder?"

"No. The problem is the body was moved and no one saw a thing. I figure Tim was placed in your showroom between three a.m. and five a.m. There's never any traffic on Main Street at that time of the morning. It's too early for bakery and newspaper deliveries although we talked to everyone with a route in the area or an early morning shift. Tim sat somewhere for at least four hours before he was moved to the Ferrari, but there's not enough forensic evidence to tell us where.

"I also got the guest list for these parties at the club. Most of the town was at one or the other party, including Mr. Hughes. The staff at the club remembers parking his Rolls right in the front row where it didn't move until three a.m., so he's off the suspect list."

In the back of my mind, I hadn't really believed Mr. Hughes would whack Tim just for the building lot any more than I would, but weirder stories than that appear in the newspaper every day now. I decided to ask Ray about Rowe's whereabouts. "Was Brennan Rowe at the party, too?"

"No. He was home alone, just like you." Ray made it sound like we'd both actually been out killing Tim. I decided to change the subject.

"What about the money missing from the town treasury?"

"I talked to Henry Hart. He said Tim proposed hiring the auditors to figure out a discrepancy. Hart's pretty confident Tim didn't take any money, based on that."

I knew Tim was honest.

"So what more do you know about Tim's death?"

"Tim's car was found in the middle of the woods near the freeway access. The interior was so clean it must have been detailed."

Another car that looked detailed. As far as I knew, Cory did the only detailing work in town. The next closest company offering the service was the car wash in the city. I don't think the killer took Tim's car there, but who knows? I did know Cory was not a killer.

"What do you make of that, Ray?"

"You tell me, Jolene."

"I don't understand, Ray. Are you accusing me of something?" Or Cory? But I didn't want to give Ray any ideas.

"I'm just waiting for someone to step up and tell the truth."

When I failed to reply, he disconnected, leaving me with the distinct impression that I, at least, was still on his suspect list.

The fax had started to hum and emit its burning smell. Now I watched as the first page of the list printed out. I picked it up eagerly and studied it. Tim's name was not on it.

The lists were spreadsheets with names, addresses, phone numbers, amounts owed, how long the debts had been outstanding and a miscellaneous column that held the names of wives, children, pets, etc. I didn't realize organized crime was so … organized. I knew enough to be afraid when I saw family members listed. A threatened family member is a powerful motivator.

Page two printed out, then three and four and on up to twelve. I didn't recognize any of the names. I got the phone book out and spent two hours comparing the names on the list to the names in the local directory. None of them matched. If Tim's death was tied to gambling, this list didn't prove it.

I folded the list and stuffed it inside my purse, then picked up the envelope containing Mr. Oliver's demands. The clock tower at the local savings bank struck noon as I drove through town to Greg Doran's office, admiring his neighborhood, which was dominated by the whitewashed wooden houses with the grand old porches of yesteryear. Taking a walk through Wachobe was like stepping back in time a hundred years when people spent their free time sitting outside chatting with their friends. Many of the townspeople still enjoy talking with the passersby in the summertime. This time of year, only the shoveled walkways and Christmas decorations hinted the homes were inhabited.

Greg Doran's office was on West Lake Road in his elegant 1899 Queen Anne Victorian home, painted an interesting shade of lavender with darker purple, gold, and brown accents, and surrounded by a browning boxwood hedge. Inside, the hardwood floors shined with loving care and the home smelled of lemon oil. His secretary greeted me and ushered me into his office where he rose from behind his antique desk to greet me.

"So you've gotten yourself into another mess, eh?" Greg gestured to the armchair in front of his desk.

"I hope not." I sat and hit the highlights of the situation with the DeLorean.

Greg leaned back in his executive chair. "Any chance you'd like to have your sister arrested for theft? Might help our case."

"I'll keep that option in reserve."

"All right. I'll call Oliver. I've had dealings with him in the past. He's not an entirely unreasonable fellow, just mostly so."

"That's very comforting."

"I'm sure he'll settle for less than ten thousand. How much can we offer him? Five?"

I felt tears welling in my eyes. I didn't have five. I shook my head. "Can't you make this go away?"

"Only through insurance if we have your sister arrested."

I sighed. "Offer him five with my sincerest apologies. Cory will check the car over to make sure no damage was done to it while it was not in our possession."

"Fair enough."

"I'd like to get it out of my garage. I was going to call him and ask him to pick it up."

"All contact with him needs to go through me from now on, until the issue is settled. We don't want to escalate this into a lawsuit. Let me know when Cory is finished looking it over, and I'll notify Oliver to pick the car up."

Why did everything have to be so complicated? "Okay."

"I'll be in touch."

I stepped back outside into a light snowfall. I caught a few flakes on my tongue for fun and wished Erica and I had been able to sled the other night. Maybe I would spring her from the psych center to sled with me when all this was over.

I stopped to buy myself lunch at Simply Divine Burgers. They served Black Angus beef, the best burgers in town. They were also the priciest, but this would be my main meal of the day. I sat at a long picnic bench in the restaurant that served family style and watched the other diners enjoy their food and each other's company. It made me feel very much alone. I choked down the burger as quickly as I could to get out of there.

When I pulled out of my metered parking spot, I heard honking behind me. A maroon minivan had attempted to pull out as well, and the black Mercedes he'd cut off had objected and refused to give way. Talk about a clash of the classes.

Cory strolled into my office around three o'clock and dropped into the side chair, just as I was working up enough nerve to call Brennan Rowe and offer him the roadster at his original authorized price. I'd toyed with the idea of selling Dad's house all afternoon to make up the difference and start my new year off with cash in hand for a change. Then it occurred to me I should ask Erica before selling our childhood home. I couldn't predict how she would react to the idea, so giving Rowe a discount won out.

After unbuttoning his navy peacoat, Cory brought me up to date. "Matt Travis is transferring the money to a bank in Albany tomorrow and nine hundred to your account as well: five to pay Dudley and four for us."

"Perfect. Thank you for taking care of it."

"My pleasure. The seller bought me lunch."

"That's nice of him. Listen, I wanted to ask you about detailing. It seems Brennan Rowe's Mini Cooper may have been used in a robbery and returned to his home in a cleaner state than it left. And Ray says Tim Lapham's car looked detailed when it was found as well. Who else besides you does that kind of work around here?"

When Cory answered, he pronounced each word slowly and carefully. "No one. Am I a suspect now?"

I balanced honesty with a desire not to alarm him. "Brennan Rowe said Ray was going to ask you about it. Did he?"

"Not yet."

"I guess that means Ray knows you're not involved."

"I hope so." Cory stared at me.

"I know you're not involved."

"Okay. It's just that I had opportunity. I know the garage code."

"But you didn't have a motive to kill Tim, right?"

"Right."

Glad we'd cleared that up.

Cory folded his hands and looked down at them. "You know how you asked me if I was keeping any more secrets about the men in your life?"

"Yes?" I tried to keep the tinge of irritation out of my voice. I knew I wouldn't like where he was headed.

"I thought of something while I was driving to Albany this morning. Something that struck me as weird at the time but then I dismissed it."

"Okay, go on."

"Remember the day Tim Lapham came in the shop and asked you out?"

"Yes." It had been early spring. I had just sold a Porsche 911 to the bakery owner down the street.

Cory leaned back in the chair and met my gaze. "Well, you were on the phone when he first arrived and we started talking in the showroom. I thought he was feeling me out for a date until you came in the room."

"What?"

"Truthfully, I thought he'd come in to ask me out."

"No." I thought back. I'd come out to the showroom to say hello to Tim. He said he'd heard about a new restaurant in town he wanted to try out. Then he said, "I'm hoping you'll want to join me."

And then he'd looked at Cory. I'd assumed Tim was embarrassed to ask me for a date in front of Cory, so I'd immediately said, "I'd love to join you." Tim then said he'd pick me up at seven.

But had he missed a beat before he responded to me? Had he meant to invite Cory all along and I misread the cues?

Now it was my turn to be embarrassed.

TWENTY-FOUR

On Wednesday, I arose determined to sort out the truth about Tim Lapham. If he was, in fact, a closet homosexual, then he could have been blackmailed into voting against Mr. Hughes or blackmailed into embezzling from the town—although I couldn't imagine why Tim would initiate an investigation of the missing funds if he had been involved in embezzlement.

I knew only one place more to look for the answers, but it would have to wait until after seven o'clock that evening. In the interim, I planned to visit Erica and Brennan Rowe, the mystery man I'd only spoken to on the phone when I offered to sell him the car of his dreams at a personal loss. I wanted him to know who he had hurt. But first, I wanted to ask Erica about selling our family home. If she didn't mind, I'd feel like I was in a better bargaining position with Brennan Rowe. The price for the roadster would be seven hundred and fifty thousand and not a penny less.

On the drive to the psych center, I got stuck in a line of stop-and-go traffic due to flooding from what must have been a burst water pipe. I could see a geyser shooting at least twenty feet into the air from my position at the end of the line of cars. While I waited my turn to accelerate past the mess, I relived my embarrassment over and over again. It wasn't so much that I minded Cory knowing what a goof I'd made, but I wondered if the rest of the town knew about Tim while I didn't. Had they all been laughing at me for dating a homosexual? Becky didn't seem to know. She assumed Tim actually liked me. I was sure he did like me. He just didn't *like* girls. Not that there was anything wrong with that.

I got a sick feeling. What if Ray knew? He knew everything. Had he been laughing behind my back too? Maybe it was a case of it takes one to know one, so only Cory knew. But somehow I had a feeling everyone else would know before this was all over.

I gave myself a mental smack. Tim was dead. Compared to that, my embarrassment was not even worth mentioning, but I would have to take another strike for not being a good judge of men.

The signalman motioned to me. I stepped on the gas.

I arrived at the psych center, which seemed remarkably calm today. At least, I didn't see anyone swinging from the light fixtures. When I arrived on her floor, Erica and Sam were in the midst of a fierce Ping-Pong battle with a handful of onlookers cheering them on. I marched to the nurse's desk and looked questioningly at Tommye, who stood counting pills into little paper cups.

She held up her hand. "Don't start with me now. They didn't have any open rooms on another floor. We've got a waiting list, you know. Mainstreaming some of these babies didn't work."

"Someone should be watching Erica and Sam."

"Wheels, we don't have the staff to do suicide watches, let alone keep Romeo away from Juliet. You're going to have to speak sharply to her, that's all." With a wave, Tommye took off down the hall with a tray of meds in hand.

The Ping-Pong war had ramped up by the time I returned to the rec room. Erica beamed from ear to ear as she scored another point, but Sam's expression caught my attention. His face was flushed, his brow furrowed, and his lips moving without any sound. She scored three more points and threw her arms up in triumph. "Yes!" Her fans roared their approval, stomping their feet and banging their hands on the table.

Sam took aim and beaned her in the forehead with his paddle.

"Ow! Hey!" Erica fingered the red spot on her forehead.

Sam stormed out of the room and the rest of the peanut gallery faded into the woodwork.

I approached Erica and put my arms around her. She had tears in the corners of her eyes. "Are you all right?"

"No. I'm going to have a lump. What'd he do that for?"

I pulled her over to a vacant couch and settled her. "He's a sociopath. He doesn't really care about anyone else. He's not capable of it."

Erica began to sob. "I know. I know. But I thought he loved me."

I held her hands in mine. "He's not capable of love. I love you, if that makes you feel any better."

She buried her face in my chest, hiccupping and stroking my pink fuzzy scarf. "I like this. Is it new?"

"Yes." I resolved then and there to go to Talbots and buy her one for Christmas. "Listen, now may not be a good time, but I have to talk to you about our house."

Erica drew back and wiped her nose on the sleeve of her yellow blouse, leaving a trail of glistening mucus. "What about it?"

"Ray moved out, and I don't want to live there anymore. The shop is struggling financially and I could use the money from the sale of the house to bail it out. Would you mind terribly if I put it on the market?"

"Where will Mom's ghost live?"

Oh, well, there was a party I hadn't considered. "I think she could stay on with the new owners or maybe she'd like to move on." I breathed in deep and plunged. "Do you need to talk to her about it before we decide?"

"No. Go ahead and sell it. I'll tell her to move over to your apartment."

And here I was trying to rid myself of old ghosts. But I didn't really believe in ghosts, so Erica's ramblings didn't bother me. Not much anyway.

"I was thinking of selling most of the furnishings. I planned to hire one of those services to run an estate sale. Can you think of anything you want me to set aside for you? Something to keep for your children, maybe?"

Erica burst out laughing. "If you're afraid you're going to pass on mental illness to a child, what makes you think it's safe for me to have one? I can't even take care of myself."

A very insightful observation for a mental patient. "Okay. I'll pick something special out for you and pack all your stuff that's still there."

I walked her to her room. She greeted a dark-haired boy of around eighteen in the hall. He wore a Syracuse Orangemen sweatshirt and jeans that hung off his boney butt to reveal plaid boxer shorts.

"Hey Mikey, you remember my sister, don't you?"

He held out his hand and shook mine. I couldn't place him but he said, "Nice to see you" and ambled off toward the rec room.

"I don't remember Mikey, Erica. Who is he?"

She flicked on the television and flipped through the channels until she found a Meg Ryan movie. "He's Walter Burnbaum's kid. He's in here for drug addiction."

At least he hadn't stabbed his mother in the hand over pork chops.

"Why didn't he go to a regular detox place?"

"His dad wanted him close so he pulled a few strings. His friends can all visit him here. He's been here a couple weeks."

I supposed if I were on the town grapevine I would have known about this sooner. No wonder Walter looked so down in the dumps the other day.

"Who are his friends?"

"Sam's brother, for one. He visits Sam and Mikey at the same time."

How convenient for him that all his closest associates gathered here.

I sat with Erica, watching Meg Ryan and Tom Hanks take one step closer and two steps back, until she said it was time for her to go to group therapy. I left the psych center after filing a complaint in the main office, documenting Sam's assault on Erica. I wasn't taking any chances with him. In the parking lot, I dialed Brennan Rowe's office number, connecting with his secretary.

"He's not here, Miss Asdale. He's on a job site. He'll be there all day."

"Can I see him there?"

"Sure. Just go straight to the trailer on the building site. It's not safe to walk around in the building without a hard hat." She read me the address and gave me directions.

The building site turned out to be an old farm they razed in order to build a new retirement home development, according to the big wooden sign next to the road. The development would be called "Apple Creek," since the site used to be an apple farm. I remembered coming here with my parents every fall and riding the hay wagon into the orchard to pick Cortlands and Macouns, a treasured family memory that sprang to mind as I pulled off the main road. I was inordinately pleased to realize I had more than one treasured memory. But now all the trees had been plowed into a heap near the road, and a massive backhoe was loading them into a dump truck.

Another backhoe was knocking down the walls of one of three barns on the property. The din from the backhoes striking the dump truck and the barn made my ears ring. Toward the middle of the lot, what looked to be a community center had been framed and sided and yet another backhoe was smoothing the basement of the first residential dwelling.

I knocked on the door of the white house trailer labeled Rowe Construction in big red block letters on the door. No one answered. I turned the knob and stepped inside.

The front half of the trailer held two desks and an architect's drawing board and smelled of sawdust, but held no occupants. I followed the murmur of a voice to a second area where a man sat at a desk with his back to the door. As I got closer, I recognized Brennan Rowe's voice and knocked on the wall.

He swung around. My mouth dropped open.

He was the best-looking man I'd ever seen. Slender with streaked sandy-colored hair. He had a tanned face and light blue eyes that reminded me of Robert Redford. When he smiled, his square white teeth only enhanced the similarity.

He lowered the phone to its cradle and stood, extending his hand. "Brennan Rowe."

I darted forward and shook his hand. "Nice to meet you."

His grin widened. "Nice to meet you too, Miss …"

I felt my face flush. "I'm sorry. I'm Jolene Asdale."

His head jerked back as though I'd caught him by surprise. "Yes, of course. What brings you here, Miss Asdale?"

"Jolene, please." Now that I'd had a look at this guy, I knew I didn't want to stand on formalities.

"Brennan, then. Please." He indicated the armchair in front of his desk and I settled in it, unbuttoning my coat.

"Well, let me get right to the point. I'd like to offer you the roadster at the price you originally authorized, seven hundred and fifty thousand."

He leaned back in his chair and folded his hands on his stomach. "You'd be taking a loss."

"I would, but it's the end of the year. I have two unsold cars that I need to move. You were quite clear in your instructions to me. I failed in the bidding. It's only fair I take the loss."

He continued to look at me with surprise and something akin to respect. "All right, sold. I'll draft a check for you and deliver it tomorrow. But let me arrange for the car to be shipped here. It's the least I can do."

"Agreed." I made no move to get up. Neither did he.

"So tell me, am I still on your husband's suspect list?"

"I have no idea, but I doubt it very much." If Ray had proof of Brennan's involvement, he would have slapped the cuffs on him by now. Besides, the only thing this man could be guilty of was being too handsome.

"Well, that's a relief. I didn't want to spend the holidays in jail."

I saw my opening. "Are you spending the holidays with your family?"

"No, my parents have been dead for years. I'm an only child."

I checked his ring finger but these days one can never be sure without asking. "What about your wife's family?"

His smile said he was on to me and found it amusing. "I'm not married."

"Oh."

His smile broadened.

It hit me then that I looked like I was on the make for an affair. Brennan Rowe knew me as Ray's wife. Hell, I knew me as Ray's wife, but his looks had gotten to me. Yet another embarrassment. "So how long have you been working on this development?"

"We started about six weeks ago. We'd hoped to get more done before the snow started to fly. Pretty soon the ground will be too frozen to dig cellars but we can at least finish the demolition and the main building over the winter. If it warms up a little, we might be able to pour one more basement and start the first set of townhouses."

I gazed out the window and spotted a group of workers approaching. I decided to take my leave. Standing, I held out my hand. "Well, a pleasure to meet you, Brennan, and congratulations on your new car."

"You're more than generous, Jolene. Thank you. I'll be sure to refer all my friends to your dealership."

I refrained from asking if they'd all be as good-looking as him.

—

By six-thirty I'd forgotten all about Brennan Rowe as I hopped in the Porsche and headed toward Bowl-A-Roll, the bowler's Mecca and the one place I might find answers about Tim Lapham.

Bowl-A-Roll was lit up like the Fourth of July with those blinking, color-changing lights that can blind a person. The inside of the bowling alley was no better. It was Saturday Night Fever on Wednesday night and the disco balls twirled colored lights over the twenty-four full alleys as "Staying Alive" played in screechy tones over the sound system. The loudspeaker cut the music off to announce ten cent drafts and I almost got trampled by the crowd as they stormed the bar. The whole place smelled like stinky feet and overcooked hot dogs, a potent combination.

I fought my way through to the main desk.

The grungy fellow who looked to be in charge slammed his hands on the counter when I stopped in front of him. "What size shoe?"

"I'm not here to bowl."

He leaned over the counter and leered at me. "Are you the stripper for the bachelor party?"

"No!" *Ew* and in a bowling alley, no less. "I'm looking for Tim Lapham's bowling team."

"They're not here tonight. They're league bowlers. League bowling starts again in January."

"Can you tell me who bowls on his team?"

He slammed his hand on the counter again, apparently prone to talking with his hands. "Teams change all the time. I don't know who's playing next year yet."

I gazed around the room and spotted Celeste with a group of women bowling in lanes fifteen and sixteen. When I turned back to the guy, he'd already moved on to the next person at the counter.

Maybe Celeste knew some of the members of Tim's bowling team. Although I was kind of surprised she bowled. It was a sport where broken nails came into play. I wouldn't have thought she would stand for that.

She caught sight of me as I dodged a drunken man holding two very full pitchers of beer, and a wary look settled on her perfectly made-up face. In a room full of sweaty people, Celeste wasn't even glistening.

I greeted her pleasantly. She replied in kind. One of her friends jostled past me to take her turn throwing the ball, pushing me into Celeste. When I got my footing again, Celeste smoothed her hot pink bowling shirt and asked, "What brings you here, Jolene? More questions about your dad?"

I was glad the music drowned her words so that none of her friends heard. I didn't want to discuss my dad in front of the whole town. "I wanted to know if you knew anyone on Tim Lapham's bowling team."

"Oh, sure."

"Can you name them?"

She reeled off the names of three guys in Tim's high school graduating class plus the brothers who ran The Dream Team, Dave and Riley Nelson. "There were two other guys I didn't know. One was older, I think maybe from Tim's accounting practice, and the other was very good-looking, but unfriendly."

I interpreted her statement to mean she'd hit on him and been shot down. Silently I applauded the man.

Celeste's friend, Mindy Something, tapped her on the shoulder. "You're up. Hey, Jolene."

"Hey, Mindy." I watched Celeste line up on the pin and let loose with a big wind-up. Her ball flew down the lane and the pins scattered. A strike. All the women cheered for her, each giving her a high five as she basked in their admiration.

I realized one woman wasn't cheering. It was Martha, Walter Burnbaum's wife. The disco lights lit up her face every few seconds, but each time her expression was blank. It didn't even seem like her eyes were focused.

Celeste reappeared at my side.

I tilted my head toward Martha. "Isn't that Martha Burnbaum?"

"It is, poor thing."

"What's wrong with her?"

"For starters, her son's impossible to handle. He's in drug rehab now. Then Walter had to go and try to cheer her up by having their old carpet pulled up and wood flooring installed on their entire first floor. Martha hates wooden flooring. Thinks it's cold and hard on her feet. She's been complaining about her feet all night, as a matter of fact. And she hasn't bowled worth a damn, either."

I watched as Mindy and another woman prompted Martha to take her turn. She rose, stumbled to the ball return, put her fingers in the holes of her orange ball, and threw without any preparation, splitting the pins and leaving a couple on each side of the alley. Her spare rolled through the middle of them, leaving them untouched. Martha assumed her seat, still staring blankly at the room.

"Are you sure she's not on drugs herself?"

"She's depressed. You should know depressed when you see it." Celeste's face turned smug.

Our détente was over. Time to leave.

I drove to my dad's house, wondering who the two mystery men were on Tim's bowling team. I could try the direct route and phone Becky to ask, but I didn't want to set her off. Bowling had seemed like a touchy subject for her. In the morning, I would phone The Dream Team and ask them instead. One of them was married to a woman who ran an estate sale business. I wanted to hire her to dispose of the contents of Dad's house so I could put it on the market.

As I pulled into the driveway, I noticed headlights down the block from a car that had made the turn onto our street after me. It had stopped when I put on my turn signal. I got the uneasy feeling the driver was watching me. I pulled out my cell phone and entered 911 just in case. Before I punched the send button, the car accelerated and blew by me. It was a dark-colored minivan, its driver hidden in the shadows of the car. I shook off my nerves and headed inside, rolling my eyes at the ludicrous thought of a criminal driving a soccer-mom car. Probably just some kids out on a lark.

The rest of my evening was consumed by sorting through the contents of the attic. By ten, I had one box of Erica's things, another of my old books that merited a second read, my father's box of papers including my mother's letters, and two items for Erica and me as keepsakes: my mother's sterling silver engraved mirror, comb, and brush set, plus my father's family bible, its last notation my mother's death. It wasn't much but it would be enough. If neither of us had children, we would have no one to pass things down to anyway.

I expected to feel sadness at leaving this house for the last time, but I felt only relief. After all these years and tears, the bad memories outweighed the good.

I was ready to make new memories elsewhere.

TWENTY-FIVE

First thing in the morning I phoned The Dream Team, but not early enough to catch them. I left a message on their machine and ended up doing the same for the wife who ran the estate-sale business.

The town and county tax bill for Dad's house remained in the unpaid bill drawer of my desk. After I opened the shop and chatted with Cory for a few minutes, I pulled it out and verified online that Mr. Travis had made a deposit in my bank account for his candy apple red Jaguar. The profits would just cover my tax bill.

Since the shop was dead, I left Cory in charge and walked to the bank. Then I continued on to the town hall tax office. The clerk was available.

"Taxes went up this year, didn't they?"

The clerk stopped filling in my receipt and bobbed her cottony head in reply. "They went up five percent. We hated to do it, but the cost of living goes up each year along with everything else."

A man walked into the office and slid into position beside me at the window. "Excuse me, is this where I pay my parking ticket?"

"Yes. I'll be right with you. I just have to make a copy of this woman's tax bill." The clerk shuffled off.

The man turned to me. "I took my kids to the Rotary Club to see Father Christmas yesterday. I parked on a meter. The waiting line for the guy was ridiculous. By the time we got back to the car, we had a parking ticket."

I could sympathize. "The meters are a pain."

The clerk reappeared at the window and held out my bill stamped "Paid" in red letters with today's date.

"Thank you." I folded it in half and smiled at the clerk. "I'm curious. How much money do the parking meters and tickets add to the town's revenues in a year?"

"About twenty-five thousand."

"Is that all?"

The man held out his ticket and check to the clerk. "Isn't that enough?"

I gave him an apologetic smile. "You're right. It's more than enough. Too much in fact."

On my walk back to work, I did a little window shopping, still in need of gifts for Cory, Isabelle, Jack, and my goddaughter Cassidy. Each year I closed the shop between Christmas and New Year's Day. Cory would head home to spend the week with his parents and married brother. Erica and I usually spent Christmas Day with Isabelle's family, but I had a feeling Erica would not get her furlough this year after her recent escapades.

I wouldn't press the issue with the psych center. The last thing I wanted was for her to lose her spot there. We were very lucky they'd held a room for her this time with so many on the waiting list, especially since she didn't appear to be an immediate threat to herself at present. Sometimes I wondered what would become of her if the state refused to accept her as a patient any longer. Then, other days, I wondered why she couldn't just snap out of her bipolar disorder. I knew this was impossible, but still I hoped.

Cory swung his feet off my desk and turned off SPEED-TV when I entered my office. "Did you see the police blotter in the town newspaper?"

"No."

"It's all about you. Dead body found in sports car boutique on Main Street. Woman abducted from funeral home and dragged behind car for blocks. Home intruder escapes police detection."

I grabbed the paper and read the blotter. Cory was right. It was all about me. "I guess I should start campaigning against crime."

Cory stood and brushed the wrinkles out of the tails of his dress shirt. "Good. Then Ray will have his D.A.R.E. campaign, and you'll have your own campaign." He headed toward the door, pulling his ski jacket off the coatrack without breaking step. "I'm going down to the sub shop. You want anything?"

"Tuna, please."

He waved and seconds later a blast of cold air let me know he'd left the building.

My phone rang. I crossed my fingers, hoping it was someone in search of a nice red Ferrari, an old Magnum P.I. fan, perhaps. Instead, it was the woman who ran estate sales, Sarah Nelson.

I explained my need to clear out Dad's house. She agreed to pick up the key from me later in the day to start arranging and pricing items right away.

"Oh, and Sarah, I left a message for your husband this morning, too."

"He's on a job. He'll be home around three. Can I help you?"

"You're going to think I'm crazy, but I heard he was on the same bowling team as Tim Lapham. I was curious who else bowled on that team."

"No problem." She reeled off the six names Celeste had provided plus a Peter Davis.

"Who's Peter Davis?"

"He worked in Tim's office."

"Was he Tim's partner?"

"Tim didn't have a partner. As a matter of fact, his whole business is a little up in the air right now. Peter may buy it from the estate."

"So they only had seven guys on the bowling team?"

"Oh, no, eight. Who'd I forget? Oh, Brennan Rowe."

I shook my head because I couldn't believe my ears. "Brennan Rowe bowls?"

"He's got almost a three hundred average. Only Tim bowled better."

Bowling did not fit the image I had created for Brennan. "So your husband must know Brennan Rowe fairly well?"

"Yes and no. Tim invited him to be on the team a few years ago. They all got along okay, but then Brennan hired my husband and his brother to repaint the trim on the garage that houses his car collection. They had an accident and broke a window with a ladder, setting off his alarm. Brennan was so mad that he threatened to withhold payment for the job."

So Brennan Rowe had a temper and was vengeful. Interesting.

I thanked Sarah Nelson and hung up. Cory carried a bag full of subs, chips, and iced tea into my office and set it in front of me.

"I had them put lettuce and tomato on your sub, just the way you like it."

"Perfect."

We unwrapped the subs and ate in companionable silence. When we finished, Cory crunched up the garbage and bagged it. "I'll take this right outside. We don't want mice."

"Noooo, definitely not. Thanks."

My conversation with Sarah Nelson plagued me, especially learning Tim's relationship with Brennan Rowe. As his bowling buddy, Tim might have been more inclined to vote against Mr. Hughes' proposed grocery store if he'd known his friend Brennan wanted the lot for an office complex. But since the vote went in Brennan's favor, he'd have no reason to kill Tim, unless he needed to cover up something else. I had no idea what that might be.

Or did I?

Cory came back in the office and flopped onto the chair. He realized I was staring at him and wiped nervously at his mouth. "Do I have food on my face?"

"No. I have a question for you."

"Okay." His knee started to bob up and down.

"You know Brennan Rowe."

He froze. "Sort of." His tone held caution. "I've serviced his car."

"Is he gay?"

Cory burst out laughing.

"Is he?"

"Oh, you're serious. Sorry. Well, let's see. He's really hot, unmarried, and completely off the radar screen of all the single women in this town. What do you think, Jo?"

I gasped. "No. I flirted with him."

"Girl, you need to get your radar fixed. He's so not into you."

I buried my face in my hands. "Oh, my God, I'm such a loser. I should have dated more guys before I married Ray. Maybe I wouldn't be so naïve." I took a deep breath. "Is he openly gay?"

"He's like me. We don't flaunt it, but we're not hiding it, either." Cory leaned forward and patted my hand. "Don't be too hard on yourself. I think it's nice that you take people at face value."

Cory's words brought me some comfort. "Have you ever dated Brennan Rowe?"

"No. I'm not sure who he dates, Jo. He keeps it all close to the vest, but then he is in construction. It's not exactly an environment to fly the pride flag."

"Could he have been dating Tim Lapham?"

Cory's eyes widened. "There's an idea. I don't know. I guess anything is possible."

"Can you ask him the next time you see him?"

"No, Jo, I can't ask him. That's not a guy thing to do. You ask him."

"All right, I will." I didn't quite know how or where to broach the subject, but I would figure it out. Brennan Rowe was still on my suspect list. Actually, he was the whole list. I hoped Ray's list was longer and didn't include Erica and me. I was still hoping he would pin everything on an out-of-towner.

In the meantime, I would go over to Talbots and buy Erica a scarf to match my new one. It would afford me the thrill of seeing

Celeste again. I wished I'd thought to ask Erica if she'd known about the affair between Celeste and Dad. I couldn't believe she'd keep it from me.

I stepped through the slush piled at the curb of Main Street and jaywalked to the door of Talbots. Celeste was dressing a mannequin in the window and gave me another of her wary looks as I opened the door. I skipped the greetings and got right to the point. I didn't want to be in her space any more than she wanted me there.

"Erica loved my scarf. Is there any chance you have another?"

Celeste jumped down from the platform under the window. "I do. I have pink like yours or a white one. Which do you prefer?" She held them up.

I couldn't decide. I liked them both.

"Take the pink. Erica's color is pink." Celeste headed for the cash register with me trailing meekly behind. In truth, she made all my clothing selections.

"I heard you got the missing DeLorean back." She cut the tags from the scarf and wrapped it in tissue paper.

"Yes." I didn't care to elaborate. Celeste probably knew more about the whole thing than I did, anyway.

"What's the latest on Tim Lapham's murder? Has Ray got a suspect?"

I watched as she slipped the scarf into a bag and held out my credit card. "Not that I'm aware of."

"It's funny how the rumors fly around. I heard again this morning that you were a suspect."

"I told you, Celeste. I was pointing, Tim was pointing, and I bumped him." Why did I even lower myself to talk to this woman?

Celeste waved her hand. "Not that. One of Walter's deputies told his mother about more evidence."

I thought about the knife sheath planted in the garage and the money from my apartment. But Ray didn't know the knife sheath came from my purse. He thought the Beak had dropped it on the floor of my car, and he still seemed to think the money came from the convenience store robberies. Or did he? "Maybe I'm a suspect because Tim was found in my showroom."

"I heard it had something to do with Tim's appointment book. The initials J.A. were written on his calendar for seven o'clock the night he was killed. Did you have a date with him that night?" Celeste glanced at me out of the corner of her eye as though she already knew my answer.

A lump formed in my throat. I could scarcely choke out the word "No."

Celeste handed me the bag and my credit card. "That's so weird."

I tried to be nonchalant. "Was this appointment book in his office?"

"No, they found it in his car that they recovered from the woods."

Ray had never asked me about this book. It seemed like an awfully important fact for him to ignore. In fact, the appointment book with the knife sheath, the money, and my alleged fight with Tim over zoning was enough to arrest me on suspicion of murder, I had no doubt. Yet, here I was walking free. Maybe Ray did have another suspect in mind. But who?

Celeste continued and answered the question for me. "I think they ought to be looking at Tim's partner."

"Tim didn't have a partner. He owned the accounting practice by himself. One of his associates is looking to buy it now."

Celeste gave me a condescending look. I remembered her asking me about Tim's partner the night of the Christmas tree lighting ceremony. "Not that kind of partner, Jolene. His boyfriend kind of partner."

I tried not to let my expression give anything away. "What do you mean?"

She shook her head and her expression changed to pitying. "I know you dated him, but he was into boys, not girls. He had a boyfriend. That's why he left Becky. They just didn't spread it around."

"How do you know?"

"I suspected for some time, but Becky finally told my sister Chrissy her suspicions a couple days ago."

"Did she know the name of his boyfriend?"

"No, but looking back, I'm sure it's that guy that used to come to bowling with him. They were always touching each other in more than friendly ways."

Of course. Brennan Rowe.

TWENTY-SIX

I DEBATED MOST OF the night whether to call Ray to ask him about my status as an official suspect. To tell the truth, I was too afraid because I knew I was guilty of obstruction of justice by not telling him about the knife sheath in the first place. But mostly I was afraid to have him confirm that he doubted me. If my own husband didn't know I was innocent, forget about a jury of my peers.

The rest of the night I tried to make a case against Brennan Rowe. Had he murdered Tim and tried to place the blame on me? I couldn't figure out a motive unless they had broken up and Brennan didn't take rejection well. I wondered if Ray had made all these connections, but didn't dare call him to find that out either. I figured if anyone knew, he did.

I unlocked the showroom at 9:45 a.m. Cory strolled in at one minute before ten and entered my office to hang his coat on the stand. "I feel like donuts. Talk me out of them. I have to run three hours at the gym to burn off the calories from one."

All my fears must have shown on my face because he reached for my hand as soon as he turned around. "What? What is it? Did somebody die?"

I held onto his fingers as though they might keep me from drowning in my fears. Then the whole story poured out of me. Cory never interrupted, not even once, but his fingers did tighten around mine a bit when I mentioned the notation in Tim's appointment calendar.

When I ran out of words, he released my hand and leaned back in his chair, staring up at the ceiling. "Let's think about this, Jo. Someone planted evidence in your house. Maybe they planted the notation in the date book as well. How hard would it be to jot your initials in the book?"

"Not very."

"It had to be the killer."

I left his words suspended in the air because he was right. It had to be.

"Do we have any irate—and murderously insane—customers that I don't know about?"

"Mr. Oliver is the angriest customer we've ever had and everything occurred before he got mad at me." His demands seemed trivial now in light of a potential jail sentence for murder.

"You have any enemies I don't know about?"

"No. The only people in my life are you, Erica, Isabelle and her family—and Ray."

Cory picked up my hand and toyed with my ring finger which still bore the slightest indentation from the wedding ring I'd worn until the day I left Ray. Well, maybe it was the day after when I found the signed divorce papers here on my desk.

He shook his head as though dazed. "Let's go over it one more time. The only people who knew the alarm code for the shop were you, me, Erica and Ray. Correct?"

"As far as I know."

He released my hand. "Call Erica right now and ask her one more time if she gave the code to anyone, ever."

Tommye answered the phone at the nurse's desk and agreed to summon Erica to the phone. I waited for five minutes with the anxiety growing in the pit of my stomach. Finally Erica's breathless voice came on the line.

"No, I never gave the code to anyone, not even Sam."

"Are you sure? None of your friends, boyfriends, fellow patients, no one?"

She huffed into the phone, sending static over the line. "Jolene, what good would it do them?"

"All right, but when you brought back the car, it looked detailed. Who spiffed it up?"

She was silent so long I thought she'd hung up. "Sam's brother and Theo. They looked over the engine and everything. They want to open up their own garage."

"Is that why you took the car?"

"Not exactly."

"Then tell me exactly why you did, Erica. I'm in a lot of trouble here."

"Theo wanted to drive it. I let him as part of the payment for your gift."

"What's the gift?"

"It's very special and it's a surprise. But I swear it has nothing else to do with the car, or any other car for that matter."

"Erica, are you sure Sam and your friends didn't rob the convenience stores?"

Again, silence filled the line. "I'm sure about Sam and his brother's friend. I'm not sure about Theo or Sam's brother."

"What's his friend's name?"

"Mikey."

Why did that name sound familiar? "Are you talking about Mikey Burnbaum, Walter's son? The one in the room next door to you?"

"Yes."

I tried to connect the dots and ended up with a big question mark. "Who did you bring to my apartment with you the first time? I saw four dishes on the table."

"Sam, Theo, and Theo's girlfriend Abigail. She went with us to the casino."

I wrote all the names down and pushed the paper toward Cory. He picked it up to read while I finished my conversation.

"Erica, is there anything else you haven't told me?"

"Just one thing. I heard the voice again last night."

I sighed. This would not be helpful. "What voice?"

"The one that damned you and said you would pay. I heard him again in the hallway last night."

"Did you look to see who it was?"

"I looked. He was gone."

Gone or never even there. So hard to know for sure when it came to Erica. "Okay, thanks. Let me talk to Tommye again, please."

I heard the scratch and fumble as she handed the phone to Tommye.

"Erica says she's hearing voices again. Is she heavily medicated?"

"No, she's been doing really well, Wheels. She's a little paranoid, but the doctors were optimistic that she did so well on the outside last week. They took it as a sign of improvement in her condition."

I could barely hear Tommye's next words. "She did tell me about the voice last night."

"What time was that?"

"I had just said good night to Mikey's father who was here visitin'. It must have been around nine."

"Nine? I thought visiting hours were over at eight."

"We let the chief come and go as he pleases. He works odd hours."

Could Walter be the voice? "Any chance the chief was there the night of Friday, December 1 at the time Erica first heard the voice?"

Tommye must have had the same thought because she didn't express any surprise at my question. "I would have to go downstairs and check the logbook that the guard keeps. I can't do that until someone comes to relieve me for my break. Let me call you back."

I thanked her and hung up, then filled Cory in on the conversation. He leaned back in his chair and put his feet up on my desk. "So we know Brennan Rowe and Tim had a relationship that no one in town knew about."

"No one except Celeste."

Cory pointed his finger at me. "Celeste. Did your dad tell her the alarm code?"

"I asked her. She said no."

"Maybe she lied. She knew about Tim's partner. Maybe she was blackmailing him."

I swiveled my chair from side to side, tapping my knees against the side of my desk. "I can't picture her carting Tim's stiff body in here alone. She's fit, but she's not muscular. Besides, she might break a nail."

Cory cracked a grin. "You have a point, but we're missing something obvious, Jo. I don't know what it is. My advice is to come clean with Ray about the knife sheath and let him figure it out. He's not going to arrest you, but he's going to be mad as hell, that's for sure."

I sat in the office while Cory headed out to the garage to do a year-end parts inventory. Ray would be angry, maybe so angry he'd never want anything to do with me again, but I knew Cory was right. I had to tell him.

As I reached for the phone, it rang. I jumped in my chair. Could Ray be psychic? No, it was Tommye.

"Walter was here that night. He left around seven."

"Did you make a note in the chart as to when she heard the voices that time?"

"Hold on." Tommye set the phone down with a thunk and returned moments later. "I don't know what time she heard the voice. She told me about it at eight and started pestering to call you. I made her wait until the next day."

The day I found Tim dead in my showroom.

After I hung up with Tommye, I tried again to connect all the dots. Could Walter be involved in Tim's death? Why would he want to kill Tim and blame me? The whole idea didn't seem very likely to me. Ray would find it laughable, no doubt.

I would never figure it out alone, though. I put my pride aside and dialed Ray's cell phone number. It went to voicemail. I dialed his number at the sheriff's office. Gumby answered just as I heard the second line into the shop ring. I let Cory answer it and asked Gumby if I could talk to Ray.

"Ray's testifying this morning. I'm not sure what time he'll be done."

"Can you have him call me right away? Tell him it's important."

"It's always important when you call, sugar, but I'll tell him."

Sugar? I hung up rolling my eyes in disgust. Line two was still lit so I wandered into the garage to see if it might be a customer hot to buy a used red Ferrari. Cory dropped the receiver in the hook as I approached.

"That was Sarah Nelson. She needs you to stop by the house. She found some paperwork she wants you to take a look at. It was mixed in with all the estate sale stuff."

I checked my watch. Almost noon. "All right. I took your advice and left a message for Ray. If he calls back, tell him where I am and to call me."

The driveway at the house was empty when I arrived. I parked in the street and walked around to check behind the house. No sign of Sarah's car. I unlocked the kitchen door and stepped inside. "Sarah? Sarah?"

My voice echoed through the house. No response. I could see Sarah had been busy at work pricing all the items in the kitchen, which were now laid out on the countertops ready to sell. The living room was in a similar state, but I spotted a note propped up on the dining room table.

It read: "Jolene, I had to run my son's lunch over to him at school. Be back soon. The items you should look at are in the filing cabinet in the garage. Sarah "

The garage. A feeling of dread washed over me. I walked out of the house through the kitchen and stared at the yellow-sided one-car garage that I had not entered since the fateful day twenty-five years ago when I discovered my mother's dead body inside.

No way was I going in there now.

I stood staring at the building and the smell of the exhaust came back to me. Then the sound of the engine. I started to shiver, and not from the cold. I turned my back and squeezed my eyes shut, willing the memories away and trying to find my happy place as they had suggested all those years ago in the hospital.

"What are you doing, Jolene?"

I opened my eyes and found Ray standing a few feet in front of me. "Trying not to remember."

He tipped his head to the side and examined my face. "Remember what?"

"Sarah Nelson is running an estate sale for me. She found some papers in a filing cabinet in the garage she thought I might want to keep. I can't go in there. It reminds me of Mom."

Ray lifted his head and looked at the garage. "Okay, I'll get them for you." He took three steps and was past me. I grabbed his arm.

"No, wait." I took a deep breath. "I have to face this sometime."

He turned, blocking my view of the garage, and placed his hands on my shoulders. "It's good to face your fears, Jolene. This is not just a fear, though. This is a horrible memory, one you don't need to relive, in my opinion. Let me do this for you."

A heavy feeling washed over me. I recognized the feeling as guilt. Here was Ray, once again, riding to my rescue, and I hadn't even confided in him yet about the knife sheath I'd been hiding. "I'm afraid of the memories, which is silly. I know she died and I know how. I'm the one who found her. I should be able to walk into that garage today without any problem at all." I shook off his hands and took five steps in that direction before my legs refused to go any farther.

Ray moved up to stand next to me again, gazing with me toward the garage. "Okay, you might be right, but be advised you may have to face two of your fears. The last time I was in the garage, I found two mice nests."

I saw those familiar fire-engine red lips again with a mouse tail wiggling. My gaze shot to Ray's face. "You go."

He smiled, chucked me under the chin, and took one step before I grabbed his arm again. "Why are you always here when I need you?"

He slid his arms around me and squeezed me tight to his chest. "You're still very important to me."

I didn't want to let go of him for fear he'd never take me in his arms again, but I had to know. I pushed on his chest. He released me. I gazed into his eyes. "I'm sorry, Ray. I never should have left you. We could have worked it out then. But what about now? I still love you. Do you still love me?"

He gazed over my shoulder, unwilling or unable to meet my eyes. "It's been three years, Jolene. I waited for you to come home for two years. You never did. I tried to move on. That didn't quite work out either." He raised his eyes to mine. I saw the pain in them. "We can't go back. We can only go forward. I know I want children. The question is: what do you want?"

I sniffled and rubbed at my nose with my fingers, smearing a thin film of mucus on my upper lip. "I'm thirty-seven, Ray. If I get pregnant now, not only do I have a chance of passing on mental illness but the likelihood of birth defects is higher."

"It doesn't have to be our biological child. It doesn't even have to be a baby. But I'd like at least one child." Ray released me and took hold of my collar, pulling it around my neck as though to warm me. "This isn't the time to hash it out. Think about it. When you know what you want, we can talk again."

He kissed me gently on the nose.

I reached into my purse for a tissue and blew my nose in a long and very unladylike manner.

Guilt enveloped me like a blanket. I had made so many mistakes, not the least of which was withholding evidence from him. Ray deserved to hear the truth about the knife sheath, even if he never spoke to me again. "Before you brave the mice, Ray, I have to tell you something."

He looked at me out of the corner of his eye and apparently didn't like the change in my expression. He turned to face me head on, folding his arms across his chest. "What?"

"You're going to be mad."

"Just *tell me*, Jolene."

"I wanted to tell you before, but I was trying to protect Erica. I think I'm the one who needs protecting now, though."

He growled, "Just tell me."

"Remember the knife sheath the state police found in Cory's car?"

"Yes?"

"I found it in the Miracle-Gro box in the garage behind my apartment the same night I found the fifteen thousand hidden in my apartment and car. I put it in the baggie, then in my purse. I know Erica didn't put it in the box, so it had to be the killer."

Ray stared at me, then turned and took two steps away. He swung around and came back, opened his mouth, and let out a puff of breath that formed a cloud in the cold air. His neck flushed bright red.

He turned around again and took five steps away, then circled back and opened his mouth again. No sound or air came out this time. He raised his arms in the air in the surrender position and walked all the way to the garage door this time, bending down to grab the handle and lift it upward. The door banged against the roof of the garage as he disappeared inside.

Seconds later, things began to fly out of the garage door. A plastic pail, a watering can, cans of pest control spray, a rake, a broom, a crow bar, a tire jack. Every tool in my father's toolbox, one at a time, then the black Craftsman tool chest itself—all of these items neatly labeled with a half-inch-square price tag. Sarah really had been busy.

When the recycling bin flew out, I dodged it and watched it roll to a stop a few yards away. The garbage can followed and slammed into the basement window, shattering it. I began to grow concerned.

The lawnmower rolled out with a price tag on it. The bag of fertilizer that followed split open when it landed on the ground, spraying pellets of weed control everywhere. The bottles of car wash bounced twice before splitting open, their blue contents coloring the remaining snow on the drive and mixing with the weed pellets to make a clumpy mess.

He appeared in the doorway to the garage with the three-drawer filing cabinet over his head as if it weighed nothing. He hurled it out and it crashed to the ground, slid five feet on the icy drive and came to a stop inches from the toe of my black boot.

"There's your papers." His voice was calm and controlled, too controlled.

"Thank you." I didn't dare say anything else.

The crash landing had dented the filing cabinet. I doubted it would sell for the twenty-dollar price Sarah had placed on it, either. I had no right to complain.

"I'm sorry, Ray. I know I should have told you everything right from the start, but I thought at first I was protecting Erica."

"Erica, Erica." Ray walked out of the garage and came to a halt with his face inches from mine, his hot breath singeing my face. "It's always Erica. Do you realize I could lose my job over this? Do you realize the Sheriff didn't want me on this case when he found out Tim Lapham's body was found in your shop and that you'd been dating him? I told the Sheriff I could be objective. I told him I would solve this case. Do you realize how this is going to look?"

This time I'd gone too far. "I didn't know. I'm sorry, Ray."

"Where's the box of Miracle-Gro now?"

"In the garage at my apartment. I didn't touch it."

"Is the garage locked?"

I swallowed. "No."

"Thank you for protecting the evidence, Jolene."

I repeated my mantra. "I'm sorry, Ray."

"I could lose my job, Jolene. I could go to jail for obstructing justice."

I tried to think of a way to soothe him. "Wait a minute, Ray. How did you obstruct justice? I only told you about the knife sheath today. You can tell the Sheriff when you get back to the office."

Something akin to regret and guilt sparked in his eye.

"Ray, what did you do?"

He shoved his hands inside his jacket pockets. "It's more what I didn't do, Jolene. I didn't tell the Sheriff about your argument with Tim Lapham or the money in your apartment."

"It was not an argument. I was pointing, he was pointing—oh, never mind. Does he know about the notation in Tim's appointment book?"

Ray's nostril flared. He didn't ask how I found out about the date book. "Yes, but only because Walter discovered it."

"So let me get this straight. You've been concealing the evidence against me from your boss?"

"In a word, yes."

TWENTY-SEVEN

RAY LEFT IN A fury, tires squealing. I decided against chasing after him. I'd forgotten to tell him about Walter Burnbaum's presence at the psych center, but Ray was too mad to listen to me right now anyway.

I stood on the filing cabinet trying to pry the top drawer open with a crow bar. Sarah pulled into the driveway in her gold soccer-mom minivan. She was a petite blonde with wide dark eyes and a beauty mark smack dab in the center of her right cheek. If she were a little taller and more buxom, she might be Marilyn Monroe. In her work overalls she looked more like Green Acres today. Her eyes grew wide at the scene before her.

"What happened?"

I couldn't tell her about Ray, because I didn't want to taint his reputation any further than I already had. I didn't think she'd buy a microburst as an explanation for the mess. I took the blame, instead. "I got a little carried away. It's an emotional time for me."

She gazed wide-eyed at the disaster. "I understand. I'll clean it all right up."

"I'll help." I took one last tug on the top drawer and it popped open, sending scads of photographs swirling into the air and me flying backward onto the corner of the filing cabinet. A shock wave shot up my spine.

"Jolene, are you all right?" Sarah rushed to my side and knelt to look into my eyes, which were now welling with tears.

Breathless, I could only nod.

"Are you sure? Maybe I should call an ambulance."

I managed to croak out the word "no."

She gripped my arm and waited. After a minute or so, I worked my way to my feet with my tailbone smarting every inch of the way.

"Are you sure you don't want to see a doctor?"

"No, I'm fine." I started to giggle. Sarah joined me. We both knew I was lying.

Sarah began to gather up the photographs. "Well, at least the police didn't need to come."

I wanted to help her, but I couldn't bend over. "What are you talking about?"

"I had a sale last month for a family who moved out of town. They had an alarm system I turned on and off every time I went over to the house. The night before the sale, it went off in the middle of the night for some reason. Maybe someone was trying to break in since the house was vacant. Anyway, the next day the neighbors yelled at me like it was my fault. The police had to come in the middle of the night and shut the alarm off because the family who owned the house was six states away and hadn't left a forwarding number. But before the police got permission to shut it off, the neighbors had to listen to the alarm for over an hour."

"You know my husband Ray is with the Sheriff's Department. Did he respond?"

Sarah handed me the photos. "Oh, no, it was Walter Burnbaum. Apparently any activated alarms within the town limits fall under his jurisdiction. I saw him a few days later. He wasn't too happy to have to get up in the middle of the night either." She moved off and got to work collecting Dad's tools.

I'd scarcely heard the end of Sarah's reply. I'd glanced down at the photograph on top of the pile she placed in my hands only to find my mother staring back at me. She had a broad, toothy smile and her arms were wrapped around a roughly six-year-old me. The sight took all thoughts, not to mention my breath, away. I flipped to the next picture: my mother and me on the first day of school. She'd made me a cotton print dress with pink ribbons for my hair, and I recalled feeling like the most special girl in the whole world. Maybe that was because my mother had told me I was.

I continued scanning the photographs. They covered the first twelve years of my life. Erica appeared five years in—an adorable baby with blond curls and a toothless smile, then later a rail-thin child who was forever holding a ratty old bear. I remembered packing the bear for her the other night. In almost all the photos, my mother stood smiling proudly, with no hint of the mental illness that would later claim her life. My father appeared in the remaining photos, including a picture at a church picnic with Martha and Walter Burnbaum.

My head snapped up from the photographs. "Sarah?"

She moved to my side and looked over my shoulder at the photos. "Great photos, aren't they?"

"Yes. Thank you for saving them for me."

She beamed. "I knew you'd want them."

"I do, but I just wanted to ask you about what you said a moment ago. Walter Burnbaum responded to the false alarm at your estate sale and turned the alarm off?"

"Yes, Walter. He's such a nice man."

I used to think so. "You said the alarm went off at Brennan Rowe's garage, too. Was he home to shut it off?"

"Nope, Walter did it." Sarah picked up the broom and began to sweep up the fertilizer pellets. "I think it happens fairly often. Walter's amassed quite a list of alarm codes."

Walter Burnbaum. He was ever-present, wasn't he? I tried to sit on the stoop. My back resisted. Instead I leaned against the house and thought.

Walter had been first on the scene when we discovered Tim's body. He hadn't even been armed. Was that because he knew the situation he was walking into? And on the night of the Christmas tree lighting when Ray and I discovered the money, I waved to Walter as he drove by me. Was he coming from my apartment where he had left tire tracks in the drive, hidden the money, and planted the sheath from the knife he used to kill Tim? Had Walter's voice been the one Erica heard both times at the psych center? For once, had she not been hallucinating? And why had Walter suddenly decided to install a wood floor in the middle of the winter when Martha hated wooden flooring? Isn't that the sort of thing a husband would know? And how come the police blotter in the local paper didn't mention the robbery call Walter had been on supposedly three blocks away from my apartment the night I surprised an intruder? I laid down the photographs, pulled out my cell phone and started to dial Ray, then changed my mind and dialed the shop. I needed one more piece to solve the puzzle.

Cory answered before the phone had a chance to ring. "Hey, Jo, I was going to call you. Brennan Rowe called. He's got the check ready for the roadster if you want to pick it up."

"Sure, fine."

"He said he'd be at the construction site until around two o'clock."

"Okay, great." I had more important things on my mind than money. "I have a question for you, Cory. Has the shop's burglar alarm ever gone off?"

"Ah ... we've never been robbed."

"That's not what I'm asking you. I'm asking if the alarm has ever been activated, especially at a time when none of us were available to turn it off."

"Oh." I heard Cory sigh. "Well, just once. You all went to a family wedding and left me in charge. I decided to stay overnight with a ... new friend. The town plow lifted a manhole cover and it flew through the front window. The alarm company tried to get in touch with all of us but we weren't available." He paused then rushed to the finish. "I paid for the new glass to be installed so you guys wouldn't know I messed up."

My cell phone started to beep, indicating a low battery. "That's fine. But who turned the alarm off?"

"Walter Burnbaum. He was giving me dirty looks for weeks afterward."

I slumped down onto the step, scarcely feeling the pain in my back as my mind reeled with the implications of Cory's statement.

"So why are you asking me about this now, Jo?"

"I think Walter killed Tim."

"*What*?"

I replayed my thoughts for Cory, who punctuated each one with an exclamation of "Holy shit!"

"So I'm thinking it's Walter."

"I can maybe see opportunity and means, but what's his motive, Jo?"

I thought about the cash in my apartment and the town's missing money. The woman at the town clerk's office said we made twenty-five thousand a year in parking meter fees and parking tickets, but that figure sounded low given the volume of tourists. I'm sure we'd discussed higher numbers than that in past business association meetings. It was Walter's sole responsibility to empty the meters. What if Walter had been skimming for years? What if Tim had done the math and come to the same conclusion? Would he have requested an audit team to prove his suspicions? Would he have been foolish enough to confront Walter privately first?

"The meter fees."

My cell phone beeped incessantly, breaking up Cory's reply. "Wh … fe … Jo?"

"I'm calling Ray right now, Cory."

I hit the end button and tried to dial Ray's number. My battery was now dead. I stumbled to my feet and darted into the house, using the phone on the kitchen wall. Ray's cell phone rang straight to voicemail. I wouldn't have been surprised if his message said, "If this is Jolene Asdale, I'm never speaking to you again." But it didn't.

"Ray, I think I know who killed Tim." I asked him to try my cell phone or come see me when he got my message. Then I dialed the sheriff's office. Ray wasn't there either. I asked for Gumby. I hesitated to give him all the details, because if I was wrong, everyone in town would hear about it, including Walter and his family. I wasn't confident enough to take that risk with anyone but Cory and Ray. Instead, I told Gumby that I needed to speak with Ray a.s.a.p. about Tim's death.

"What for, Jolene?"

"I just need to speak to Ray. It's very important."

"It always is. That man drops everything for you, except not his pants anymore, right?"

I hung up the phone in disgust. How Gumby ever got to be on the force was beyond me.

I wanted to drive around and see if I could spot Ray somewhere, but his territory covered almost a six-mile radius. No way would I be able to locate him on my own. I would just have to wait.

I checked my watch. Brennan Rowe had said he'd be around until two. It was almost two now. I would drive by his construction site to pick up the check and ask him if he had in fact been Tim's boyfriend. He may have been the one who accompanied Tim to Vegas. I could see why Tim found it easier to let Becky believe that it was me. If Brennan was Tim's boyfriend, then Tim might have confided his suspicions about Walter.

After apologizing profusely to Sarah for destroying all of her hard work, I lowered myself painfully into the low-slung seat of the Porsche, and hit the gas.

When I pulled off the main road onto the construction site, I didn't see any sign of activity. No cars or trucks, no demolition work, no nothing, but it was Friday. Maybe his workers cut out early for the weekend, too. Or maybe it was just too cold to work.

I parked next to the trailer and knocked. When no one answered, I tried the handle, only to find it locked. I walked around the back of the trailer to look for Brennan's car. The site was indeed unoccupied by man or car. A quick check of my watch confirmed I was only five minutes late, but I hadn't called to say that I was coming. Apparently, Brennan didn't wait around.

The crunch of wheels on the gravel road into the site brought me back around to the front of the trailer. A maroon minivan glided up and parked. Not exactly the kind of car I pictured Brennan Rowe driving, but then, minivans are common on the road. This one was the same color as the ones I'd noticed at least twice this week.

The thought no sooner crossed my mind than the man stepped out of the van, a gangly man wearing black, a man with a hawk nose. The Beak. He had his switchblade in his hand.

The Beak sauntered over and came to a stop about two yards from me. He flicked the switchblade back and forth. The sun glare from it made me blink.

"I thought you were in Arizona." I pressed my fingers over my mouth to prevent further nonsense from blurting out. Clearly he had been following me around town all along.

"I never left here. I tapped your phone and I stayed to monitor the wire." He held out his empty hand. "I'd like my list of gambling debtors back now."

"I don't have it."

"Liar. I heard you talking to the truck driver. Give me your purse."

"If you tapped my phone, you know the Sheriff's Department already has a copy of this list."

"They can have a hundred copies as long as I have one to collect on."

"Don't you have the original on a computer?"

The Beak's lips formed a grim line. "Computers got seized in the bust. I'm working on my own now."

Great, his boss had been busted but he soldiered on like some militant, only to his own benefit. And my detriment.

I didn't think I could dodge him and reach my car in time to escape, and of course, my cell phone was still plugged into the car charger and lost to me. He probably wouldn't appreciate being hit in the head with my purse again, either.

I dropped it to the ground and tried to remember what we'd learned in self-defense class about disarming an attacker holding a knife. Something about grabbing the weapon in my hand and holding the blade in the curve of my fingers so it wouldn't cut me. It had sounded good at the time, but we never practiced that move.

The Beak took two steps forward and brandished the blade. I jumped back. He knelt and picked up my purse, retreated to his van, and set it on the hood to dig through it. I watched, happy he'd left me behind and intact. He pulled the lists from it and shook them in the air triumphantly. Throwing my purse on the ground, he pulled open his door and paused as we both heard the crunch of another vehicle's tires on the drive. I looked up to see a brown Crown Victoria approaching.

It came to a stop directly behind the minivan. No one got out. The Beak's car was now trapped between it, my car, and some huge black plastic piping undoubtedly waiting to be installed as the sewage system. The Beak could still make it off the property if he didn't mind a little bumper car action. Apparently he came to the same conclusion because he turned his back on the new arrival and bent as though about to climb in his car.

I heard a rifle cock. The Beak must have, too. He looked at me. I was looking between him and Walter, who had stepped out of the unmarked car, armed with a hunting rifle.

"I got plenty of shots, boy, and I never miss. Drop the knife and move over by Jolene, please."

Any relief I'd felt at the sight of Walter died as soon as he looked at me. I could see rage and determination in his eyes.

The Beak tilted his nose into the air defiantly, then continued to slide into his car. A shot rang out. He screamed and grabbed at his ear. Blood appeared between his fingers.

I jumped back. Walter swung the gun my way. "Stay right where you are, Jolene."

He swung the rifle back toward the Beak.

"I repeat, drop the knife and move over by Jolene."

The Beak walked over to my side, shooting daggers my way like it was my fault he'd been shot. In a way, I suppose it was. Blood dripped from his ear, coating his jacket in a brown polka-dot design.

I watched it drip and had to pry my gaze away as my stomach started to churn.

Walter approached us and stopped. He had the rifle at his right shoulder and his eye trained on the sight. He appeared calm and in control except for the slight flutter of his left eyelid. I couldn't believe it was the same mild-mannered man I'd known for years. Ray always did say to watch out for the quiet, polite ones.

"My son heard that nurse talking to you, Jolene. He asked me a lot of questions. The questions end here and now."

Walter wasn't in uniform. He was in hunting camouflage. For a brief second, I wondered if he'd been the one robbing all the stores, but then I realized Ray and I would have recognized his distinctive strut, a cocky walk he'd developed when his wrestling team became state champs.

He raised his head and seemed to have half an eye on us as the other half scanned the construction site, weighing the possibilities, no doubt. I decided the best option was to start talking and keep him talking. Maybe someone would happen by and spot our plight from the road.

I fumbled for words to placate him. "I'm sure Tim's death was an accident, Walter. We'll talk to Ray and work it out."

He pointed the rifle barrel at my throat. "Shut up, Jolene."

Walter was not going to be placated. I tried a different approach. "If you're going to kill me, the least you could do is fill me in on why."

The Beak piped up. "Is this the guy who stuffed the stiff in the boss's Ferrari?"

I let him join in the conversation, feeling more confident with his presence than I would have alone. We outnumbered Walter. Perhaps we could outtalk him, too. "Yes."

"The one who's been robbing parking meters?"

"The same."

"Man, you gotta rid yourself of the public service mentality. You should try gambling and extortion. Pays a lot better than a few grand a year."

Walter flushed and the creases in his frown deepened. I wanted to smack the Beak because he'd further irritated Walter.

"Shut up, both of you. Start walking toward the barn." Walter pointed toward it with the rifle barrel.

Neither of us moved.

"Now!" Walter shrieked and fired a warning shot into the air.

We scrambled to obey, with me in the lead, the Beak following. I had visions of Walter shooting me and blood draining from my chest. My heart started to pound. I sucked in air and pressed my hand over my heart, trying to remain calm and think. But all I could think of was Erica. Would she now talk to both Mom and me from the grave?

The snow had made the ground muddy. I slipped a few times in my high-heeled black boots. Several times the heel stuck in the ground and I had to jerk it out. Once, the Beak even grabbed my bicep and yanked me out.

I couldn't see any weapons except gravel on the ground ahead of us. The sound of Walter's heavy breaths behind us only made my heart beat faster. He sounded like a bull about to charge. My gaze darted, looking for something, anything, to help us escape.

Ten feet from the decaying barn I caught sight of something hopping and springing across the snow, leaving a trail of tiny tracks. It was a tan field mouse, no bigger than my fist.

He stopped to chew on something he held in his forefeet then wiggled through a hole in the base of the fire-engine red barn. The last thing I saw was his tail flick through the opening. I froze. The Beak slammed into my back, propelling me forward onto my knees and splashing my new white coat with mud.

Walter fingered the trigger. "Get up, Jolene. Stop screwing around."

"No." I folded my legs and crossed my arms. "I'm not going in that barn. I'm not doing another damn thing you ask." I looked at the bank of melting snow next to me. "As a matter of fact, I'm leaving a note." I took my finger and wrote in the snow "Walter killed Tim."

Walter shoved his rifle in the Beak's back and pushed him aside to shuffle through my words, destroying them. "Cut it out, Jolene."

My anger overcame my good sense. "You're going to have to shoot me now, Walter. Right now, right here."

He pointed the rifle at me but didn't seem prepared to shoot. "Damn you, it's all your fault."

I struggled to my feet. "My fault? I didn't kill Tim Lapham, you did."

Walter began to alternate pointing the rifle barrel at the Beak then me. It occurred to me that he couldn't shoot us both if we tried to rush him.

"You couldn't leave it alone. You had to ruin everything." Walter's one eyelid was now fluttering out of control but his other eye remained firmly fixed on us.

"Walter, I don't know what you're talking about. Can you explain?" I folded my arms to hide their shaking and waited.

When Walter spoke again, his voice sounded strangled. "I had to put Mikey in the psych center. Martha was beside herself and left for her mother's. Tim came over to my house that night and accused me of embezzling the parking fees and padding my expenses. He said you had pointed out to him that the town must make an awful lot of money on the meters."

I gave myself a mental slap in the head. The Beak frowned at me.

Walter continued, "When he did the math and checked the records, he realized I was skimming. He was going to tell the town board. If he did, I would lose my job, Martha, everything. I panicked. When he stood up to leave, I grabbed my hunting knife and stabbed him." Tears rolled down Walter's face. "I didn't mean it."

The Beak shifted as though uncomfortable. "Oh, man."

I was more than a little uncomfortable. I had gotten into a bit of a rant that day in my showroom when Tim told me about the zoning board's complaints. Apparently, I really had killed Tim Lapham in a way—I'd opened the door to his investigation of Walter. Guilt filled my veins and slowly turned to ice. It was too late for Tim, but I'd applaud the installation of more meters on the streets now if Walter would promise not to kill me.

Walter swept his hand over his face, drying the tears. "I didn't want to dump Tim in the lake. I wanted his family to be able to bury him. I needed a place to put him where he'd be found, but it wouldn't point to me. I decided to make the evidence point to you, Jolene." He met my gaze. This time his eyelid wasn't twitching.

I swallowed the saliva that had filled my mouth. "Why me, Walter?"

"Because it was all your fault. Besides, I knew Ray would be involved in the investigation. I knew he would never believe you did it. And even if he did, he would never let you go to jail. Never."

"You're awfully sure of yourself, Walter. Ray's an honest cop. I think he'd put me in jail if he had to."

Walter shook his head. "Never. Everyone in this town knows Ray loves you way too much."

Everyone but me. I almost asked Walter to shoot me right then and there to put me out of my misery. But first I needed to grovel at Ray's feet for his forgiveness.

I turned to the Beak and whispered, "What do you say we rush him? Only one of us would get shot. We might not even die."

The Beak's eyebrows flew up. He grinned, revealing stained teeth. "I like you. Too bad you're already married."

Walter took a few steps back from us, moving the rifle even more rapidly between us. "Stop talking. Stop talking!"

A vein pulsed in his temple. His face turned beet red. I hoped he might have a heart attack on the spot and save us the trouble of fighting our way out. He didn't.

The Beak breathed, "On the count of three. One ... two ... three."

I rushed forward. So did the Beak, only he was screaming like a maniac, surprising the shit out of me and Walter, who jumped backward. His rifle wavered. I grabbed hold of it, pushing it skyward. I tried to pull the rifle from his hands. He butted me with it in the stomach. I clenched my teeth and swallowed the pain and nausea as I continued to struggle for control of the weapon. It didn't take Walter, a trained wrestling coach, long to knock me flat on my ass and leave me gazing at the clouds.

It did take me a couple of seconds to realize the Beak was high-tailing it across the site to his car instead of standing to fight with me. I should have known better than to trust a convicted criminal.

Everything went into slow motion as Walter brought the rifle to his shoulder and squeezed the trigger. The Beak dropped to the ground and didn't move.

"Walter!"

He swung around and pointed the gun directly at me. "I'm sorry, Jolene, but I'm a police officer. Do you know how long a policeman survives in prison? And what happens to him before he prays for death? Now, get up. We're going in that building." He gestured to the new community center with the rifle.

I looked back at the Beak. He still wasn't moving. Walter would shoot me, too, no doubt about it. I glanced at the building a hundred yards away. A hundred yards to think of plan B.

I got to my feet and started walking. I could hear Walter lumbering behind me, his change jingling in his pockets and the leather of his polished black boots creaking with each step. He was murmuring something under his breath that sounded like "Damn you, Jolene Asdale." Now I knew Erica wasn't hearing things after all. I guessed I owed her an apology, too, if I ever got the chance.

We were within a yard of the open doorway. I bolted inside, darting around the first wall I spotted. I heard a shot splinter the framing behind me. The drywall was already up on the first floor. Walter could no longer see me.

I darted around another corner. A second shot rang out. He was catching up fast.

That drywall concealed a stairwell. I took the stairs two steps at a time, snagging my heel in the hem of my pants. I fell to my knees. I struggled to my feet, ripping my pants and feeling as though my heart would burst from my chest. I clawed my way to the top of the stairs.

I stumbled onto the landing, falling again, and took in the sights quickly. This floor was only partially drywalled. I could run, but once Walter made it up the stairs, he'd have me in his sights.

I heard him pounding up the steps. My gaze settled on a length of two-by-six abandoned on the plywood floor. I pushed to my feet, scrambled, and grabbed it. I swung just as the rifle barrel came into sight, striking Walter in the forehead. He fell backward down the stairs, tumbling over and over and slamming into the exposed metal beam at the base of the stair. His rifle discharged, the bullet whizzing by my head and embedding in another two-by-six inches away from me, sending slivers of wood flying through the air. The rifle came to rest at his still feet.

After a moment of studying Walter where he lay, I tiptoed down the stairs and stepped with care over him. Blood trickled from a cut in his forehead. He moaned. I grabbed his rifle and raced out the entryway onto the gravel outside. I hoped to reach my car and speed off before he managed to get to his feet.

"Jolene!"

Twenty yards away, Ray stood behind the open door of his sheriff's car, his radio in his hand. I started running toward him, got a few yards, slipped in the mud, and fell, sprawling flat out and dropping Walter's rifle.

As I pushed to my knees, Ray reached inside his car, pulled out his shotgun, and pointed it in my direction. I couldn't believe my eyes. I froze and opened my mouth to scream his name.

A shot rang out. I looked down at my chest, expecting pain and blood and wondering why in the world Ray would shoot me.

I didn't feel any pain. I did see blood, but not until I looked behind me reflexively when I heard gasping. Walter had managed to rouse himself and follow me out of the community center. A large rose formed on his camouflaged chest. His right hand lowered, releasing his sidearm, which embedded in the mud and gravel. He fell to his knees. His now empty hand moved to his chest as though he were saying the pledge of allegiance before he dropped face forward into the rocks and lay silent and still.

Ray lowered his shotgun as he stepped away from the open door of his sheriff's car. He crossed the ground between us in seconds and pulled me up against his chest. He whispered my name and kissed my hair. I slid my arms around him and buried my face in his jacket, smelling gunpowder and sweat. Nothing had ever smelled better to me.

We heard a car door slam and looked up in time to see the Beak making a run for it in his minivan, denting Walter's car in the process.

Ray pulled his radio from his belt. "This is car 42. I have an officer down at 912 Whipple Road. Send an ambulance. And put an APB out on a maroon Dodge minivan, license plate Alpha Lima Whiskey Six Two Three Nine, heading north on Whipple Road.

The driver is Fitzgerald Simpson, a.k.a. the Beak. Suspect is armed and dangerous."

I frowned. "They're going to think he shot Walter. They're gonna kill him."

Ray shrugged. "They're going to do their job, Jolene. That man dragged you behind a car and almost killed you. I'll let him take his chances, but I'm stacking the deck against him."

He crossed the gravel and knelt beside Walter, checking for a pulse. "He's gone."

I hadn't expected any less. Ray was a damn good shot. Walter didn't stand a chance. I wasn't sure how I felt about that, but I was happy to be alive. "How did you find me?"

"I listened to your voicemail, tried to call your cell, then talked to Cory at the shop. He told me your suspicions about Walter. They matched mine. Cory said you were headed out here. I figured I might be able to catch you."

Ray looked over my shoulder at Walter's body. "Lucky I did."

His gaze returned to me. He brushed a lock of hair off my face and smiled. Once again, he was here for me.

Good thing a crying woman never bothered Ray.

TWENTY-EIGHT

I SPENT THE MAJORITY of Christmas Eve day assisting Father Christmas at the VFW Club, something I had done for the last three years since Ray and I separated. It made me feel good to volunteer, and this year spending time with happy, healthy children, making them even happier than they were before, eased my conscience about my role in leaving Tim's kids fatherless.

Father Christmas wore a curly wig of white hair, a matching beard, and a full-length red velvet coat with a black fur collar and gold and red trim. The coat had a matching red rope belt tied over his dark green and gold waistcoat. He had a wreath of red berries in his hair. I sported a matching one with the dark green dress the town costume closet had ready for me in the morning.

The snow had stopped falling and melted, ruining the white Christmas effect. An enterprising young woman in a tartan cap and white scarf strolled the street in front of the temple, selling snowballs off a tray. Apparently she'd had the foresight to store snow in her freezer. For five cents, a few lucky children were allowed to buy enough for a brief snowball war while they waited their turn to see Father Christmas.

Several of the littlest darlings cried as soon as their parents brought them in range of Father Christmas. Some of the bigger children almost broke the poor man's leg when they climbed onto his lap. A two-year-old peed his pants, leaving a spot on Father Christmas' leg. Each one received a candy cane from me. All in all, it was an exhausting but satisfying day. And it kept my mind off Ray. He had to work double shifts on Christmas Eve and Christmas Day, punishment from his boss, the sheriff, who didn't appreciate learning that Ray had found large amounts of money in my apartment and didn't tell him.

Ray and I had enjoyed two dinner dates since he saved my life, two dates where I spent plenty of time apologizing for my failure to tell him about material evidence as well as my error in judgment for ever leaving him. We hadn't tackled the kid thing yet. We did make use of our marital bed one more time before Sarah Nelson sold it during the estate sale. Call it a celebration of life.

On my way home from helping Father Christmas, I averted my eyes as I drove past the showroom window where the Ferrari sat with a great big green bow across its windshield. No one had expressed interest in buying it, but the sale of my home would more than fund another year of operation, including Cory's salary. My New Year's resolution would be to get in the black and pay myself back for the loan.

The zoning board wouldn't meet again until the New Year. When they did, I would be ready for them.

I also kept my eyes off the line of parking meters on Main Street. They were a daily painful reminder of how I had contributed in my own inimitable way to Tim Lapham's death. My donation to his children's college fund did little to assuage my conscience.

My phone rang at eleven o'clock Christmas Eve. I lay under the tree staring up at the lights glinting off the red and gold balls and the handmade decorations Erica and I created as children. I did this every year because when we were children, my mother slept with us in sleeping bags under the tree after we opened our presents on Christmas Eve. It is my fondest memory of her and the only reason I could bear the holiday without her now. Of course, we missed the year she died and I went to the hospital. But the very next year, my father made us start the tradition again, only then he slept under the tree with us. I think it made all of us feel closer to my mother.

"Merry Christmas." Erica wasn't allowed to leave the psych center to spend Christmas with me this year because of her excellent adventure with Sam. She still sounded happy and excited. Good.

"Same to you. Did you guys have a party?"

"We had lasagna, salad, and Christmas cookies, plus eggnog. I hate eggnog."

"I know." We had that in common. It was why I always made hot chocolate when we decorated the tree.

"I called because I have a surprise for you. You have to go get it right now."

"What are you talking about?"

"Your Christmas present. We always exchange presents on Christmas Eve."

When she said this, I felt guilty. I'd planned to bring hers to her tomorrow. Given her ongoing status as a mental patient, I thought we might need to start a new tradition this year.

"I'm coming to spend the day with you tomorrow. Can I pick it up then?" I heard someone in the background tell Erica to hang up the phone because her time was up.

"No, it's not here. It's under the Christmas tree in the park. You have to go get it RIGHT NOW." Erica raised her voice two octaves.

"Okay. I'll go get it." I didn't bother to ask her how my present got there. Maybe she'd left it there earlier in the week, like I left the money I'd found in my apartment.

"RIGHT NOW!"

Apparently, the gift was a perishable. "Right now, I promise. I'm hanging up and going right now. Merry Christmas, Erica."

"Merry Christmas, Jolene. I love you."

"I love you, too."

If Erica weren't a mental patient, I would have questioned this phone call. But in the scheme of things, I found it rather charming and harmless enough.

I parked on a meter for free, given the time of day. I wondered for the millionth time how everything had gone so wrong for Walter and his family. I felt sorry for them, but even sorrier for Tim and his family. Tim had tried to do the right thing by everyone and ended up getting killed for his efforts. According to the auditors that Tim had insisted the town hire, Walter had embezzled over a hundred thousand over the last five years. He had fallen into the parent trap of trying to bribe his son to stop using drugs with the promise of gifts like a big screen television and a car. Drug rehab would have been cheaper and more effective, but Walter didn't learn about the tough love school until it was too late.

Come to find out, Theodore Tibble had been robbing convenience stores with Sam's brother, the armed gunman, so they could get enough money to open a garage and detail shop. Heck, if they'd asked me about it first, we might have been able to strike a deal for them to rent space in my garage for their new endeavor. I didn't know how many cars they would get to work on in prison. The only good news was the expected full recovery of the convenience store owner whom Sam's brother shot. The trial was scheduled for January. Theo was out on bail at present.

As I neared the tree in the park, still brightly lit at this hour approaching midnight, I saw a shape beneath it. From a yard away, I realized it was an infant car seat, zippered almost closed. What had Erica done now?

I knelt beside it, took a deep breath and pulled the zipper open.

A little red face appeared, cheeks like roses and lips like cherries, all snuggled up in a pink fleece snowsuit. The baby's eyes were closed, but I could tell from the gentle but rapid rise and fall of her chest that she was breathing just fine. She was the most perfect baby I had ever seen.

A Christmas card, an empty bottle, three diapers, and a can of baby formula were tucked at her feet. The can had a sticky note with the instruction "Feed her in two hours."

The Christmas card with a picture of the star of Bethlehem on the cover read:

"Dear Jolene,

Mom and I talked it over and we think a baby is the answer to all your prayers. Her parents are Theo Tibble and his girlfriend Abigail. They can't take care of her. They have to leave town. I called Greg Doran. He'll be in touch to take care of all the paperwork to make her yours.

Her name is Noelle. I'm hoping Noelle Parker. You have to do the rest.

I love you best. Always.

Merry Christmas, Erica

I brushed my finger over the baby's cheek. She squirmed, smacking her lips and fluttering her spiky eyelashes. She didn't awaken.

A car engine turned over nearby. I spied a dark-colored Lincoln pulling away from the curb. The face in the passenger window was too far away for me to make out the features. I saw a hand wave.

Theo Tibble. He asked to drive the DeLorean in exchange for his baby. Now that's character. The name Abigail was familiar, too. I thought for a moment. The tattooed, pregnant clerk at the 7-Eleven three weeks ago came to mind. Could she have been the girl in the second robbery? Great, I had custody of the child of two armed robbers on the run from the law. The baby certainly didn't have much of a future with them. Had Erica known what was going on all along and tried to save this child?

I looked at the beautiful baby before me. Noelle opened her eyes and tried to focus on me. In the dim lights from the Christmas tree, I must have looked like a monster because she started to cry. I rocked the car seat. She screamed. I was going to have to pick her up.

The only baby I'd ever held was Isabelle's daughter. I hadn't felt any pressure because Isabelle had been beside me as backup. I was flying solo this time and feeling woefully inadequate. But when I lifted Noelle from the seat and pulled her to my chest, my body automatically started to sway side to side. After a moment, she fell silent.

I took another peek at her adorable little face and felt a rush of emotion I couldn't name. I knew I would probably have to give this child back. Who would expect two wayward convenience store robbers to keep their word to give her up for adoption? And what mental patient was competent enough to arrange an adoption? But in the meantime, what was a woman to do?

I pulled out my cell phone and called Ray.

THE END

ACKNOWLEDGMENTS:

First I have to thank my parents, Bill and Gini Pierson. They instilled in my brother and me a love of books, reading to us nightly as children and taking us to the library until we were old enough to drive there ourselves. They also assured us that we could do anything. For a while, I wasn't sure "anything" would include getting published, but the proof is in your hands.

All my love and greatest appreciation to my husband and children. Tom enabled me to write full-time, and he took me to my first "sports car boutique." My children let me "work" in peace and relinquished computer time. I couldn't ask for three better or more lovable cheerleaders.

Thank you to my critique group, the LadySleuths: Kelly Hackel, Teresa Inge, Shelley Shearer, and Kathy Whelan. They read not only this book and its sequels but the three prior attempts that will never see print. Their feedback, support, and friendship continue to make a difference. Thanks as well to Jared Case, Trina Riggle, and June Shaw who provided feedback and encouragement on this book and others.

I also thank my agent, Eric Myers. I think he works twenty-four hours a day. I know he never gave up.

Finally and especially, thank you to Bill Krause and all the team at Llewellyn Publications and Midnight Ink.

Book Club Questions: *For Better, For Murder*

Ray Parker was first attracted to Jolene Asdale in high school because she looked like his favorite actress. What first attracted you to your spouse or significant other?

Town gossip paints Jolene as a murder suspect but also helps solve the case. Discuss how gossip can be both destructive and constructive.

It has been said that sisters butt heads more often than any other family members. Have you found this to be true? What do you think of Jolene and Erica's relationship? Are they better for having each other, or worse? As a grownup, should Erica still be Jolene's responsibility?

Discuss Jolene's reasons for not wanting to bear a child and Ray's response to her decision. Did that decision lead to their breakup, or something else?

What did you think about Ray's relationship with Catherine and how Catherine handled herself?

Who did you first believe had committed the murder and why? How did you feel when the murderer was revealed?

Common mystery elements include: suspects (each with means, motive, and opportunity), clues, and red herrings (false clues). How many of these can you identify from the story?

So where does the story leave Jolene and Ray? Is it where you hoped?

Jolene likes to live her life without drama, rumor, or fanfare. What kind of a life do you like to lead?

Jolene and Ray had a tradition of attending the lighting of the town Christmas tree each year. What traditions do you have with your spouse or significant other? What holiday traditions does your home town have that you enjoy each year?

Jolene sells "pre-owned, but pristine" foreign sports cars. If you entered her showroom with cash in hand which make(s), model(s), and color(s) would you want? Why?

For Better, For Murder is a cozyish mystery with a number of underlying themes. What makes it cozyish? Identify the underlying themes.

ABOUT THE AUTHOR

Lisa Bork worked in human resources and marketing before becoming a stay-at-home mom. When her children entered school full-time, Lisa turned to writing to fill her days and exercise her mind. *For Better, For Murder* grew out of her family's love of the Finger Lakes region and her husband's obsession with cars. Lisa is a member of the Authors Guild, Mystery Writers of America, Sisters in Crime, the Guppies, and the Thursday Evening Literary Society. Lisa resides with her husband, children, and the family dog in western New York. She has a B.A. in English and an M.B.A. in Marketing.